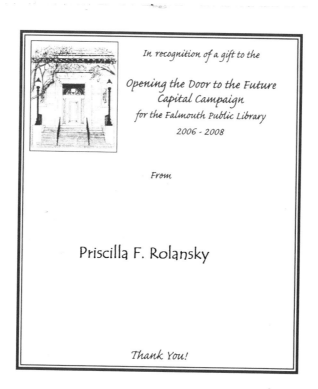

IN THE MOUTH

IN THE MOUTH

Stories and Novellas

Eileen Pollack

FOUR WAY BOOKS
TRIBECA

EDITORIAL OFFICE
Four Way Books
POB 535, Village Station
New York, NY 10014
www.fourwaybooks.com

LIBRARY OF CONGRESS CATALOGING-IN-PUBLICATION DATA
Pollack , Eileen, 1956-
In the mouth : stories and novellas / Eileen Pollack.
    p. cm.
ISBN-13: 978-1-884800-82-5 (pbk. : alk. paper)
ISBN-10: 1-884800-82-3 (pbk. : alk. paper)
1. Jewish fiction. I. Title.
PS3566.O4795I5 2008
813'.54--dc22
2007037691

This book is manufactured in the United States of America and printed on acid-free paper.

Four Way Books is a not-for-profit literary press. We are grateful for the assistance we receive from individual donors, public arts agencies, and private foundations.

 This publication is made possible with public funds from the New York State Council on the Arts, a state agency.

 Publication of this book is made possible in part by an award from the National Endowment for the Arts, which believes that a great nation deserves great art, and by a generous grant from a private foundation.

Distributed by University Press of New England
One Court Street, Lebanon, NH 03766

[clmp]
We are a proud member of the Council of Literary Magazines and Presses.

This book is dedicated to my agent,
Maria Massie,
and to the memory of my father,
Abraham J. Pollack, DDS

CONTENTS

vii

ACKNOWLEDGMENTS

I want to express my gratitude to all the friends, colleagues, family members, and students who kept me going while I wrote these stories and who provided invaluable suggestions for revising them, with especial appreciation to Charles Baxter, Suzanne Berne, Noah Glaser, Marcie Hershman, Marian Krzyzowski, Maxine Rodburg, Adam Schwartz, and Therese Stanton.

Also, many thanks to the editors of the literary journals and anthologies in which these stories first appeared:

David Huddle, Devon Jersild, and William Lychack, *New England Review*, "The Safe"; David Leavitt and Mark Mitchell, *SubTropics*, and Stephen King and Heidi Pitlor, *Best American Short Stories 2007*, "The Bris"; Laurence Goldstein and Vicki Lawrence, *Michigan Quarterly Review*, "Milt and Moose"; Don Lee and James Welch, *Ploughshares*, and Bill Henderson, *Pushcart Press Anthology XX*, "Milk"; Hilda Raz and Kelly Grey Carlisle, *Prairie Schooner*, "Uno."

And, of course, my never-ending devotion to Martha Rhodes, Vesna Neskow, Ryan Murphy, Lytton Smith, Sally Ball, and the rest of the crew at Four Way Books.

IN THE MOUTH

The Safe

MY FATHER WAS BORN not far from Blessington, but my mother didn't move there until after they were married. She was motherless and pregnant and so developed friendships with the other young women on her street. Unfortunately, these young women were even more superstitious and less informed about procreation than she was. When a friend named Cissy Flyte suffered a miscarriage, Cissy blamed herself for indulging in the pleasure of gloating about her blessings—a comfortable well-furnished house, a successful devoted husband who couldn't keep his hands off her, and the baby growing inside her womb—before the child was born. Later, when she became pregnant a second time, Cissy told no one but my mother, and even then she made my mother swear she wouldn't breathe a word to another soul.

I'm not sure why my mother betrayed her best friend's confidence. She was perfectly capable of keeping a secret. She didn't enjoy poking fun. And yet, when my father came home from his dental office that night, she told him that Cissy was pregnant again.

As it happened, Cissy had an appointment with my father two days later. He isn't given to playing jokes. But on this one occasion, he apparently couldn't resist.

"Why, Cissy!" he exclaimed, peering down her throat. "Did you know that you're expecting?"

Too shocked to say anything, Cissy opened wider.

"There is no doubt about it. You ought to call Sol and let him know the good news."

"But, Boris," she said. "You don't mean to tell me you can see the baby that way, down my throat?"

"Certainly I can. There's a membrane protecting the fetus. But in just the right light . . ."

He meant to end the joke there and wish Cissy all the best. But she begged him to look down her throat a second time and tell her if the child was healthy or not. Cissy's hunger to be reassured was so apparent on her face that my father said yes, she would have a healthy child—a boy, he suspected, although at this stage, the genitals were so tiny it was risky for him to guess.

When both prophecies came true, Cissy called my father to thank him for sparing her those five dreadful months of anxiety, and he never did bring himself to confess the trick.

* * *

Two years ago, when I was pregnant with my own son, I drove home to Blessington on the pretext that I wanted my father "to take a look at my teeth." While my mother sat behind the desk, entering payments in the ledger and writing out bills, my father snapped on his white jacket, started the water swirling in the cuspidor, and poked his mirror around my mouth.

When he asked what the trouble was, I told him to please keep looking, didn't he see anything odd?

"No," he said. "Your teeth and gums are fine. Now tell me what's wrong. You know I hate mysteries."

"Did you look down my throat?" I asked.

My mother caught the joke first. She came to stand in the doorway, a gaunt pallid woman in a navy blue skirt and white silk blouse. The plastic pen from the desk set was tucked behind her ear and she was clutching a card that read YOUR ACCOUNT IS PAST DUE. "Look harder, Boris! Tell me what it is, our first grandchild, a girl or a boy!"

And my father, befuddled, fell back a few steps, then thrust out his arm and patted me roughly on the head, tears shining in his eyes. As I lay in that chair, with the glow from my parents' faces as bright as the incandescent light from the lamp above my head, I realized I had been rehearsing this joke not only for the three-hour drive from Boston, but for most of my life. I had become a radiologist and specialized in obstetrics because the idea of glimpsing a fetus in the womb had haunted me since I'd first heard the story of my father peering down Cissy Flyte's throat. (I was five at the time and didn't understand the joke, I only pretended I did, so thrilled was I to hear my parents' laughter, so afraid it would end with a question from me.) Sometimes I think I convinced my husband, Grant, that we ought to have a child because my mother was dying and I couldn't bear to miss the chance to act out this brilliant reprise of my family's one joke.

* * *

Now my father is retiring, and if I ever find the courage to get pregnant again, I will need to reveal my secret in whatever

5

mundane way other daughters use. Last week, my father sold the house in which he had lived with my mother for thirty-nine years before she passed on and in which he has lived alone for the past eighteen months. Ostensibly, I have come home to help him run a yard sale. But both of us know he could do that on his own, and in fact would prefer to do so.

It is early on a Friday night. His office light is on, so I park and go in. The building used to belong to the Blessington mortician, a man with the truly remarkable name of Mortimer Bury, who died the week my father came home from World War II. In the foyer stands a naked winged boy, so innocent and plump he might be a cherub, although his smile is so coy he ought to hold a bow and arrow. As a child and adolescent, I passed this statue so many times I must have stopped seeing it. But today, as I enter, I reach out to stroke an alabaster knee.

A door opens. I drop my hand.

Dr. Paxton, who rents an office from my father, stands in the hall before me. A short man with a ropy mustache and a wide down-turned mouth, he resembles the catfish lurking in the murky tank he keeps in his waiting room. You might assume such a man would scare children too much to be a pediatrician, but as soon as a patient steps into his lair, Dr. Paxton pops up, throws out his arms, and grins, so every child assumes he or she has some special power to make this grown-up smile.

"Sharon!" he cries. He takes my hand in his and rubs his thumb across my knuckles, then flips my hand to inspect the palm. "How are you? Not still nursing that bruiser of yours, I hope." His gaze travels to my feet, then back to my face. I wonder how many times he saw me naked as a child. "Is something bothering you?" he asks. "Stop me if I'm prying, but you seem sad."

I would explain to him what's wrong, but I'm not sure I know. I loved my mother and I miss her. But she was dying for many years and wracked by suffering at the end, and we were relieved to see her go. This other loss, this grief, seems to me uncaused. What else do I have to mourn? My husband is loyal and kind. I love my son so much, and so unexpectedly, it's as if I had awakened to discover a valuable object in my house and I could spend the rest of my life giving away portions of my wealth to all those in need without becoming poorer myself.

"So how is little Paulie?" Dr. Paxton asks, as if my son's image has burned through my skull. "Your dad can't get enough of seeing him, I'll bet."

When I tell him that I've left Paul at home with his father, I brace for a scolding.

"Just the two of them? Your mother would no sooner have left you alone with your father than left you lying out in the street. The men of my generation, they have no idea what they missed."

Thinking of Ed Paxton, childless himself, yet the only man in Blessington to know the satisfaction of spending his days with kids, I feel my old affection for him surge back. I want to ask what my mother said and did when she brought me in to see him. Did she ever talk about her own parents? Did she ever talk about my father? I never once saw them touch. Was something wrong in bed? Was that why I'm an only child? They belonged to a generation that kept their problems to themselves. No matter what happened, there was a dignity to be gained by silence. I'm not certain my mother even discussed such matters with Cissy Flyte.

The tips of Dr. Paxton's whiskers brush my cheek. "Keep up the good work," he says, as if being a mother were a matter of diligence, like brushing one's teeth. Then he goes out the door before I have a chance to ask why I've always felt so uneasy around my father and whether my feelings for my own child are perverse.

7

* * *

Before Paul was born, I assumed a parent could violate a child only from hate. But now I'm not sure. I nursed my son for a year, and I can't deny that the suck of his lips and the warmth of his hands kneading my breasts brought me great joy. But the feelings that disturb me began several months later, when I no longer feared I might damage or even kill him through my neglect. I could leave him unclothed without worrying that he might contract a chill. I could allow my mouth to linger on his fragrant neck and scalp as he lay sprawled across my legs, limp and sweaty from his nap. Only when I knew that he wouldn't slip from my hands and drown could I revel in the smoothness of his sweet unblemished skin, the indentation of each armpit beneath each pudgy arm, the curves of his belly, the puffy brown buds on his chest. And later, when he lay glistening from his bath, pink from the water's heat, this child I could devour bite after bite like any cruel witch, I would lean down and blow kisses on his navel while he giggled, screeched, and squirmed.

And once, a few days ago, he was laughing so hard I couldn't bear to stop. His head was thrown back. His mouth gaped so wide I could see the pendulum of flesh swaying above his throat.

I rubbed my lips across his belly. Inside were his intestines, stomach, liver, spleen, all those nerves, veins, and bones so exquisitely fashioned, cell upon cell, from my own blood and milk. Before I knew what I had done, I had moved my lips lower to kiss the small penis and soft wrinkled scrota that grow between his thighs like some precious pink fruit.

I took a step back. I would have run from the room, but he couldn't have climbed down without getting hurt. Instead, I diapered and clothed my son, telling myself that I hadn't done any harm. It was just a one-time slip. And yet, at odd moments—talking to a colleague, watching Paulie play, driving here from Boston—I have again felt the urge to cover him with kisses, to press my lips against the soles of his smooth white feet, the hollows behind his knees, his delicious cherry mouth.

* * *

My father's waiting room is furnished exactly as it was when Mortimer Bury worked on corpses in the back. The same heavy wood chairs with green leather seats, the same maple pie-shell table with the swan-shaped lamp on top. Each piece is perfect Art Deco, and the set would bring hundreds, maybe thousands, of dollars, if only my father would allow me to haul it to a dealer. If I cared enough to insist.

I walk softly to his office. The girl reclining in his chair is twelve or thirteen. He towers above her—six feet four inches, two hundred and twenty pounds. By all rights, a man that large ought to be clumsy. When he tried to enroll in dental school, the dean forced my father to undergo a dexterity test. But his hands might be the claws of a praying mantis, that's how graceful they are.

When he finally looks up, he stares at me a moment, then shakes his head to clear his sight. No doubt he was expecting to see my mother, bringing him a question from a patient on the phone. He jabs his index finger in my direction, then down at the girl in the chair, then at his own jaw. I understand this dumb show only because I can guess what he wants to say: *Wait until I'm done and I'll check your teeth, too.*

I go back to the waiting room and sit behind the desk my mother used to occupy from the year I entered kindergarten until a few months before she died. This was their bargain: in return for the security and love he gave her, my mother would sit behind this desk and translate my father's rough, clumsy gestures for the world.

Though my father is usually prompt about removing the records of patients who have died to the drawer marked EXPIRED, I find my mother's card in the file for the living. It begins with a list of the nineteen teeth my father filled before their marriage—he did the work in two days, without using Novocaine, a drug he believes is only for dentists so inept they shouldn't be allowed to practice—and ends with a cleaning two weeks before her death. On the back is a diagram on which heavy black Xs, etched deep with regret, mark the three teeth he couldn't save.

My father comes out, holding up his hands to show they're sterile and I mustn't hug or kiss him, although I hadn't planned to do either.

"What are you looking for?" He is trying to whisper, but his voice comes out harsh.

I close the drawer and ask how much longer he will be.

He motions toward the chair. "It's a sin," he hisses. "She ought to be shot." He is referring to the fact that the girl's mother feeds her sugary foods and doesn't make her brush. "If you want, you can go home and I'll check your teeth later."

"I'll be fine," I say. "I'll just go in back and freshen up." I slip past his patient—she reclines on her pedestal, eyes shut, neck exposed—and enter the dental lab in the back. A row of plaster teeth sits grinning on the shelf. To give my lie veracity, I enter the tiny bathroom and flush the toilet. My father's drill is still squealing, so I tiptoe down the stairs.

As a child, I was always curious as to what the cellar might hold. Cissy's son, Myles, once told me that a stack of bodies had been lying in the cellar waiting to be embalmed when Mr.

Bury died. I longed to go see them. Like most children, I felt the urge to stare at someone else's body so I would better understand what was normal or abnormal about my own. And who will let us stare at their bodies with impunity except other children and the dead?

At first, I wasn't tall enough to reach the light. Then I forgot what Myles had said. When I finally did go down there, I found nothing more morbid than a barrel of de-icing salt, boxes of toilet tissue, bibs, and paper towels, and in one corner, a lacquered Chinese screen with white cranes and scarlet poppies.

It was June, I remember, but the cellar was so cool I got goose bumps on my arms. I had recently turned fifteen, and in the previous few months, I had shot up several inches and gained twenty or thirty pounds. The skirt I was wearing was short and tight. My blouse gaped across my chest, the armholes chafing the newly shaven skin beneath my arms. Earlier that afternoon, when I had come to see him for my checkup, my father had told me to go home and tell my mother to buy me some clothes that fit. I tried not to feel embarrassed. But that must have been why I reacted so strangely when he came down to get more paper towels and noticed me by the screen.

The room suddenly seemed too small. I felt queasy and hot. I couldn't have said what scared me. When my father demanded to know why I was down there, I couldn't really tell him. Dead bodies in the cellar? I no longer believed what stupid Myles Flyte had said. Confronted by my silence, my father seemed to think I was searching for some kind of evidence with which to incriminate him. The idea that I was doing exactly that upset me so much I burst out crying. My father stood and watched. Then he rushed across the room and engulfed me in his arms. His fingers gripped my shoulder blades as if he were wrenching them from my back. He prob-

11

ably wanted nothing more than to make me stop crying. When I cried harder, he let me go and retreated up the stairs. I walked slowly up behind him, leaving the screen where it was.

Today I don't hesitate. I walk to the screen and fold it back. Behind it stands a safe as squat as a bull, with a dusty black hide and a silver handle like a horn. I drop to my knees and twist the dial, listening for the tumblers. But the handle won't budge. I think of asking Dr. Paxton to lend me his stethoscope, but I remember he's gone home.

"Sharon? Are you down there?"

"Yes! I'm coming right up!" I pull the screen in place, then run up the stairs and join him. "Dad," I say, "that safe—"

He turns to the sink, squirts yellow soap from a spigot, and begins lathering up his hands.

"Was it there when you bought the building?" I ask. "Didn't you ever bother to open it?"

He keeps washing his hands. No one but this man could make me feel like a woman who chatters too much. With tongs, he lifts his instruments from their steaming bath and lays them across a towel. I fill my own cup, clip my bib around my neck, then ease myself back in the reclining chair as my father leans close to my wide-open mouth. Water swirls in the cuspidor. His mirror clicks against my teeth, sending circles of light across the ceiling. His face is enormous. He is holding his breath. I study his cheeks, those stump-covered plains. The caves of his nostrils. The mole on his chin. Seeing him this close, I think I should be able to learn something about him that isn't so obvious from a few feet away. But that's as foolish as believing that he ought to be able to divine what's inside me by looking down my throat.

He re-adjusts the light. "Open wider," he commands, and those huge hands come toward me. I grip the chair. His eyes twitch, as if he's scared to hurt me. When he finally lets out his breath, the air is hot and moist on my face. It smells of anti-septic, though beneath the Listerine lies the tang of peanuts, my father's favorite food.

"Turn this way," he says, nudging my chin with his thumb, and the warmth of his touch brings tears to my eyes. I wonder what he felt on his wedding night, lying with my mother, a woman he barely knew, or later, in the hospital, when my mother or a nurse unswaddled me. I have no memory of him ever holding me. Is it possible he never did, except that one time, in the basement beneath this office?

"Rinse," he says. "Spit."

I pat my lips with the bib.

"You have a fine set of teeth. You'll have to find a new dentist and make an appointment to get them cleaned."

I nod, but what I'm thinking is how surprised I was to learn that most children went to the dentist once a year, not once a month.

"There," he says, "all done."

But I can't seem to stand. I have lain in this chair so often, I can't fathom or accept this might be the last time.

He walks around the room, cleaning up the mess and changing from his jacket to a white short-sleeve shirt. "Sharon? Are you coming?"

Slowly, I get up. He flicks off the overhead light, the swan lamp. In the foyer, we pass the boy.

"We ought to have him appraised," I suggest.

"Who?" my father says, and I point to the leering cherub. "Never mind that," he says, then goes outside and locks the door. I expect him to lead us downhill to a restaurant in town, but he remains standing where he is. "If you don't mind, I'd rather eat at home. I've already cooked our dinner."

When my mother was alive, we ate out once a week, my mother smiling pertly at everyone in the restaurant while my father hunched above his plate, hoping none of his patients would stop by to talk. But two or three of them always did, turning their cheeks inside out to reveal an abscess on their gums, a broken bridge, a swelling. Sometimes, they would hand my father their dentures right across his plate.

Tonight, my father is even less keen on looking into someone's mouth than having one of his patients stop by to thank him for caring for their teeth or to wish him luck on whatever comes next.

"I know you have the car," he says, "but if it's all the same to you, I'd rather walk."

He starts striding up the hill, moving so quickly I barely have time to get in my car and drive home before I see his shirt bobbing through the dusk at the end of our street. From a neighboring yard, a child shouts: "No! Go away! I can't!" I walk to the edge of the driveway. A burly man with a ponytail seems to be punching his son in the mouth. I step closer and see that the man's fingers are forked inside the boy's teeth, as if to yank out his tongue.

"Blow!" the father says, and a whistle tears the air. "Again!" the father says, and the boy swats away the hand, hooks his own fingers in his mouth, and whistles a note so much softer and higher, so achingly pure, he seems to be an angel in a choir, lifting his voice to God.

* * *

When I follow my father into our house, the emptiness is shocking. He has donated the sofa, dining-room table, beds, mattresses, and pillows to a home for retired vets. Everything else is packed in boxes for the yard sale. He has kept almost nothing. Doesn't he want to hold onto anything that reminds him of my mother? Or does everything remind him of her too much? I have no idea where he intends to go when he moves. He hasn't mentioned plans to travel or take up golf.

The table is set. It must have been set since he left for work. I make small talk about the clinic while my father heats aluminum pans of beef and macaroni—three for him and one for me—and a pan of potatoes au gratin. With my mother's flowered mitt, he carries the pans to the Formica table. Then he lunges forward, grabs me against his chest, and plants kisses on my neck. He is so big, and his mouth on my skin is so warm, I find myself wedging my hands between our bodies. Still he holds on. His belt buckle presses against my ribs. I can hear his stomach grumble, hear his heavy heart thud.

Finally he lets me go, rushes to his chair, and starts forking macaroni in his mouth, as shaken as a soldier who has darted across a field to grab a fallen comrade. We eat our meal in silence. After watching the evening news, he informs me that he's tired and begins to climb the stairs. He stops on the landing and leans forward, as if he intends to dive toward me again.

"The towels in the bathroom are clean," he says. Then he climbs to his room and shuts the door.

* * *

The telephone rings. The clatter is so vicious, echoing against the bare walls and floors, I hurry to answer. Even before my husband says hello, he's complaining that he's exhausted. Paul has been crying ever since Grant picked him up at day care.

(Most afternoons, when Paul notices that I've come to get him, he runs across the yard and wraps his arms around my legs and buries his face against my thighs, sniffing the skin as if I give off some irresistible scent, like fresh bread.)

"We should have come with you," Grant is saying. "If you needed time away, you should have gone somewhere more relaxing. But if you wanted to see your dad, we should have come along."

What he really wants to know is why I suddenly stopped wanting to dress or bathe our son, why I won't take Paul swimming or let him climb in bed and cover me with pillows, as he so loves to do. But Grant isn't able to find the words to ask. To Grant, a boy's body is what it is. He loves to tell stories of his summers at Scout Camp and the gymnastic tournaments he won at school. He enjoys nothing better than wrestling with Paul. He plans to toilet train our son in the same manner his own father trained him—by lining up tin cans across a field, peeing in the first one, then moving Paul closer and challenging him to fill the next.

Even if Grant manages to ask me what's wrong, how can I say that I'm no longer able to watch our son play in the tub without feeling shame? From this far away, it's absurd to think I would ever hurt our child. Then why am I so afraid?

"Your father," Grant says, "does he talk about your mom? How can you live with someone for that many years and not, you know . . . "

What he means is whether there might be some connection between my father's almost pathological reticence and my own odd behavior. *Of course there is,* I think. Connections like that are easy to make. *My father never touched me, so I slept with eight men my first year away from home. My father is huge and moist, so I married a man as slight and papery as a twig.*

"I miss you," I say. And really, I do. There is something about Grant—who is after all a botanist—that makes me feel as if everything in nature had evolved to the point that he and I could make love and bear a child. But later, as I lie on the floor of a room whose bed now belongs to a retired veteran, it's not my husband but my son I imagine in my arms, and so manage to drift to sleep.

* * *

The next morning, I awaken early, but my father has already left. AT OFFICE CLEANING explains his note. I spend the morning and afternoon preparing for the yard sale. Hour after hour, I snoop through my father's boxes, though I doubt I will learn anything I didn't know before. My parents lived as if their house were a ship and if it weren't kept in order, with each cooking pot in place, each coil tightly wound, a single strong wind might send us to the deep. No souvenir of their courtship survives. In a way, they never had one. A year or so after he opened his dental practice, my father asked his supply man if he knew a single woman who might make a good wife. The salesman suggested his own younger sister, a girl with no parents, little formal education, and extremely bad teeth. They met. Then they married. Did they learn to love each other? Or did that joke they played on Cissy arise from some barely acknowledged jealousy of what she and her husband had that my parents didn't?

I sift through a box, but it's not as if my mother kept a diary. Neither of my parents was much of a letter writer. When I went away to school, my father sent me notes scrawled on prescription forms with his name across the top. His advice was so terse, I felt I ought to take his letters to a pharmacy to fill.

In an alphabetized cardboard file, I find the manuals for

every appliance and car my parents owned. The appliances themselves should be in glass cases in a fifties display: the shiny chrome toaster; the iron, sleek but heavy; the mixer, with its twisted wire whisks and nested bowls; the blender; the rotisserie; the electric razor my mother gave my father a few years before my birth. In a box in the garage I find three snapshots labeled in my father's block print: MARTHA AND CHRYSLER 1952; MARTHA AND HOUSE 1953; MARTHA AND SHARON 1954. In this last photo, it is winter. My mother is wrapped in a camel's hair cape, and my face is barely visible in the quilted bundle in her arms. Our yard is so desolate she might have brought me home to the moon, with no one to help take care of me—or, for that matter, help take care of her—except the man whose shadow nearly reaches her galoshes in the snow.

Also in the box is the only home movie my father ever took, with a camera borrowed from Cissy's husband. We owned no projector, but often, as a child, I held this roll of film to a light, unspooling it slowly, the way I do now. We are gathered around the kitchen table—my mother, Cissy, Myles in Cissy's arms, and me, on my chair, standing above a cake. Frame by frame, I bend forward and plunge my hands in the cake up to the wrists. My mother rises from her chair, jerks me back, and wipes my arms. Cissy laughs and claps her hands and kisses me on the cheek. The next few frames are blank. Then I run toward the camera, arms lifted high and wide, and just as my upturned face fills the negative, the strip of plastic ends.

* * *

By nine the next morning, the temperature is eighty-two degrees and cars are lined up in front of our house, although

18

the sale isn't scheduled to start until ten. Families from the boondocks think that anyone who lives on our street must be rich. Our neighbors want to see my parents' belongings strewn across the lawn, a sight as intriguing as a cadaver sliced from sternum to navel for embalming. My father is in his office. Yesterday, he carted home the furniture from the waiting room. He's already sold his equipment for scrap. What could possibly be left to clean?

The rotisserie goes first. The washer is hauled away by a redheaded farmer who wraps his arms around its bulk and walks it to his pickup as he might walk a drunken friend. After that, I lose track. People carry off my parents' possessions like looters at a riot. I thought I would be sorry to see so many familiar objects go, but I feel secretly gleeful, as if these were siblings I had hated since birth.

When the frenzy finally dies, only a few of the smaller items remain—my mother's plastic fruit, the shoeshine kit and birdhouse my father made as a teenage boy. A child whines for lunch. "No," her mother snaps, then pulls a bag of Hershey's kisses from her purse. The child's hands and face turn a syrupy brown. She begs for more kisses. Her mother slaps her hands. "Not on my new white pants!" Then she grabs the girl by the wrists and sucks the chocolate from her fingers. I stand transfixed until the last smear has vanished beneath the mother's tongue.

An old-fashioned station wagon pulls up and Dr. Paxton gets out. My father unfolds from the passenger seat, walks around the back, flips down the rear fender, and, with Dr. Paxton's help, eases the safe from the rear compartment, which opens like a hearse.

"What's in that?" asks a man who has been pushing our ancient manual mower back and forth across the lawn.

My father leaves the safe beside the curb, shrugs, and stalks off. The other shoppers drift over until twenty-odd people crowd around the safe.

"It's locked," a neighbor says. "Hey, Sharon, what's in it?"

I hold up my hands.

"What do you mean you don't know?" This comes from the farmer who bought the washer. "This some sort of trick?"

I tell them how my father found the safe but never opened it and now wants to sell it. Several heads nod—that's just what he would do. They jiggle the handle and twirl the dial. Someone kicks the walls and asks, "Weren't the Burys rich?" An elderly man mentions a rumor that when bodies needed to be exhumed, the remains were found without the jewelry they ought to have been entombed with. And didn't Mortimer Bury die quite suddenly? Without a wife, and without an heir?

"What's the price?" a woman asks.

I start to say I've decided to keep the safe, but the farmer interrupts. "I'd give fifty bucks just to find out what's inside."

"Fifty?" someone else says. "Safe alone's worth more than that. I'd give seventy-five."

By then it's too late.

"Hundred fifty!"

"Two hundred!"

What do they think could be inside? Wedding rings? Stocks? Silver fillings from the dead? I don't believe the rumors. So why do I want to know what's inside that safe as badly as they do? Because it's locked? Because my father wants to sell it?

"Four hundred dollars." This comes from a man with reddened skin and silver hair so sparse his scalp shows. Earlier today, he bought the pie-shell table, the swan lamp, the chairs with green seats, the magazine rack and desk, the Formica table, and my mother's clock radio, which runs on tubes. He's probably made such a killing already he can gamble on the safe. Maybe he'll take it back to his antique shop on the Cape, serve wine and hors d'oeuvres, and hold an auction himself.

"Here's the money," he says and hands me four new bills. Before I can tell him it's all been a mistake, he announces he'll be back later to collect his purchases, then climbs in a green sports car and zooms off.

The losing bidders mutter angrily, as if they plan to break open the safe and carry off its contents. In the midst of this anger, Cissy Flyte wanders up. This isn't so odd. The owner of these objects was her best friend. Cissy is thin and well preserved, with whitish-yellow hair and an innocent trusting face. For all I know, she still believes it's possible for a man to look down a woman's throat and see what's in her womb.

She walks across our lawn with a man who must be Myles. Cissy and her husband, Sol, who died the year before my mother died, raised four children besides Myles, but their daughters are the kind of kids who live on ashrams in remote villages in Bangladesh or run fishing camps in Alaska. I haven't seen Myles in years—he spent his twenties in the Navy and his thirties in South America, strung out on booze and coke, and my parents and the Flytes rarely if ever mentioned him. He hasn't aged as badly as might be expected given the life he's led, but he's gained a lot of weight. Twice divorced and now remarried, he cradles a baby girl across his girth.

"Sharon," Cissy croons. "Here's little Annie. After all these years, a grandchild!" The baby rubs her pursed lips against Myles's flabby chest, trying to nurse. My father reappears, looking pale and dazed, as if he can't figure out why his possessions are scattered across the lawn. Cissy, meanwhile, has picked up the white porcelain basin in which my mother kept our rags. "Sharon, Sharon, you don't know how often I'd come over and find you in this tub! And Boris, do you remember that time Martha was away, in the hospital, that first time? Sharon, you won't believe this. I came over to see if your dad needed a hand, and guess where I found you? In that tub! By yourself! A six-week-old infant! And there was your father, standing in the corner, as if he expected you to take your bath yourself."

If Dr. Paxton's frown extended any further, his chin would drop off. "You poor lamb." He squeezes my arm. "We're lucky you're even here."

Cissy holds the basin toward Myles. In all the years that it sat in our basement filled with the family's rags, I never noticed that there was a little pink rocking horse painted on the rim.

"Let's take it for Annie," Cissy says. "That way, she won't have to bathe in that nasty kitchen sink when she visits her Gram."

"Give me that!" My father snatches away the basin, nearly twisting Cissy's wrist. "What do you know about bathing a child? You don't even know where they come from." He turns and shoves Ed Paxton. "And you. If you're such an expert on how to raise a child, why didn't you have one?"

Dr. Paxton flinches. My father has voiced the doubt every parent in Blessington must have felt when this man pooh-poohed their concerns about a newborn with colic, a teenage girl who wouldn't eat, a boy who insisted on wearing his sister's clothes. Even men like my father could reassure themselves they knew one thing that Ed Paxton didn't know: what it was to love a child.

Though I chastise my father, this is only halfhearted. His cruelty was meant for my sake. And I don't like the way Dr. Paxton pretends that he's always been this wise. He once told my mother it was healthier for a baby to drink formula from a bottle than be suckled at her breast. And he never said or did anything to disabuse my father of the notion that he shouldn't touch his female child.

"Here." My father hands me the basin. "Take it back to Boston for Paul."

"It's not big enough," I whisper. "He takes his bath in the tub now."

"Then we'll save it for the next one."

That's all it takes, "we," and I have to admit what I've known all along—that my father has been waiting for Grant and me to invite him to live with us. And the thought of my father swooping from the shadows to grab my son—or grab me— makes me so nervous I want to demand that all these people return his possessions so he can stay and live here.

Then I imagine my father washing my son in this basin with the rocking horse on the rim, and I can't help but wish I were pregnant again. I imagine my father in his twenties, giving me a bath. Gingerly, he unswaddles me and lowers me in the water. But how can he wash me? How soap between my legs or cradle my buttocks in his palm? He sets me in the tub and takes a few steps back.

That's when Cissy Flyte barges in. *Boris, what's the matter! Here, let me do that. You can't be trusted with that child!* After that, he never touches me again, except once a month, when he summons me to his office and examines me in his chair. And this must be the source of the sadness that haunts me: that my father loved me with the same helpless passion I feel for my son, and his passion scared him so much he couldn't let it show.

He takes the basin and goes inside.

"Really," Cissy says, "he still thinks he fooled me with that silly trick."

But I know she's lying. Maybe Cissy is less naive than my parents once thought she was. But she did, in her dread, believe my father's joke.

The mother of the girl with chocolate hands has turned on our sprinkler. The girl pulls off her T-shirt, then her shoes and shorts and underpants. While her mother picks through a box of spatulas, the girl straddles the spinning sprinkler, pushing down at the spray like Marilyn Monroe pushing down at her dress. I start to turn away. The cleft between her legs is so unprotected that my mere gaze seems an assault.

Then I turn back. What sight will I ever see as lovely as this? It's all I can do not to leap in my car and drive home to Paul before he won't let me hold him, before he demands to bathe and dress behind a locked door. That I have missed even this many days of his childhood seems intolerable to me now.

The man from Boston comes back, driving an enormous van. At least a dozen people offer to hoist the safe. With so many hands, they swing it too quickly and something inside goes *clunk*.

The man from Boston climbs in the driver's seat. The van thunders down the hill. When it reaches the stop sign at the bottom, the crowd turns to me as if demanding that I run after it and bring back the safe. *Something is inside! Didn't you hear it rattle? How can you live without knowing what it is?*

But I would no more want to open that safe than I would want to dig up my mother's coffin, pry open the lid, and see if her diamond ring is still on her finger and my father's perfect silver fillings still inside her teeth.

The Bris

WHEN MARCUS PACKED FOR FLORIDA, he harbored no illusions about what would happen when he got there. His father's liver soon would fail, and, without a transplant, he couldn't survive the week. "Why waste a miracle on an elderly man like me?" his father scoffed. He pooh-poohed the new liver as if it were a slightly used sports car Marcus insisted he buy. "At least let me put your name on the waiting list," Marcus said, but his father blew raspberries through the phone. "Give that same liver to someone young, and he or she could get another fifty years out of the goddamn thing."

And so, with a heavy carry-on and an even heavier heart, Marcus flew to West Palm Beach. He rented a car and drove to the hospital in Boca Raton where his father had been taken after his last collapse. As he checked in at Registration and followed the arrows to the room, he prepared for the likelihood that in another few days he would be arranging his father's funeral. What he couldn't have predicted was that first he would be called on to arrange his father's *bris*.

"Your *bris*, Pop?" Marcus laughed, although his father rarely joked; for a former hotelkeeper in the Catskills, he was a singularly humorless man. His request that Marcus find a *mohel* who would circumcise him before he died could only be an effect of the drugs he was taking or the poison seeping from his liver. "Don't worry, Pop. All of that was taken care of a long time ago."

His father waved a bloated yellow arm. Hooked up to an IV, he reminded Marcus of an inflated creature in the Thanksgiving Day parade. "A lie," his father gasped. "Everything has been a lie."

"What, Pop? What lie?" If there was one thing Marcus knew, it was his father didn't lie, any more than he ate shellfish or pork. When Marcus was a boy, his father made such a *megillah* about never telling lies or playing tricks that Marcus imagined he must have been the victim of some terrible prank or hoax. That his guileless, defenseless father had been wounded by someone's lie made Marcus resolve never to lie himself. When he started his first accounting job in Manhattan in the eighties, he couldn't bring himself to fudge even the tiniest account his employer expected him to fudge. A quarter of a century later, he still had trouble living in the world of shaded truths most New Yorkers lived in.

"Don't talk to me about lying," he told his dad. "You're the most truthful man I know."

His father squinched his lips and shrugged, a gesture meant to convey he wasn't the saint everyone took him to be. "They won't let me be buried—" He sucked oxygen from the tube inside his nose. "In the plot. Beside your mother."

Marcus was seized by the premonition that his father was

about to reveal a sordid and completely out-of-character affair with the woman who used to be the social director at the family's hotel. While Marcus's mother was still alive, his father treated Liddy Newman's voluptuous advances as a burden to be endured rather than a pleasure to be pursued. But Marcus's mother had dropped dead of a heart attack while working in the kitchen one particularly stressful night when Marcus was fifteen, and he'd never understood how or why his father found the self-control not to fool around with Liddy after that.

When his father finally sold Lieberman's—gave it away was more like it, to a group of Brooklyn Hasids who promised they would use it as a camp for retarded teens, then used it as a get-away for themselves—he moved to a retirement community in Boca, where the widows hounded him so ferociously he took a few to lunch. Maybe he took a few to bed. But how could that deny him the right to be buried with Marcus's mother?

"The cemetery," his father rasped. In his younger days, he had been a tall fair broomstick of a man, with mild blue eyes and a generous expression—he'd reminded Marcus of a scare-crow begging the crows to take his corn. But this last bout of hepatitis had puffed his face and limbs and turned his irises and skin such a bilious yellow-orange he looked as if vandals had stuffed him with extra straw and jammed a rotting pumpkin on his neck.

"The cemetery," Marcus repeated dully, the reality sinking in that within a few days both his father and his mother would be lying in the ground.

Although apparently not together.

"The cemetery is only for Orthodox Jews." Marcus's father's hand drifted to his groin, which he clutched as if it pained him. "And that is something I am not. Not only am I not an Orthodox Jew, I am not a Jew of any kind."

Marcus hadn't been aware he'd been holding his breath until he let it out. "Pop, if you haven't been a good enough Jew, no one ever has." He recited his father's acts of charity— his quiet beneficence to the poor, his selfless attentions to Marcus's mother and her parents, the litany of favors he had extended to the guests, employees, and various hangers-on at Lieberman's Mountain Rest.

His father chopped off the recitation. "None of that is relevant. You might as well say actions such as these make a man a good Christian."

Marcus rubbed his eyes. He had been up late the night before deciding whether to propose to his girlfriend, Vicki, despite her desire to have a child, something Marcus was loath to promise. His flight from LaGuardia had left at six. On the plane he couldn't sleep, mostly because the harried young man beside him couldn't control his son. The boy kept vaulting Marcus's knees and bounding down the aisle, colliding with the flight attendants; Marcus took this as a sign that he was too old to have a child. Not that Vicki had made having a child a prerequisite to getting married. But how could he live with the knowledge that he'd deprived the woman he loved of what she wanted most?

"I wasn't born a Jew," his father cried. "And I never converted. It was such a little thing. But I couldn't face the prospect of anyone coming near me with a knife. The very thought made me woozy."

The force of his father's revelation set in. Short and solid as he was, Marcus swayed like a beachfront high-rise in a hurricane. He sat heavily on the bed. "This isn't making sense. All these years and, what, you've only been pretending to be a Jew?"

His father nodded and turned away. What little Marcus knew of his father's early life came back to him. Orphaned young, he'd deserted his rural Texas town to escape "a lack of opportunities" that Marcus had always assumed to be the result of anti-Semitism. His father lied about his age, enlisted in the Army, spent two years overseas, and suffered a minor wound. A veteran at nineteen, he'd landed in New York and found a job in the garment district, winding ribbon on card-board spools; he'd gone to school at night and earned his diploma, then used his GI loan to finance a few semesters at NYU, after which he'd taken a summer job waiting tables in the Catskills, where he fell hopelessly in love with the owners' daughter, married her, and never left. Now, as Marcus listened to a revised and expanded version of those events, he under-stood that the astonishing gaps in his father's history—Marcus never had seen a photo from the years before New York, never had met a Texas relative—disturbed him so much he'd never dared to ask for an explanation.

In truth, his father had been the only child of narrow Bap-tist parents who were indifferent to his survival, let alone his desire to find a less restricted, warmer, more cosmopolitan way of life. "It was one of those Christian homes where the only book is the Bible. They were scornful of anything that brought comfort to a boy. Music. Art. A kind word. A pat on the shoulder. One time, my father found a drawing of a pretty girl, a classmate, I had sketched in a notebook. It wasn't meant to be crude. I had never seen a naked female and I was trying to visualize . . . My father beat me and broke my hand." He teared up even now. "To draw a beautiful girl is a sin, but breaking a young boy's fingers isn't?"

He took another gasp of oxygen. "That was the first instance I ran away. I hid in the back of a bus to Lubbock, which was the nearest big town, and I sneaked in a theater to see my first show. I was so sick with guilt that before the picture started I

29

needed to go to the men's room and vomit. But it was entirely worth the fear. The movie was a Marx Brothers feature. Can you imagine what it was like for me to see those four brothers act in such a way? In the movie, the brothers live in a made-up country, but in my mind, they might have lived on Mars."

That his father had once had his hand broken for sketching a female classmate and run away to see *Duck Soup* filled Marcus with a pity so profound it nearly burst his chest. Certainly, this explained why his father used to drop whatever he was doing, even on the busiest weekend of the year, to turn on the little black-and-white set in Marcus's room and spend two hours watching whatever Marx Brothers movie happened to be on. Until now, Marcus had attributed his father's fondness for the Marx Brothers to the fact that only these four comedians could make him laugh. And yet, thinking back on those after-noons when he and his father had sat at the foot of Marcus's bed watching *Horse Feathers* or *A Night at the Opera*, he felt sadly left out, as if his father and the Marx Brothers, instead of playing their tricks on some overly zealous cop or a wealthy snobbish matron, had been playing a trick on him.

His father wiped his eyes. "You can imagine the beating I got when I returned home. My father could only think I had gone to town to visit a house of prostitution. Prostitutes! It had taken all my courage to sketch that naked girl! I can't imagine how I made it through another year in that house. But where was I to go? This is a terrible thing to admit, but I was glad there was a war. How else could I have gotten away so young?"

Here, the new version of his father's autobiography merged with the version Marcus already knew. "I was so tall I had no trouble passing for two years older. But what a shock, meeting those older men. The way they cursed! What they said about women! Imagine what I felt, finding myself among people who believed Christ was no more than a carpenter who had lived in Galilee a long, long time ago." Not that the conversion had been immediate. He'd simply felt so much more at home among the Jews he met in the army and in Manhattan that he absorbed their culture and religion, their love for music, art, and books. "I had been told that Jews were stingy. But to my way of thinking, they gave too much of everything. They talked too loudly, too much. They studied too hard, made too much fuss about their health, about everyone's health, about this or that injustice. They made a lot of money, but they gave so much away. And food! The mountains of food they ate! It came to me that Christians lied about Jews to hide their own guilt at being so stingy, not only with their money but with their love."

He hadn't taken the job at Lieberman's with the intention of passing as a Jew. It was just that once he got there, everyone assumed he was one.

"I told your mother. *She* knew the truth. And I would have converted. For your mother, I would have done anything. I *wanted* to be a Jew. In my heart, I already was one." He rose from his pillow. "But every time I thought of being circumcised . . ." He turned a paler shade of yellow. Beads of oily sweat popped out on his brow. "Your mother, *oleha ha sholem*, took pity on my dilemma. She wanted to be married to a Jew, but she loved me too much to insist I suffer anything I couldn't suffer willingly."

It came to Marcus that he'd never seen his father's genitals. For all the years they'd shared a house, for all the times they'd changed together in a locker room, he'd never caught his father naked. If Marcus thought anything, it was that his father was excessively shy or afflicted with some embarrassing deformity—his balls were strangely shaped, his penis small or oddly bent. The realization that his father's obsessive modesty had been a deliberate sham made Marcus feel as foolish as a *shtetl* wife who's just learned that she's been the dupe of a Yentl-like deceiver, so ignorant of the facts of life she couldn't figure out that her "husband" was a woman dressed up as a man.

His father's eyes were closed. The tracings on the monitor flowed as quietly as the ripples on a pond. Marcus jostled his father's hip. "Pop, it's all right. Whatever it is, I forgive you."

Without opening his eyes, his father patted Marcus's hand. "For your forgiveness I thank you. But what I need from you now is not your forgiveness but your help."

Not ask his forgiveness? He remembered all those Saturdays when his father had carried him to *shul*, slipped a yarmulke on his head, wrapped him in a *tallis*, then sat beside him on the bench and helped him follow the Hebrew prayers. (Did his father even know how to read Hebrew? When would he have learned? More likely, he'd glanced at their neighbors' books, spied the right page, and followed as best he could.) When Marcus had lost his faith and considered canceling his bar mitzvah, his father listened to his objections and quietly and persuasively reinstated his belief, if not in God, then at least in being Jewish. None of this had done Marcus any harm. Yet there seemed something unsavory about these acts having been performed by a gentile. It was as if a man pretending to be a doctor had removed Marcus's appendix, and even though the operation had proved a complete success, Marcus couldn't help but be shaken to learn that the surgeon had been a quack.

"In other ways I'm not a coward," his father said. "In the war, I ran across a field while bullets were being shot and dragged a man to safety. I saw terrible bloody sights a man ought never see."

A long time went by. The elderly man in the next bed passed gas so forcefully that Marcus jumped. "*Oy, gevalt*," the man moaned. "Tell me, dear God, what I did to deserve such misery!" As if every human fart were under God's control.

Marcus plucked a Kleenex and wiped his father's brow. His father opened his eyes and pressed Marcus's palm to his lips. "You are a good boy, and I am sorry if I failed you. What little I know about being a parent I had to teach myself. My own father cared only that I never drink or dance. He died a few months after I ran away. My mother couldn't be bothered to make inquiries. She died when you were four. Who was there to say I wasn't actually a Jew?"

The onslaught of revelations, including a gentile grand-mother who'd still been alive in Texas when Marcus was a child, rendered him mute. He wanted to get away and think. Or rather, he wanted to call Vicki and ask her what he ought to be thinking. "Pop," he said, "this isn't doing either of us any good. Why not take a nap? I'll drive to the condo and eat a bite, then I'll come back and see you later."

His father grabbed his wrist—it felt as if Marcus were being touched by a rubber glove full of lukewarm water. "We don't have much time."

"Time? Time for what? Don't tell me that you intend to get circumcised now."

"That is exactly what I do intend."

"Oh, Pop, can't we just get the folks who run the cemetery to make an exception? Would they actually refuse to allow you to be buried with Mom?"

"Of course they would refuse! Ahavath Yisroel is only for Orthodox Jews. And to be an Orthodox Jew, a man must be cir-cumcised. The night before the funeral, the members of the burial society must sit up and wash the body, and the individuals on that particular committee would immediately notice what was what. If they made an exception for me, why not make an exception for everyone?" He shook his head miserably, the plastic tube from the oxygen mask waving like a tusk.

Marcus had never seen his father's face so troubled. His lips were dry and rough and he kept licking them as he spoke. "Pop, I don't get it. Why did you bury Mom in Bubbe and Zayde's plot if you knew you wouldn't be allowed to be buried there with her?"

The tracings on the monitor erupted, as if a meteor had hit the pond. "You know how much your mother loved her parents! How could I deny her the right to spend eternity beside them?" And—what he didn't mention—how much he'd loved them, too, the Jewish parents he'd never had. "They gave us those spaces as a wedding gift. If we'd refused to be buried in their plot, we would have needed to explain the reason. I was still a young man. I thought I had all the time in the world. I assumed there would be advances."

"Advances? You were expecting the doctors were going to come up with a pill you could swallow and your foreskin fell off? Believe me, Pop, that sort of research is not high on the list of medical priorities." The mere mention of someone's foreskin falling off caused his head to swim. The two times he'd been invited to a *bris,* Marcus had needed to sit on the stoop outside until the cutting part was over. "There's no use discussing it. Your body couldn't stand the shock."

His father wrapped his hands around the rail and pulled himself to sit. "I'm going to die anyway. I might as well die a Jew."

"Pop, I can't."

"Have I ever asked anything? Have I ever, in all your years, asked you a single thing?"

34

No, Marcus thought, he hadn't. His father had taught him how to swim—albeit so Marcus could supervise the hotel pool—and his happiest memories were of his father and him washing off the stink of serving the evening meal by taking a midnight dip. His father had bought a book and used it to teach the two of them to hit a tennis ball on the single cracked court at Lieberman's. True, this was partly so Marcus could provide a partner for the guests, but he and his dad had enjoyed many a cutthroat set in the mystical pre-dawn hour before the guests got up and started clamoring for their lox and eggs. His father had given Marcus everything a father could give—and what a mother could give as well. He had cooked for him and cleaned. He had nursed Marcus through the mumps, mononucleosis, diarrhea, and upset stomachs. Marcus felt like a gambler who could never repay his bookie. Better to change your name and run away, start a new life, put your debts behind you.

Which, except for the name change, was exactly what Marcus had done. He'd moved to Manhattan, gotten his degree in accounting, and set up the kind of life in which he was free from obligations, even to himself. Rather than cook, he ate out. He sent his dirty clothes to a laundry and hired a maid to clean. He lived within his means and paid off his college loans. For Christ's sake, he didn't even own a cell phone. He owed nothing to anyone. Except, it seemed, his father.

"Pop, if the people in the burial society see a recent scar, won't they be suspicious?"

His father held up a finger, as if Marcus had finally asked a question worth answering. "If the foreskin has been removed and the survivors of the deceased can provide a certificate of conversion, the officials must accept that the individual is a Jew. As it happens, I have a friend who is a rabbi. Twice a week

I attend the services that Rabbi Dobrinsky conducts at the condo *shul.* Three times a week, we play tennis as partners. At first, he wasn't so enthusiastic. But I kept speaking from the heart and he began to see my point. Also, I agreed to leave my money to his synagogue. If you add your plea to mine, he won't refuse."

Marcus was incensed that his father had pledged his few hard-earned dollars to bribe some unscrupulous rabbi into performing a rite he ought to perform for free. He wondered if his father meant that he, Marcus, ought to add his own money to his father's "donation" in the hope that this larger bribe would persuade the rabbi to do their bidding.

"Once the rabbi is on board," his father went on, "all that remains is finding a *mohel* who will perform the circumcision."

"Sure," Marcus said, "that's all. And who do you suppose is going to circumcise a dying man?"

His father motioned toward the cart beside the bed. Marcus opened the little drawer and found a newspaper clipping about a pediatrician named David S. Schiffler, who, in his spare time, performed ritual circumcisions for the newborn Jewish males of Boca Raton. "That's quite an interesting side-line," Marcus said. "And lucrative as well."

"Don't make fun. You think a man like this, a professional man, needs what he earns performing a *bris?* He donates his fee to the Boca March of Dimes. Also, he is performing a service for the community. He comes in the home, but he does the proce-dure in a sanitary modern way, the baby isn't traumatized."

Marcus was about to remind his father that he wasn't a baby when a nurse bustled in.

"Now we will be having a soothing, refreshing bath," the woman said with a Jamaican lilt. "We can't let a man get all smelly, now can we?"

"The rabbi," his father said. "You can find him on the tennis court. He plays a doubles match at four."

The nurse drew the curtain around the bed. "First we will wash down as far as possible." She dipped a sponge in a pan of soapy water and squeezed out the excess. "Then we will wash up as far as possible." Giggling, she reached for his father's gown. "And then we must wash possible!"

As thoroughly as it irked him that a stranger would get to view what had been hidden from him for so long, Marcus was horrified at the prospect. In his mind, his father's penis grew and grew until it was a pointy-headed rocket zooming toward outer space. Before the nurse could expose his father's "possible," he dashed out in the hall. Weaving to avoid the patients and their relatives, who hobbled along the corridors three- and five-abreast, he headed for the lobby. Outside, he found his car and reached for the key, only to find the clipping about Dr. Schiffler still crumpled inside his fist.

* * *

During his father's previous bouts with hepatitis, Marcus had become acquainted with the route from the hospital to the condo. Still, he lost his way. He pulled off on the shoulder near an intersection where a cheerless man in overalls was selling the *Homeless Times* and a girl in a green bikini hawked hot dogs from a cart. The father he had known for forty-eight years was dying, as was the father who'd grown up in a poverty-stricken Baptist town and had his hand broken for drawing a picture of a girl, then glimpsed redemption in a universe ruled by Groucho Marx. In the months and years to come, whenever a question about this gentile Texas father sprang to Marcus's mind, there wouldn't be a soul to answer it.

How could such an honest man have lived such a whopping lie? And how could he have made such a *tsimmes* about the shame a lie could bring? Then again, who else was qualified to issue such a warning? For thirty-three years, the poor man had lived without sex to avoid the need to explain to a Jewish woman why he wasn't circumcised. Marcus almost wished his father had been the kind of man who would sleep with a woman he had no intention of ever marrying. *Oh, Pop, wasn't the urge to make love stronger than your fear of having your foreskin cut off?*

He knew he ought to go. With the way the retirees down here drove, if he sat here long enough someone would plow into him. Bits of red plastic from an earlier victim's taillights still littered the intersection. But Marcus couldn't move. His poor mother! It must have made her sad to know she wasn't married to a Jew. Or a man who loved her enough to face his worst fear for her sake. How isolated she must have felt, how cut off from her parents.

Unless her parents knew. How could they not have known? Now that he thought about it, his father didn't look Jewish. His name was James Sloan. What kind of Jew is named James Sloan? There had been so few available Jewish men during the war that Marcus's mother was twenty-seven when she met his father, six years older than her suitor. How could his grandparents have objected to a handsome generous man who was willing to marry their spinster daughter, live a Jewish life, and run the hotel they all loved? The only detail they hadn't guessed was that, unlike most American men, their son-in-law wasn't circumcised. Marcus did the math. Was it possible his father had only been forty-three when Marcus's mother died? Then again, Marcus had been so absorbed in pretending his mother's death hadn't nearly killed him that he'd barely noticed his father's grief, let alone his age.

Once a week, on Sunday, after the guests checked out, they'd driven to the little Jewish cemetery on the outskirts of town, where Marcus had shuffled down the path with the feigned indifference of an adolescent hiding his bitter urge to fall on his mother's grave and weep. Even now, he sometimes rented a car and drove up to visit the plot where his mother and grandparents lay beneath a monument engraved with the family name. Most of the surrounding monuments also bore the names of Catskills resorts, which reinforced Marcus's notion that owning a hotel and serving people killed you. Certainly it had killed his mother. She might have been overweight, but trying to feed two hundred and fifty guests without a salad man or a dishwasher would have killed a much thinner woman with a healthier, younger heart.

Yet who was he to say? His mother had loved running Lieberman's so much that if such interments had been permitted, she would have asked to be buried on the front lawn. Marcus missed the hotel, too. Whenever he visited his mother's grave, he sat with his back to his grandfather's headstone and imagined they were waiting for his father, the way they used to wait for him to finish some repair or settle a dispute and join them in the dining room for the *erev Shabbos* meal.

And his father had screwed it up. He'd had thirty-three years to muster the courage to check into a hospital and allow the doctors to trim his foreskin—under anesthesia, after all— and he'd put it off and put it off. Maybe it wasn't only the fear of the operation. Maybe he hadn't been able to face the idea of giving up that last little bit of the man he used to be.

But did his father actually believe this Dr. Schiffler would agree to perform a circumcision on a dying man? For a moment, Marcus wondered if a *mohel* would circumcise his father *after* he was dead, but the notion made him ill.

39

The homeless man tapped on his window and Marcus shook his head to indicate he didn't want to buy a paper. It bothered him that the guy wasn't allowed to beg but had to pretend to sell a newspaper no one wanted to read. These days, no one was allowed to give anything away for free, not even charity. Marcus saw the girl in the green bikini pointing to her cart and miming the act of eating a hot dog, so he pulled onto the road again. He was hungry enough that he could have wolfed down several hot dogs, but he didn't want anyone to think he was one of those men who would buy a woman's wares so he could look down her cleavage when she leaned in the window and set his hot dogs in his lap.

* * *

The condo development where his father lived was populated almost exclusively by Orthodox Jews. No rules excluded gentiles, but what Christian would want to settle in a place where the country club served heavy kosher meals and the tennis courts and pool were locked from sundown Friday to sundown Saturday and nearly all the residents attended services at the dumpy concrete synagogue within the development's walls? While the guard checked Marcus's name against a list, he felt the impulse to reveal his father's lie. He couldn't have said why. He felt no less Jewish than before. He had inherited his *zayde* Lieberman's dark Hebraic looks. That his mother had been a Jew guaranteed that Marcus would be certified as a Jew by even the strictest rabbi. He had attended Hebrew School, well, religiously, and—thanks to his father—had been circumcised and bar mitzvahed. His father had lived a completely Jewish life for seven decades. How could this one act of sacrifice—which most Jewish men had undergone when they were eight days old and drunk on the Manischewitz the *mohel* had given them to suck from a bit of cloth—count for so much?

The guard waved Marcus through. Of course he wouldn't reveal his father's origins. He didn't wish him any harm. As for his father's right to live in this development, God would be issuing His eviction notice soon enough.

* * *

Marcus parked in his father's space and let himself into the condo, which was stuffy and stank of mold. His father had never been a hoarder and, in recent years, had given away most of what he owned. Every time Marcus flew down for a visit, he flew back to New York with a moth-eaten cardigan or a set of wooden shoe-trees or a box of jellied fruit slices some kindly female neighbor had given his father for Passover the year before. Little remained on the condo's shelves except the novels of Leon Uris, some kitschy figurines of Jewish peddlers, and his grandparents' brass menorah. Marcus turned on the air conditioner, but the unit was so palsied his khakis and shirt were plastered to his skin before the place cooled down. The apartment, which until then had held only pleasant associations, now harbored a sinister possibility in every nook, as if the harmless geckos flitting here and there might suddenly hiss and bite.

He looked up Dr. Schiffler's number, picked up his father's rotary phone, and dialed. When he finally got through, he told the receptionist he needed to discuss a circumcision. "There are . . . let's call them complications," Marcus said, and she agreed to let him speak to the pediatrician at 6:15, when his regular appointments were done.

Marcus lingered by the phone. If only he could talk to Vicki.

But he needed to get to the tennis courts in time to catch Rabbi Dobrinsky before his doubles match.

* * *

The air was so humid Marcus could hardly catch his breath. He crossed the parking lot and reached the pool, which shimmered seductively in the sun, then walked along the path that skirted the development's man-made lagoon. The water was a sludgy brown that concealed who-knew-what creatures. Alligators? Snakes? From earlier explorations, Marcus knew the shore was lined with the mounds of fire ants. Yet he entertained the fantasy of running down the bank and diving in.

Finally he reached the tennis club, whose palm-shaded courts and coolers of icy water beckoned like an oasis. Marcus had played his father here three times, and all three times he'd lost. As kind as his father was, he turned fiendish on a tennis court. No matter where Marcus hit the ball, his father, with his willowy arms and legs, managed to reach it and return it. Even in his seventies, when his ground strokes had lost their force, he could still slice a ball so deftly that it traced corkscrews in the air before landing just shy of Marcus's racquet.

He stepped into the clubhouse and the air conditioning froze his sodden clothes. Beyond the racks of colorful nylon shorts, he found a woman in her fifties standing behind a desk. She had brassy red hair and blue-framed glasses. Racquet-shaped earrings dangled from her ears.

"Excuse me," Marcus said. "I'm looking for Rabbi Dobrinsky. My father said he always plays a doubles match at four."

The woman startled Marcus by reaching across the counter and taking his hand in hers. "You must be James's son. How is he? What a dear man. Please, next time you see him, tell him Rita Crookstein sends her love."

She wasn't his father's type, but it pained Marcus that Rita Crookstein probably felt real affection for his father and had little or no idea why he never asked her out. The clubhouse door swung open and three leathery, fit old men came in. All three wore white shorts, white polo-shirts, white cotton knee-highs, and bandages and supports around their limbs. Two of the men had fluorescent green yarmulkes bobby-pinned to their hair.

"Excuse me," Marcus said, "I'm looking for Rabbi Dobrinsky."

The shortest of the three lifted the tinted lenses that were clipped to his regular frames. He looked Marcus up and down.

"My father is in the hospital," Marcus said. "He's very ill. He sent me to ask a favor."

The rabbi took out a handkerchief and blew his nose. "I'm sorry he's in the hospital. But your father already asked his favor, and already I told him no."

Marcus rose to full height. Even at five-foot six he was taller than the rabbi. What kind of spiritual leader would act in such a peremptory way to the son of a dying man? Extortionists like Dobrinsky were exactly the reason Marcus didn't belong to a congregation. You joined, and right away someone demanded to see your tax returns and dunned you five percent, then hit you up for pledges to the building fund and the mortgage fund, donations to the UJA, service on committees. In return, all you got was a seat for Rosh Hashanah and a place to say *kaddish* when one of your parents died. Like Diogenes with his lamp, Marcus longed to find a spiritual leader who didn't see his position as an opportunity to take advantage of a person in need.

"My father told me you'd consented—" He glanced at the other men, who were making a show of examining a rack of shirts. "To do what he asked."

The rabbi unzipped his racquet. "Your father believes what he wants to believe." He said this in such a loud voice the other men and Rita Crookstein couldn't pretend they hadn't heard. "What I told him was, I will come when he is dying and offer what prayers I can. If he takes this to mean I will issue some sort of paper that says he is a Jew, he is badly misinformed."

"But if a dying man wishes to convert to Judaism? If he wishes to be buried beside his wife? After all, my father lived most of his life as a Jew."

Dobrinsky bounced his racquet against his fist. "I have known your father nine years. We play tennis. We play golf. We discuss politics and theology. More than that, we are friends. So, you don't think it's a shock, all of a sudden he tells me he's not a Jew? Against non-Jews I have nothing. But against non-Jewish friends who pretend to be Jewish . . . Pardon me if I do not believe that the reward for so many years of deceit should be an easy deathbed conversion." The rabbi flipped down his lenses and started toward the courts.

"Rabbi Dobrinsky." Marcus raised his voice. "My father is dying. You say he is your friend. Yet you can't find it in your heart to stretch the rules?" Something came back to him from his years in Hebrew School. "I thought any rule could—and should—be broken to save a dying man."

Rabbi Dobrinsky stopped. "To *save* a dying man. Not hasten his death. If this truly were a matter of bringing about *shalom biet*, peace in the family . . . But it is only about allowing your father the convenience of being buried as a Jew."

"But think of the peace it will bring my mother. Think of the peace it will bring me!"

"I am not entirely without sympathy for your case. *Your* case, not your father's. But a conversion must come about as a complete change of heart. The act of circumcision, followed by immersion in the ritual bath, the *mikveh*, must be experienced by the convert as a blessing. Your father wants his conversion should entail a sleight of hand. He wants the *mohel* and I should say *abracadabra* while he's lying there unconscious and suddenly he's a Jew. And not just any kind of Jew, but an Orthodox Jew, an observant Jew—"

The telephone rang and Rita Crookstein answered it. "Yes," she said, "the three of them are here. I'm so sorry. I'll let them know." She hung up and primped her hair. "Rabbi Dobrinsky? That was Mr. Markowitz. His wife suffered another stroke. He's calling from the hospital. He can't make your doubles match today."

All three men looked as disappointed as if the messiah weren't coming. Then they turned to Marcus.

"If you are your father's son," Dobrinsky said, "you know your way around a tennis court."

Marcus almost said no, but his vanity wouldn't allow it. "I play. But tennis wasn't on my mind when I packed to come down here." Nothing his father owned would fit. The sneakers would be too tight, and the ancient racquet his father still played with was made of some heavy metal Marcus could barely lift.

Dobrinsky motioned to the desk. "Racquets she has plenty." He looked at Marcus's feet. "Size nine, a common size. There is a dress code at this club, but I am sure you will find a suitable shirt and shorts in Ms. Crookstein's lost and found."

"You expect me to play tennis at a time like this?"

"Let me put it this way. If you fill out our fourth, I will see what I can do about your father's request."

It took Marcus a while to get the rabbi's point. Already this Dobrinsky had extracted a donation to his *shul* from Marcus's father. Now he was trying to extract a doubles game from Marcus. "Fine," Marcus said, "but only for an hour."

"An hour is all we play. In case you hadn't noticed, we are not such young men." He introduced Marcus's partner, Victor Eisen, and the rabbi's partner, Isaac Karsh. Rita Crookstein loaned Marcus a shirt and shorts. The racquet's frame was dented, as if someone had smashed it against the court, and the strings were strung too loose, but as keyed up as he was, Marcus felt confident he could beat the rabbi and Isaac Karsh with a fly swatter.

Yet once they were on the court, he muffed shot after shot. The ball failed to clear the net or went sailing out of bounds. He dribbled in serves so weak they could have been returned by a crippled Girl Scout. Sweat cascaded down his brow and made the racquet slip inside his grip. He rarely played on clay, and this threw off his rhythm. His opponents' yarmulkes were the same fluorescent green as the balls and misled his gaze. (No doubt this was intentional. Who had ever seen yarmulkes in such an obnoxious hue?) Worse, his mind was on his father. Marcus would have given anything—gallons of blood, a kidney, the very marrow from his bones—to save his father's life. Instead, he had been asked to play a game of tennis in the Florida heat so his father could have a *bris*, and this he couldn't do.

In no time, Marcus and his partner were behind five games to love. Marcus found it difficult to hit his most powerful shots against two such frail old men. What if Rabbi Dobrinsky ran for a shot and fell? What if Isaac Karsh suffered a heart attack and died?

Nor was Marcus's partner in healthy shape. When Dobrinsky tossed up a lob, Eisen shaded his eyes, scuttled backward like a crab, then shrugged and let the ball drop without trying to smash it. "Stenosis of the spine," he explained to Marcus. "I lean too far back, I could snap something in my neck and be paralyzed for life." When Eisen played at net and a shot came whizzing toward him, he stepped aside and let it pass. Worse, he was nearly deaf and couldn't hear the strategies for a comeback Marcus whispered in his ear when they switched sides between games.

Karsh was no Rod Laver, but Dobrinsky must have known he was giving Marcus the weaker partner. Marcus suspected the rabbi would try to cheat, but if anything, he was a stickler for the rules. Repeatedly, he called foot faults on Marcus, which no one had ever done, and questioned his every call, demanding to see the skid marks for any shot that landed any-where near a line. Marcus got so rattled he and his partner lost the first set six games to love, then started going under in the second set.

"Either you're not much of a player," the rabbi gloated, "or you're not trying your best. I won't even consider doing what your father asks me to do unless you win two games."

Marcus was enraged. The rabbi had mentioned nothing about how many games he needed to win to fulfill their bar-gain. As Dobrinsky prepared to serve, Marcus bent low, weaving and bobbing, forgetting everything except his desire to smash the return of serve crosscourt as deep as possible. The rabbi tossed the ball, and the serve came looping high and wide with a devious slice. But Marcus had played enough games against his father, who used a similarly deceptive spin, to know what to do. He let the ball drop, drew his racquet back and down, then whipped it across his chest.

The rabbi, who had come to net for what he assumed to be a winner, took Marcus's return in his face. His glasses went flying—the tinted lenses came off, as if a bird had lost its wings in flight—and he dropped to his knees and screamed.

Eisen helped him to a chair. Karsh doused a towel with water and laid it across the rabbi's eyes.

47

Marcus crouched beside the rabbi. "Are you all right? Can you see?" He was appalled at what he had done but couldn't keep from glancing at his watch; there was less than an hour before he was due to meet Schiffler. "You have to admit, I satisfied what you asked. If I get a *mohel* to perform the *bris*, will you sign a certificate of conversion?"

The rabbi raised his fist. "Not in a million years! This is the Almighty's way of reminding me what happens to those who turn a blind eye to deception."

"Oh come on," Marcus scoffed. "You can't seriously believe—"

The rabbi peeled off the towel, and Marcus could see red skid-marks above and below the eye. "No," he said, "I don't. But you knocked some sense back into me. I can't be party to more betrayals. I love your father. He is a very good man. But I will not sign some phony document of conversion." Squinting, he peered from the teary eye, moaned, and shook his head. "And now will someone please drive me to the emergency room before I lose what little sight God has seen fit to spare?"

* * *

Blinding a rabbi was no small matter. Had Marcus helped his father's cause or ruined it? He didn't have the time to carry out his usual calculation as to who owed what to whom. If Schiffler performed the circumcision, the burial society might assume the wound had been the result of a medical procedure in his father's final days and see no reason to ask for a certificate of conversion.

He removed his borrowed clothes, stepped into the shower, and lathered up. He soaped his belly and then his balls. How could the sight of his own circumcised prick not remind him of his father? What a little thing to have one's foreskin snipped off. Then again, what if Vicki asked that he chop off his little finger? Would he be able to do it?

No. Not even for Vicki. Did that mean he didn't love her? What would Vicki do for *him*? He'd toyed with the idea of asking her to lose a few pounds. Paula, his ex-wife, had been Manhattan thin, which at the time had turned him on. He'd never imagined he could make love to an overweight woman. But Vicki's extra weight served as an aphrodisiac. Marcus would catch himself thinking about all those rolls of flesh, the pillowed breasts and rounded thighs, the soft warm welcome of her vagina, and he would find that he was hard. Even now, his prick reared its foamy head. He worked it in his hand, then braced himself and came; a sad spurt of semen spattered the stall as Marcus wept and cursed.

By that time, he had less than ten minutes to put on his clothes and drive across town in rush-hour traffic to speak to Dr. Schiffler. He arrived twenty minutes late, parked, and ran inside. The waiting room was full; the doctor had been delayed by an emergency and was running late. Marcus was glad he hadn't missed his appointment, but it seemed a punishment that in a city reserved for the very old he should be compelled to spend an hour in a room full of kids.

He took the one remaining seat. Scattered around the carpet were miniature trucks and buses with bobble-headed passengers that fit on the pegs inside. On a table the height of Marcus's shin sat an elaborate wire structure along which a pixie-ish Hispanic child of indeterminate gender slid colorful wooden beads. When Marcus was young, doctors had provided nothing to keep a child amused except tattered copies of *Highlights*, whose goody-goody articles and harsh black-and-white illustrations had irritated him to tears; it wasn't bad enough you needed to get a shot, you also had to be subjected to pious sermons by a poorly drawn bear.

He tried to read a magazine, but the articles on newborn colic and toddlers' tantrums made him sweat. His mind wandered to his daughter, who lived on Staten Island with her mother. He loved Michelle. But she was tied up in his mind with the grudge his ex-wife held against him for not providing enough help around the house or enough money to support them. Marcus had waited to marry until he'd found a wife as self-sufficient as he was, independent to the point of fierceness, a lawyer whose job it was to ferret out fraud in the banking system of New York State. But his plan had gone too far. The day they'd moved in together, Paula had tacked up a chart on which they could record how much time each of them spent doing chores. Likewise, she insisted they spend exactly the same amount on necessities for the apartment. Marcus could understand why a woman of Paula's generation would fear that her talents might be wasted in the service of her husband's career. But he wasn't an ambitious man. He had grown up with a father who wasn't ashamed to lift a mop. The very fact that Paula felt the need to keep track of what Marcus did or didn't give made him surly and defensive.

Strangely, after the divorce, Paula's scorekeeping had grown even more precise. The amount for Michelle's upkeep was deducted from Marcus's bank account, but Paula—who earned as much as Marcus—demanded that he pay extra for his daughter's ballet and karate lessons and her stays at summer camp, and she kept track of every minute he spent with their daughter, offering monthly statements of both accounts, until Marcus felt as if the girl were a commodity in which he had purchased so many shares.

It struck him that his marriage, like most of his friends' marriages, had failed because each member of the couple had been so wary of being asked to give more than his or her fair share. What he loved about Vicki was her generosity. Like Paula, she worked hard. She was the founder of a bakery that sold muffins and croissants to yuppie groceries around the city. (As her accountant, Marcus had advised her to use less expensive ingredients, to which Vicki had replied that she would rather not bake at all than sell pastries made with axle grease masquerading as a dairy product.) But her philosophy seemed to be that if two people loved each other, they did everything possible to make each other happy. She assumed that Marcus was as generous as she was, and her love and good opinion kindled in his heart a desire to give.

"Mr. Sloan?"

Marcus looked up. The waiting room was empty. The receptionist led Marcus to an office in which a weedy pop-eyed man sat behind a desk. The diplomas on the wall were surrounded by photos of Dr. Schiffler handing oversized checks to the chairpersons of Boca charities, snapshots of children's circumcision ceremonies, and thank-you letters from grateful parents.

The doctor shook Marcus's hand. "I understand this has something to do with a circumcision. With complications, you said? An interfaith marriage, I take it? Perhaps your wife and in-laws are upset or confused about the ritual?" The pediatrician smoothed his tie, which was printed with those colorful costumed children found on products sold by UNICEF. "Tell me about your problem and I will do everything I can to make this event a *simcha*, even for the non-Jewish individuals involved."

Buoyed by Schiffler's open-mindedness, Marcus related his quandary, although even as he spoke he wondered what kind of madman would be telling such a tale. Usually, when he entered a doctor's office, it was in his capacity as an accountant and the doctor was the one who had something unsavory to explain. Now Marcus was the *shnorrer.* It wasn't a position he favored. In high school, they'd read a play in which Marcus had found a line that encapsulated his own philosophy: *Neither a borrower nor a lender be.* Yet here he was, begging favors from everyone he met. Only the fact that he was begging these favors on his father's behalf lent the begging some nobility.

The pediatrician picked up a pencil and, to Marcus's amazement, used it to clean his ears. He wiggled the pencil briskly, as if to dislodge the screwy request, then said he couldn't possibly circumcise a dying man. "I would need to put your father under general anesthesia, and between that and the procedure, I would be hastening his death. I might even kill him outright. The hospital would never allow such a thing. And my conscience would not permit it."

Marcus was reluctant to push the matter further, but he had already invested so much time in his scheme, he tried another tack. Perhaps Dr. Schiffler might be willing to perform the circumcision on his father at home? "Not under general anesthetic, but the way you do it with babies. I mean, maybe we could get him drunk?"

The doctor glanced around as if he expected Alan Funt to step out of a closet and ask him to smile. "You aren't serious. Are you? What do you think I am? I could lose my license for a stunt like that!"

Marcus raised his palms. "The joke of a desperate man. I appreciate your taking the time to listen." He reached in his pocket and removed his checkbook. "I don't suppose a donation would change your mind?"

Schiffler looked around again. By now he seemed frantic, as if he were being set up for a sting.

"What I mean is, in return for taking up your valuable time, I am happy to write a check to your favorite charity. But maybe you would prefer I send it directly to the March of Dimes rather than making it out to you?"

The doctor smiled wanly. "Yes. Certainly. Thank you. I must have misunderstood." He rose and held the door. "I'm afraid my receptionist has gone home for the day. Just follow the signs to the waiting room, then let yourself out."

Retracing his steps, Marcus passed a nurse's station on the top of which sat a cardboard box of lollipops, a pad of the doctor's letterhead, and a stack of bandages and gauze. He didn't yet have a plan. But the moment he placed the lollipop, the letterhead, and the packet of gauze in his trouser pocket, the plan began to sprout.

* * *

He found his father sleeping. His skin glowed eerily against the sheets.

"Mr. Sloan?"

Marcus turned. His father's gerontologist beckoned from the hall. "I'm glad you were able to get here in time." Marcus was suspicious of any doctor who worked in Florida—they seemed a pack of jackals that had migrated south to take advantage of the dying Jews—but his father's gerontologist, Dr. Persky, was a compassionate warm-hearted man. Boyishly thin and sweet faced, with stooped shoulders and curly silver hair, he gave the impression of eternal youth combined with extreme old age, as if he had taken on himself the burdens of his patients. "I'm sorry to have to tell you, but it doesn't look good. We don't usually suggest this, but if he continues to refuse the transplant, which, to be honest, I completely understand, there isn't anything we can do for him here. I was wondering how you would feel about taking your father home."

Home to die, the doctor meant. Marcus's stomach shrank. He had never seen anyone die. The night his mother's heart gave out, he had been at a rock concert in Monticello, his parents having granted him the evening off from his job as headwaiter in the children's dining room. At the time, he'd been relieved that he hadn't seen his mother's corpse, but later he regretted that he hadn't had the chance to ask her forgiveness for all his snotty backtalk. And the chance to say good-bye. He wasn't about to make the same mistake with his father. *Good-bye, Pop, forgive me. Good-bye, good-bye, good-bye.*

The doctor lifted his hands. "Of course, there's always the hospice center. But in your father's condition, it won't be more than a few days. And having him die at home might have certain advantages."

Advantages, Marcus thought. "Yes. I would prefer that my father die at home."

The doctor seemed taken aback at how quickly Marcus had agreed to his suggestion. "If you're sure. Perhaps you need a few days to consider all the options? Make certain you're up to the strain? Although if you do choose to take your father home, a visiting nurse will stop by every afternoon to help you keep him comfortable." He gripped Marcus's hand, and Marcus was touched to see that the corners of his eyes were wet.

Marcus went back inside the room and sat by his father's bed, stroking his yellow arm. Just as he was about to leave, his father's eyelids fluttered open.

"Hey, Pop. It's Marcus."

"Your mother . . ." He used his tongue to wet his lips. "I dreamed Claire was here. Beside me. In this bed."

Marcus shrugged to say *who knew?* "How would you like to go home?" He could see this information flatten his father's face. "Of course, if you'd rather stay here . . . Or we could move you to a hospice."

His father shook his head. "Home. No hospice." Again he licked his lips. "And the other? Dobrinsky? Schiffler?"

Marcus fought his qualms and lied. "Everyone's on board. When the time is right, they've all agreed to do what needs to be done."

His father sank back and closed his eyes. Marcus was surprised he didn't ask for details. He probably didn't want to know.

The wife of the man in the next bed reminded her daughter-in-law to bring a box of cookies for the nurses.

"What Mom is really saying," the son chimed in, "is if you bribe them with cookies, they'll come running faster if Dad needs help."

"And what's wrong with that?" the mother asked. "Just don't get the cheap ones from Publix. Go to that nice bakery in the mall. Get some elephant ears and a pound of *rugelach.* Don't skimp, we shouldn't look cheap."

Just as Marcus thought he could stand the conversation no longer, his father opened his eyes and asked, "What about the woman?"

"Woman, Pop?"

"The baker."

Marcus assumed his father was referring to the conversation about the cookies. But his father made a wavy shape in the air with one hand. "*Zaftig,*" he said, and Marcus knew he meant

Vicki. It wasn't hard to see why his father liked her. Marcus cooked so rarely he owned only two pots, but in honor of his father's visit to Manhattan, Vicki had prepared a magnificent meal, beginning with a mushroom barley soup whose flavors brought tears to his father's eyes and ending with a peach strudel so rich Marcus's father had felt impelled to kiss Vicki's hand. In Boca, Vicki had taken one peek in his father's cupboard and immediately gone out shopping; she'd returned with six bags of staples and a selection of gourmet items that Marcus was sure his father would never eat, although the next time he came to visit, all these items were gone.

"I like a woman who's got some meat and potatoes on her bones," his father had often said, a preference borne out by the fact that Marcus's mother had been anything but svelte. Which, no doubt, was why Marcus used to be attracted to skinny women. Who wanted to think he was making love to his mother?

"Marry her!" his father whispered hoarsely. "Marry that girl today!"

And Marcus didn't argue. Instead, he waited until his father's eyes had closed, got in his car, and drove as quickly as he could back to the development.

The drive seemed to take forever, as did placing the call to Vicki. *Come on*, he thought, *come on*, urging the signal north.

"Sweetheart!" she cried, her voice clotted with whatever pastry she'd been tasting. "I've been thinking about you and your father all day. How did it go? How is he?"

And out it all came, in a wholehearted, uncensored way that Paula never would have allowed. Not that she wouldn't have cared. But she would have been waiting for her turn so she could tell him what had gone wrong at her office that day.

"Oh, Marcus," Vicki said, "I can't think of anything more

upsetting. Do you want me to come down there? I could hop on the next plane."

Oh no, he said, she shouldn't even think of coming down. Whatever his father asked, Marcus had to be the one to do it. Still, Vicki's willingness to listen calmed him. When they had exhausted every possibility for solving his father's problem and had hashed out at least a few of the implications of his father's revelation about not being Jewish, Marcus felt stable enough to ask what was new with her.

"Nothing you need to worry about. That new guy I hired left a stack of towels too near the stove. You can imagine all the smoke. We lost most of a day before we could get back in the kitchen."

It touched him that to avoid upstaging his trials in Florida, she had minimized what must have been a frightening event and a serious financial strain. "I love you," he said.

"I love you, too," she said, which was followed by a pause in which she must have been wondering what he had decided about getting married. "I miss you. Call me anytime."

He almost blurted out that if having fifteen children was the price he had to pay for keeping her in his life, then fifteen children they would have. But she took another bite, and the sound of her mastication prevented him from saying any more than "I'm sorry about the fire" before he hung up.

* * *

The next morning, the ambulance drove up and the EMTs unloaded Marcus's father and carried him to his room. As his father lay in the musty condo drifting in and out of sleep, Marcus sat beside him, unable to think of anything except how much he owed this man and how little he could do to pay him back. Maybe that was the source of the resentment in so many families. The parents stewed about how much they had sacrificed for their kids while the children chafed at being saddled with all that guilt. What changed the equation for Marcus was his newfound understanding that his father hadn't sacrificed quite as much as Marcus had always thought.

For an entire day and night, his father barely surfaced from the depths. Marcus couldn't focus enough to read *Exodus* or *Reader's Digest.* He ripped the skin from a blister he must have gotten playing tennis. He bit the cuticles around his nails, peeled the calluses from his feet. To keep from giving himself a whole-body circumcision, he rummaged through the drawers. To find what, a cache of gay porn? A syringe and a vial of heroin? In the bathroom, Marcus found nothing more questionable than a pack of bubble-gum flavored floss; in the den, nothing but an envelope whose contents verified that his father had indeed left half of the few pennies in his account to Rabbi Dobrinsky's *shul.* Marcus didn't mind about the money. What made him feel cheated was the wealth of information his father would take to his grave. How had Marcus's grandparents ended up in Texas? What country had they come from? Had any of Marcus's ancestors fought in the Civil War, and, if they had, on the Northern or Southern side? What had his father's baptism been like? Had he grown up eating pork, and, if so, had he liked it?

In the kitchen drawers, Marcus found plastic forks and coupons and a stack of Christmas cards from a man who appeared to be his father's buddy from the war. The man's greetings seemed effusive. Had the sender of these cards been the soldier his father had saved? Marcus would need to let him know his father had passed away. But the cards were bare of envelopes. Hoping to find an address book, he emptied the drawer. At the bottom lay a directory of Jewish services in Boca Raton. Marcus thumbed the pages, and there, under RITUAL CIRCUMCISIONS, he saw a list of three *mohels.*

The first number was disconnected, and whoever answered the second number didn't have a clue what a *mohel* was—the directory, Marcus saw, was five years out of date. But the third *mohel* not only answered, he said he would be happy to meet with Marcus that afternoon.

"To tell the truth," he said in a heavy old-world accent, "business hasn't been so good." He laughed a wheezy laugh. "I have nothing on my agenda. I am not the type to play tennis or golf."

"I'll be there in an hour," Marcus said. When the visiting nurse stopped by, he was halfway out the door before she set down her bag.

The address the *mohel* gave him was in the only shabby section of Boca that Marcus had ever seen. The crooked mossy lanes were lined with stunted palms and flimsy pastel cottages that hadn't been painted since the fifties. Marcus's knock echoed, and when the old man let him in, the un-conditioned air, laden with pipe smoke and the odor of salted fish, nearly knocked Marcus out. By the time the *mohel* had led him to his "study"—a tiny room with a folding metal chair, a child-size desk, and shelves and shelves of books in Hebrew—Marcus was already soaked. The man offered him a glass of hot tea, but the idea of drinking anything hot appalled him. "Nothing, I'm fine, but thank you."

The *mohel* sat heavily. "*Mazel tov* on the son." He slapped his thighs, his rheumy eyes shining. But as Marcus explained the details of why he'd come, the *mohel* bowed his head—his beard brushed his chest, which was bare to the sternum, the shirt unbuttoned to either side. After Marcus finished, the *mohel* lifted his chin and stroked his beard. "So, this is quite a situation you've gotten yourself into. I suppose you would pay a considerable sum to convince me to perform this *bris.*"

Why, the wily old bastard! Of course, given the man's poverty, such a shakedown made sense. The *mohel*'s shirt was so old the fabric had turned as yellow as Marcus's father's skin. His trousers were threadbare, and he wasn't wearing shoes; his cheap white cotton socks had a hole in each big toe.

The old man grinned—gray teeth, gums an unhealthy brown. "I suppose a successful man like you has a fair amount of money in his wallet."

As a matter of fact, he did. On his way to the airport, Marcus had stopped at an ATM and withdrawn five hundred dollars, of which he'd spent only forty. He removed the wad of cash and held it toward the *mohel.* In a way, it would be a *mitzvah* to give a bribe to such a poor man. Pediatricians like Schiffler probably were putting their more traditional counterparts out of business.

Slowly, the *mohel* stood. He held out a thick-nailed hand and made a gimme-gimme motion. When Marcus didn't move, the hand darted out and snatched the cash. Marcus jumped back, and the *mohel* startled him even more by dashing the money to the floor and stomping on it as if it were a roach. With one white-socked foot planted across the bills, the *mohel* began to shout. "To be a Jew there are no shortcuts! God demanded that Father Abraham be circumcised at ninety-nine, and because Abraham agreed, God told him that his seed would be as numerous as the sands on the beach. Abraham didn't try to sneak out of the operation. He didn't wait until he was dying and no longer conscious of the pain. Think of all the pain *one* child can cause. How should Abraham have become father to *millions* of Jews with no pain at all?" Shakily, the *mohel* bent, scooped the money in his fist, and shook it at Marcus. "Get out, and take your filthy money with you!"

A moment later, Marcus stood by his car, holding the bills and trembling. It was a relief to be outside, but he was dizzy and out of breath. How was it fair to punish a person for handing over a bribe he'd been finagled into offering? And that speech about Father Abraham . . .

He dropped to his knees. *Oh, God, don't let me pass out here.* He glanced at the *mohel's* house and saw the curtain flicker. The heat blared. A lizard skittered past his hand. He touched his forehead to the sidewalk, fighting the urge to crawl back to the *mohel's* house, scratch at the door, and beg to be let back in.

That's when he heard the voice. Or rather, a wordless chant, a honeyed vibrating hum. He looked up at the sun, whose rays poured down and blinded him, wave after wave of light and heat and hum. He understood what he understood. Things were what they were. His father was what he was. *Oh, God,* he thought, *thank you.* He staggered to his feet, brushed the broken seashells from his palms, found a sprinkler on a ratty lawn a few houses down, wet his face, then drove back to his father's condo to wait and let whatever might happen happen.

* * *

He resumed his bedside vigil. And the longer he sat, the more he came to see that unless he took matters into his own hands—literally—neither he nor his father ever would have a chance to be at peace. He wanted desperately to talk to Vicki, but if he spoke to her now he would feel compelled to reveal his plan, and she would tell him that he was nuts.

"Claire!" His father's arm flailed across the mattress, groping for his wife. Then: "Reuven!" and "Hattie!"—Marcus's grandparents' names. "Reuven! Hattie! Claire!" Soon he would slip below the surface a final time. The visiting nurse arrived and left. The evening stretched ahead.

Marcus got a tumbler from the kitchen, then found his father's stash of Manischewitz and carried the bottle and cup to his father's room. He shook his father's arm. "Dad? It's time. Wake up."

Remarkably, his father opened his eyes. "Time? Schiffler's coming?"

Marcus held out the cup. "He told me to get you good and drunk."

Though his father looked frightened, he tried his best to smile. "Sure, I'm a regular *shikker*," he said, and Marcus had to laugh. Neither of his father's two religions, the real or the adopted, encouraged the use of alcohol. But Jews allowed themselves a sip of candyish wine to commemorate important rites. His father gulped down the Manischewitz, then motioned for Marcus to pour another cup and slugged that one down, too. He closed his eyes and lay back, a purple mustache above his lip, and soon he was sound asleep.

Marcus counted to a hundred, then clapped his hands by his father's ear. When his father didn't stir, he went to the den and rummaged through the trousers he had worn to visit Schiffler. He found the items he had pilfered from Schiffler's office and laid them next to his father's bed, then took a very long breath, peeled back his father's sheet, and lifted his gown.

There it was, neither overly large nor small, not so badly wrinkled, an orange-yellow mouse curled up in its nest of silky white hair. The foreskin dangled like the tip of an un-inflated condom. Intellectually, Marcus knew this was the natural state of the male organ, but the hood on his father's penis seemed somehow devious, as if it were hiding something. And the penis as a whole was nothing like Marcus's own.

How can you be my father? How can I be your son?

So it was with anger as well as love that he gripped his father's cock and twisted it, this way, then that, and then for good measure he twisted it again, as if, by sheer force, he could twist off his father's foreskin. Tears rose in his eyes. *I'm sorry, Pop*, he thought, then opened a pack of gauze. Clumsily, he stuck a pad to either side of his father's cock, which was red now as well as yellow, and wrapped the whole thing in tape so it stood away from his father's groin like an obscenely prominent erection.

Marcus printed a few hasty lines on the pediatrician's letter-head, then set it beside the lollipop.

His father jerked awake. He looked up at Marcus with pleading, befuddled eyes. "So?" he said. "Is it done?" Gingerly, he caressed his swaddled cock.

Marcus nodded.

"The pediatrician? Schiffler?"

Again Marcus nodded. Maybe, if he didn't speak, he couldn't be accused of lying. Then again, what was so awful about a lie? Maybe the immorality lay in whatever cowardice the lie was meant to hide.

"It hurts," his father said, "but not nearly as bad as I thought it would." His father smiled—a genuine smile this time—and Marcus's heart fluttered.

He handed his father the lollipop. "Here. He said you were such a good patient you deserved a treat."

His father took the candy by the stick and waved it. "A fine man, didn't I tell you? A real *mensch.*" A look of concern crossed his face. "What did he charge? I wouldn't want the fee should come out of your pocket."

Marcus picked up the sheet of letterhead and passed it to his father, who passed it back and motioned that Marcus should read what it said aloud.

"'One adult circumcision, local anesthetic. Fee: contribution in the amount of $500 to the March of Dimes of Boca Raton, Florida.'"

His father beamed. "See? This is how a real Jew behaves." He closed his eyes to savor the bliss not only of waking to find himself circumcised but also receiving proof the world held righteous men. Then he opened his eyes and moaned. "Did he by any chance leave something for the pain?"

Marcus hadn't planned another lie, but this one came out as if he'd scripted it. "Not with the shape your liver is in. Schiffler said even one Tylenol might finish you off."

His father shrugged. "My comeuppance for waiting so long. Soon the pain won't matter." He closed his eyes and, still smiling, drifted back to sleep.

Marcus used the chance to call Dobrinsky. "You can come or not come, but there isn't much time."

The rabbi's answer was noncommittal. "I'm not forgetting you nearly blinded me."

"Rabbi Dobrinsky, my father is dying. I'm calling to inform you of his condition. If you can see your way toward coming, my father would be obliged. If you can't, we'll get along without you." He hung up and went back in.

His father was awake. "I was thinking. A convert is supposed to bathe in the *mikveh*. Of course, if it's too much trouble . . . But even a dip in a tub or pool . . . "

Marcus went to the window and peered between the jalousies. The sun was almost down, but the streetlights gave off the same yellowish glow as his father's skin. "Sure, Pop. It won't be official, but we'll do the best we can." Tenderly, he wrapped his father in the sheet and lifted him in his arms. His father was so full of fluids he nearly sloshed, but Marcus had little trouble carrying him across the lot.

Unfortunately, the pool was locked. Marcus could have scaled the fence, but not while carrying his father.

He continued along the path. His father looked up with a quizzical expression, then shrugged and turned his face against Marcus's chest. Marcus saw the rabbi walking toward him. Dobrinsky wore a white shirt, dark pants, a white yarmulke, and street shoes, as if death, like tennis, had a dress code. If not for the eye patch, he might have looked like a rabbi. But the closer Dobrinsky came, the more Marcus felt pursued by a shifty old pirate determined to steal the treasure from his arms.

Marcus veered off the path, his feet sliding on the stiff slick grass. Peering at the shadowy ground to avoid stepping in a nest of fire ants, he approached the lagoon. Something in the distance splashed—a frog, he hoped, or a turtle. To be a true *mikveh*, a body of water had to be free flowing, which Marcus doubted this lagoon to be. Then again, all water came from somewhere. And flowed to somewhere else.

His shoes filled with sludge. Another step and he sank in to his calves. His father opened his eyes and looked up. Marcus looked up, too. The sky was wild with stars, the kind of spectacular array Marcus never saw in the city.

He dipped his father in the lake and bathed him the way a parent bathes his child. The way, if all went well, Marcus would soon bathe the child to whom his wife gave birth.

The sheet absorbed the sludge, and the burden in his arms grew so heavy he could barely lift it. What a bother it would be to disinter his mother and her parents from their plot at Ahavath Yisroel and move their remains to a more ecumenical cemetery where his father could join them, along with Marcus himself, and Vicki, and whatever children they might have, and, for all Marcus knew, his daughter and former wife. Let everyone in the world who wanted to be buried in the Sloan-Lieberman family plot be buried at his expense. The more guests checked in, the merrier it would be.

Above him, on the bank, Dobrinsky slipped and cursed, although the curse, being in Yiddish, sounded more like a blessing. Dobrinsky limped down to the shore and stood beside Marcus, then he adjusted his eye patch and started chanting a Hebrew prayer whose melody and words Marcus had never heard. Nothing the rabbi said or did now would exert the slightest effect on his father's religious status. But the simple fact of the rabbi's presence might bring his father peace, and for that Marcus was glad.

Oh Pop, Marcus thought, *you were such a generous man. Why did you stop a few millimeters short of doing all you could?* Because even if a person was asked to cut off his foreskin, or, for that matter, his entire cock, he needed to give and give and give, no matter how frightened the giving made him, no matter how much it hurt.

Marcus raised his face to the star-drenched sky, and even as the rabbi sang whatever prayer he saw fit to sing, Marcus composed his own prayer of thanks for having been allowed to repay even a small part of the debt he owed his father. Although really, it didn't make much sense to keep track of such matters, any more than it made sense to measure what the sun and stars gave a person as opposed to what that person gave to the sun and stars.

Milt and Moose

"Moose, Moose, they won't let me go out like a gentleman."

Milt had been a dentist for forty-one years, and today was his last day. He was selling the building, the practice, this house. He and Greta were walking away and starting over. At least, they were trying to walk away and start over.

"They won't let me leave on my own terms," he told his friend Moose. "They want me to keep working until I drop dead in the office, right beside the chair."

Moose, who owned the local milk-delivery business, had just gotten home from his morning rounds. He was heading into his house to get some sleep; Milt was heading out to drive to work.

"My hands," Milt said. "Look at them, how they shake." He held out his hands so Moose could see how badly they trembled. The dentist was tall and silver haired, with a neck rounded from years of bending over patients. He looked like one of his instruments—the curved mirror, or the explorer,

67

with its gently hooked tip. "It's nothing serious," he told his friend. "At least it's not Parkinson's. It's just some hereditary thing my father passed on." He laughed. "He didn't have anything *else* to pass on." Milt reached inside his jacket, removed the key to his Impala, and brought it toward the lock. Despite the terrible shaking, he managed to get it in. "My hands are in a patient's mouth, it's like they're too busy to shake. But people see a needle coming, or a drill . . ."

Moose chopped the air with his own hands, which were as thick and steady as spades. "Ahh, you think people care you're getting older? They call. They make appointments."

"That's the trouble!" Milt said. "They won't let me go out now, while I'm still . . . respected." He looked up at the maple at the edge of his lawn, purple-red-yellow-orange against the bright, bright blue of the morning sky, the leaves bursting with . . . *vivacity*, he thought. Why did people think autumn was a sad time? He was so happy he might have burst into a glory of colored leaves himself. The maple was taller than his house, which, admittedly, was a split-level ranch. But when he looked up at the leaves, his heart swelled, as his heart still swelled to see his wife at the foot of their bed, undressing for sleep.

He had planted this tree on a Sunday afternoon in May of '49. The next morning, he drove down to the office, and a windstorm blew up out of nowhere. When he drove home later for lunch—in those days, before the kids, Milt barely could keep his mind on his eleven-fifteen appointment—he found Greta on her knees in the battering wind, trying to wrap her body around the young tree to keep it from uprooting. The rain was wetting her thin green housedress, and her hair clung to the fabric. He had wanted to take Greta right there on the lawn. Let the tree blow to hell! But he had gotten her inside first, where she'd pulled the wet dress up and over her head, uncovering the dark moist hollows beneath her arms, and he had gone to her, nearly dying from gratitude. Her brassiere had been wet in his hands as he'd unhooked it, her nipples cold and damp to his mouth, and she had run her hands through his own damp hair and down the sides of his neck, and this had made Milt so eager to be inside her that he wouldn't let her get away to take her usual precautions and their son, Joel, had been conceived.

"You ought to be honored," Moose was saying. "Look at me. I give the dairy a year, at the outside. Home delivery? It's not as if I'm providing a product people can't get elsewhere."

Milt hadn't credited his friend with that much self-aware-ness. Greta often said it would be easier to pick up milk at the market, when she bought everything else. First you had to remember to leave the note. Then the delivery man clattered up your porch at five in the morning. If you forgot to bring it in, the milk and cottage cheese sat there all day, spoiling.

"Well, I can't stand here gabbing, I'm dying on my feet." Moose rubbed his shoulders thoughtfully. Even at sixty-nine he was built like a gallon milk-carton. That's how long they'd known each other, sixty-nine years. Their fathers had owned dairy farms on the same road, and every morning Milt and Moose had hiked to school together—skied, sometimes, in winter. Summers they drove the milk wagon to the Dairytime warehouse. They'd gone away to the war the same week, then come back the same month and built identical split-level ranches across the street from each other.

Milt knew every twitch of the other man's habits—how Moose got up in the middle of the night and drove down to the ware-house to organize the deliveries, then drove home for a second breakfast just when Milt himself was heading out to his car. They would bullshit by the curb—the weather, the kids, that putz

Reagan—until Moose started to rub his shoulders and found an excuse to go in. Milt and Moose never spoke of this, but Milt knew that Moose's wife, Cynthia, would still be in her nightgown; she had gotten the kids off to school and gone back inside to lie down, and this was the time she and Moose made love.

She had been a looker, that Cynthia. Petite, with a waist you could put one hand around—one of Moose's hands, at any rate. A sharp dresser—her folks owned the hardware store, and they could afford to keep her in those nice sweaters Milt remembered from tenth grade. He would have asked her out himself, but Moose got up the nerve first, and Cynthia didn't say no. Moose was a handsome guy then, with that build on him, and Milt so thin that he was embarrassed to look down at his own legs in P.E.

He glanced across the street now, past the unkempt shrubbery. Cynthia wasn't in their bed. No one was in their bed. What did Moose do when he awoke from his nap and there was no Cynthia? The grief of it, a man trying to rub his own back, trying to pleasure his own body.

Milt slid into the Impala and slammed the door on the thought of his friend Moose with his hands in his pants. How long had it been since he, Milt Rothstein, had laid a hand on himself? In the service, sure. In dental school once or twice, after a rough exam. But not since he'd married Greta.

Jesus, what was it with all this sex stuff? Sure, he had pleasurable thoughts if an attractive woman was in the chair. But with Greta, he didn't need to think about sex all day. It was only, well, a language, by which he meant sex was unimportant in itself, unless you had something to say and someone to whom to say it. He glanced back at his own house, and when he didn't see a light—no one in the bedroom, no one passing back and forth in the kitchen—his heart *klopped.*

No, no, it was all right. He remembered now. He had awakened that morning to find Greta up and dressed. "I have a doctor's appointment," she had said. "A check-up. You know, darling, I go every year. It's what they recommend." She fiddled with an earring. "I could wait until we move down south, but it might take a while to find someone new. And who knows what kind of doctors they have down there. Nincompoops who couldn't make a success of it up north." He had let this go as truth, returned her kiss and rolled over, but now it seemed as if she had gone on a bit longer than she needed to go on, and Greta never went on. She never fussed with her jewelry.

Moose yawned and tapped Milt on the shoulder. "So don't forget," Moose said. "There's a Rotary meeting tonight. I shouldn't tell you this, but the boys are planning a little surprise."

Just what he needed—jokes that weren't jokes, the buffoonery of old men.

"And the award!" Moose said, laughing. "Don't forget you're getting that award!"

Worse than buffoonery, a lie. Most Wednesdays, when it came time to walk to the Homestead Restaurant, Milt thought: Who needs a bunch of hick businessmen who prefer that putz Reagan to an intelligent, educated *mensch* like Carter. Better to be in his own home, eating Greta's mandarin chicken, or maybe a nice blintz and sour cream, than tearing away at the fatty prime rib in the Homestead's back room. They would have kicked him out a long time ago, but the recording secretary was one of Milt's patients, so, every week, no matter if Milt was there or not, a check went next to his name, and Andy Atkins sent the attendance records to the state chapter, and here Milt was, retiring, and the state chapter decided to honor him for forty years' perfect attendance. A certificate, a plaque—for what? For eating dinner with his wife.

Moose started up the walk to his own wifeless house, then turned back to his friend. "Meant to warn you," Moose said. "Sonny found out this is your last day. Boy, is he in bad shape, sitting on your stoop, bellowing like a *behayma*. 'Oh, how could Doc do it to me? Who's going to take care of me now?' He was yelling this, top of his lungs, five o'clock this morning."

Milt shook the Impala's steering wheel, the way he used to shake Joel by the shoulders before the kid straightened out. "Haven't I done enough for Sonny Kuppelstein? Don't I deserve a little peace?"

"I'm only telling you, it shouldn't be a shock when he's sitting there like one of those stone things with the ugly mugs, scaring away your nine o'clock appointment."

Why was Milt so irritated at his friend for saying this? It was as if Moose were using this other man, this cripple, to say what Moose couldn't say himself—*Don't go, you're deserting me, you have no right to leave.* Before Milt knew what he'd done, he'd thrown the Impala into gear and was accelerating away from the curb without so much as a wave or nod, *See you at six for Rotary*, nothing. His urgency, his fear that someone would throw a net over his car and trap him, pursued him to the corner.

He might not have stopped at the stop sign, but who should be waiting beside it but Carolyn Miller, holding up her palm, and Milt was too much of a gentleman to floor the gas and spit gravel to get away from her.

Carolyn wore a pink tennis outfit at exactly the right length for a woman in her sixties who still had nice legs, and she spoke in that sweet voice she had used all those years ago, before Milt had given her his dental school ring and she had assumed he would follow it up with a diamond, which he hadn't, and she had flushed his ring down the john.

She leaned in through the window. "Milt, I know this is presumptuous of me, but the twins are coming home for Thanksgiving."

Milt's foot twitched on the gas pedal.

"They just pleaded and pleaded. 'Ma, we know Dr. Rothstein is retiring, but maybe he could see us one last time?'"

Carolyn held out her hands as if one twin were standing in each. The girls were in their thirties, married to twin brothers in Oneonta, and they still drove down to Milt for their dental work, whether because they couldn't bear to go to someone new or because their mother encouraged them to return home and visit Dr. Rothstein. Even in their teens, Carolyn had brought them to their appointments, as if to say, *See? For all I wouldn't let you touch me, Milt Rothstein, I am not a frigid woman. Why should I have slept with a man who wouldn't promise that he would marry me?*

But Milt hadn't done much more with Greta before their marriage than he'd done with Carolyn. He had known from the way Greta kissed him that first night, on the stoop of her flat in Greenwich Village, known from the way Greta moved her lips against his, the way she curved her hand around his neck, that she didn't regard sex as, what would you call it, a trade—for a husband, a house, a child. With that kiss, Greta had set blooming in his head the knowledge of what their married life would be. He'd never even pictured having intercourse with Carolyn Tomaschevsky, or with any of the other girls from home. Except, oh, when he saw them in their gym suits and he wondered what their bare breasts might look like—large or small, round or tipped. He had grown up with these girls—they were like his sisters. But more, he sensed that none of them would do for their husbands what Greta would do for him. What she did in fact do, though he never asked her nor expected it. And she did it with such *sweetness*, such *enjoyment*, he could only moan like a schoolboy and turn and do for her what she had done for him.

"Oh, Milt." Carolyn adjusted the visor of her tennis cap and looked up at the sun. "It's all going to fall apart now," she said, "all of it, because you and Greta are leaving," as if he had punched a hole in some dam and started a torrential flood that would wash away their homes.

"What 'fall apart'? There's a time for everything." By which he meant he wasn't about to keep his practice going until he dropped dead beside the chair just so Stephanie and Lydia Miller would never have to pay ninety bucks per filling to someone who hadn't jilted their mother and still felt guilty. "Call Art Spivak, he can fix them up over the holiday."

"Oh, Art Spivak," she said. "I know all about Art Spivak," which most of them did. Ben and Adele's boy. A nice kid. All right, too nice. A *nebbish*, Milt admitted it. But who else was going to take over a practice in a nowhere town like this? Okay, so Art Spivak wasn't Mr. Personality. Milt had seen some of the kid's work—nice conservative dentistry. Artie Spivak wasn't going to ruin anyone's mouth. Art knew his limitations. He would send the tough cases to a specialist. He was a decent grateful kid; he must have thanked Milt a thousand times for putting in that good word to the admissions board at NYU and then handing over his practice for beans, not just the office and the equipment, but the patients' records, complete with a letter from Milt saying how much he hoped everyone would show Dr. Spivak the same courtesy they had always shown Milt himself.

"If the girls don't want to see Art Spivak, there's nothing

further I can say," and he drove off, feeling as if he had just escaped whatever beast he had been dreading all morning.

* * *

Sonny Kuppelstein was not, as Moose predicted, making a gargoyle of himself on the steps to Milt's office. There was only Milt's brother, Marv, an optometrist who shared the building with Milt. Marv was bending laboriously to pick up the *Times*; he might have been a hippopotamus on its hind legs stooping to pick up a newspaper with its hooves, or whatever hippos had.

"You know, Miltie." Marv grunted and snagged the paper. "You really sold me down the river. That candyass Spivak, he came snooping around here yesterday. 'Oh, hi, Dr. Rothstein, so nice to see you,' and he shakes my hand in that way where you have to wipe your palm on your trousers. Next thing, he's asking, 'So, what does your brother charge you rent?' And when I tell him my brother *doesn't* charge me rent, only utilities—what does he think, a brother collects rent from a brother?—this candyass Spivak says, 'Gee, Dr. Rothstein, I don't think I can keep up the mortgage myself. I hope you don't mind, but I'm going to have to ask you to kick in your share.' Three hundred a month! *Plus* utilities. And the plowing service in the winter, and a quarter of the property tax on top of that!"

"Damn it, Marv, you can't expect the kid to carry the building himself. I gave you the chance. You could have bought the building years ago for pocket change, and you would be charging *him* rent."

Marv slapped Milt's forearm with the rolled newspaper. "You could have kept it in your name until I closed up shop."

"I'm moving to Florida. I should have to worry the furnace here goes on the fritz some freezing night in February?"

"Florida this, Florida that. What's so great about Florida? You won't know a soul there. You'll be lonely, mark my words."

Lonely? For whom or what? Milt wanted to be rid of everything—the building, the house, the worries about malpractice. He was disencumbering himself of the entanglements of his life, Milt thought, though it wasn't a word he normally would have used. When he said that word, *disencumbering*, he saw a man struggling out of his suspenders and unbuttoning his pants, although Milt had never worn suspenders and no longer knew anyone else who did. "You'll be singing a different tune this winter," he told Marv, "when you're shoveling out from under a blizzard and Greta and I are strolling on the beach."

"Beach, beach, don't talk to me about no beaches. You bite a sandwich, a piece of fruit, what do you get except grit on your tongue?" Marv extended his own fleshy tongue and fingered it for an elusive grain. "And the filth! The bloody needles, those plastic whatyacallits, those women's things. And hot, hot. All that sun, you've got to worry you'll get a cancer. Tell me, Johnny Weissmuller, when was the last time you took a swim?"

The last time? It couldn't have been Atlantic City, a godawful honkytonk of a place even in the fifties. No, the last time had been, oh, what was it, '65 or '66. That pervert Al Marshiniac down at the Holiday Inn had told Milt and Moose and a few of the other men, "Listen, nobody much uses the pool. For a few bucks, you can have yourselves a membership, bring the wives up after work, relax, have a good time." And Milt had thought, Sure, why not, it was worth fifty bucks just to see Greta in a suit. And maybe it was the sight of her in that simple blue one-piece, the long soft beauty of her legs and arms and neck, her hair wound and pinned up, maybe that was what had put it in Milt's head to wonder where that weasel Marshiniac went after he'd greeted them in the lobby, the six or seven couples who came up every Tuesday after dinner.

Milt followed his question to the men's room, the last stall, and there was the little bastard with his eye pressed to a hole above the tank. And when Milt pulled Marshiniac away and put his own eye to the hole, at whom was he looking but his own wife, stepping out of her suit, twisting so he could see the dimpling of her shoulder, the white curve of one breast, the rich heaviness of her buttocks. He felt the way he might have felt if he'd looked through a telescope at some dazzling ringed planet, and it seemed heartbreakingly beyond any man's grasp, and yet, if Milt reached out, he could touch this planet and bring it home.

Then Marshiniac whimpered behind him and Milt turned and slugged the guy so hard his head dented the opposite partition, the first and only time that he, Milt Rothstein, veteran of some of the worst fighting in the Pacific theater of operations, had ever used his fists on another human being. And *that* had been the last time he'd seen Greta in a suit; it was as if the word *swimming* had entirely dropped out of their language since then.

"You want to lie on some beach with a bunch of strangers, fine. You still could have kept ownership of the building." Marv mimicked Art Spivak's milquetoasty voice. "'I don't mean to inconvenience you, Dr. Rothstein, but I could never rest, knowing all those newspapers are down there. They could go up by themselves, spontaneous combustion, let alone from a spark.' Candyass kid, afraid of a stack of paper."

Milt wanted to snatch the *Times* from his brother's hand and smack him on the head. *Draykopf!* Of course the papers were a

77

hazard. Marv owned copies of the *Times* dating back to V.J. Day. When Milt's cellar had filled up, about the time of Korea, Marv had begged Joe Potter, the podiatrist next door, to let him use *his* cellar. Near the start of Vietnam, Marv had slipped Eva Gorman a fifty to take over the cellar of her beauty shop, and so on down the street, through that Panama fiasco and then that Gulf thing. What did Marv think, after he retired he was going to sit around and read all the articles he hadn't read the first go-round? He would become a big-shot military strategist and consult for the Pentagon? Or maybe he would get the chance to live his life over, all the current events he'd missed? Except that the entire system of paper-filled basements might go up in flames, like one of those coal-mining towns in Pennsylvania, the houses collapsing into sinkholes, the town smoldering for years.

"Marv, Art Spivak has every right in the world to ask you to clear out that crap." Milt tried to insinuate himself past his brother's bulk. "I can't stand here gabbing all day. I've got to get ready for my nine o'clock."

"You don't think I have my own appointment to straighten up for?"

Hah! Milt laughed to himself. You *shtunk*, you haven't done one thing to straighten up that office in forty years. That fish tank, everything dead in there except the hermit crab Marv's neighbor's kid had brought home from camp in Maine, the water in the tank so black the poor creature would outgrow its shell and go looking for another and not be able to find it.

"Good morning, Dr. Rothstein." A pleasant girl in her early thirties walked up the steps. "And hello to you, too, Dr. Rothstein." She giggled at her joke. Plump, a sweet face. What was her name, Something Woods? She wore a pair of Marv's owly tortoiseshells, the kind of frames even Milt knew had gone out of fashion in the seventies. What's the matter, Milt had asked his brother, you never heard of selection? And that *zhlub* of a brother of his had picked his nose and flicked away Milt's suggestion with whatever treasure he'd excavated. "Selection? Forget selection. The patients sit there forever. 'How do you like this one, Dr. Rothstein? What about these?' Glasses is glasses. They're for how you see, not for how you look."

Marv offered only three choices—the big tortoiseshells for the women (Greta hated her pair, she only wore them because how would it seem, she didn't go to her brother-in-law for glasses), and black wire aviator frames for the men (Milt, Moose, and Marv each wore a pair), and those sparkly frames with points for kids—blue for boys and pink for girls. If you stood by the traffic light long enough, you would see nearly everyone in town go past in those tortoiseshells, or those black aviators, or those blue or pink sparklers. Marv didn't have his own kids—whether it was his fault or Flo's, Milt never found the tact to ask—but here was an entire population whose appearance Marv had influenced as surely as if he had *shtupped* every woman who sat in his chair, which he nearly did, the way he climbed in their laps with that instrument of his, peering in their eyes. *Oh Marv, Marv, with your dusty newspapers and your* farshtunkeneh *fish tank. You're my older brother, I tried my hardest to look out for you, but for Almighty sake, it's supposed to be the other way around!*

"Dr. Rothstein? Could we go in now? I have to bring some cupcakes to my son's class at ten o'clock."

"Have a little patience," Marv cautioned her. "This is my brother's last day, a man doesn't rush such a moment." He turned to Milt. "You tell that *pisher* Spivak I don't pay more than utilities, and the newspapers stay. Then you can go enjoy your retirement."

* * *

Milt's receptionist, Olivia Golden, was packing into a cardboard box the orange-juice can covered with yellowing macaroni shells her son Hunkie had glued for her in elementary
school, the golden hammer that Hunkie had been awarded
for his talents in shop, a stack of back issues of *McCall's*, and a
bag of the butterscotch candies she always sucked. She
plucked a tissue from a holder decorated with a wool jacket
she had crocheted herself, swabbed her eyes, blew her nose,
then tossed the tissue in the wastebasket. Sure Milt felt bad,
but was it his fault Artie Spivak preferred to work with a
trained hygienist instead of a receptionist who could barely
keep the billing and insurance procedures straight? Two-
handed dentistry was dead. The kid already had hired a girl
who could clean teeth in the back chair while he himself,
Artie, did the tough work out front. Wasn't that why Milt had
installed the second chair all those years ago? He just had
never gotten around to hiring an assistant. He liked his privacy. And he was too . . . sensitive to work so close to a strange
woman. Artie Spivak was a single man, no reason he couldn't
hire a hygienist. Was Olivia a slave, a concubine, that she
should be passed along from master to master? Milt did what
he could to soften the blow—salary and insurance through the
end of the year—and he tried to pull a string to get her a place
as an admissions clerk at the hospital. Was it his fault they were
laying people off?

"Oh, Doctor." Olivia plucked the last tissue, and it upset
Milt, seeing that last tissue pop up and another not take its
place. That, plus Milt felt responsible for anyone crying in his
office, as if he should have foreseen the trouble and taken the

proper prophylactic measures, or, neglecting that, should accomplish whatever restorative actions were required.

"Olivia, get a hold of yourself. Nothing is so terrible. No one is sick." He told himself to stop right there, but next thing he knew, he was telling Olivia that he had decided three months' salary wasn't enough and he was doubling it to six.

"Oh, thank you, Doctor!" she said, even before he finished, in a way that made Milt see what a pigeon he was, she'd had this show planned. He wouldn't have put it past her, the way she'd used up that last tissue at just the right moment.

"Doctor, I should tell you, there's one more thing . . ."

Which he wasn't about to give her, lay it on thick as she might.

"Sonny Kuppelstein was here this morning. Doctor, you say he's a harmless man, but this morning you might have thought otherwise. I don't know what he was shouting, but I wouldn't let him in, and he finally ran off." She unwrapped one of the butterscotch candies and palmed it in her mouth in the manner of a woman resorting to a tranquilizer. "I wouldn't be surprised if he comes back."

Was this what the cramping of his intestines had been about, the dread of Sonny Kuppelstein throwing a scene? "Please," he told his receptionist, "don't let him in if I'm working on a patient."

Tearfully, she nodded, although both of them knew how ineffectual she was in holding back Sonny Kuppelstein if he wanted to come in.

* * *

In the privacy of his inner office, Milt unbuttoned his shirt and hung it on the hook behind the darkroom door, then slipped into the white vinyl jacket that previously had hung on that hook, snapping it along the shoulder. He flipped open the sterilizer and lifted the instruments from the steam, wishing he hadn't thrown these into the deal he had made with Artie Spivak. Did a musician give away his violin just because he stopped giving concerts? Then Milt thought: Where was the comparison? A violinist could play for his own enjoyment, at home, but what would a dentist do, work on his own mouth, or his wife's?

"Miss Sink is here," Olivia said from the doorway, and she handed him the large index card on which was noted the dental biography of Generva Sink, Milt's first and oldest patient. When he'd opened his practice, he had been so grateful for Generva Sink's trust that he had charged her half the going fee. He *still* charged her half price, but whenever Olivia handed her a bill, Generva Sink stood there calculating and recalculating, as if Milt had gotten the addition wrong. She had been his math teacher in high school, and he retained the painful memory of standing before a chalked equation for half an hour, and when that didn't improve his computational skills, having his forehead smacked against the board.

"I suppose you think I'm going to offer you good wishes." She stood beside his chair, straight as a rubber-tipped pointer. *Her* hands didn't shake. "I am ninety-three years old, and the probability is high that I will not live more than a few years longer. One would think that one's dentist would have the courtesy to wait until his oldest patient died before he retired." She stood waiting for an answer, as if life were a math problem Milt was too dull to comprehend.

"Generva," he said, though he had never before called her anything but Miss Sink—"speaking as one adult to another, I have never given you cause for complaint."

82

"Now Milton. Speaking as one adult to another, I thought you would be able to tell a compliment from a complaint. I certainly didn't hear anyone begging me to stay at my post when I stepped down from teaching." She sat sideways on his chair, then, knees tightly pressed, drew her legs up and onto the footrest. "Why don't you take care of everything that might need taking care of, and I won't have to trouble Arthur Spivak, who, though he has a better head for mathematics than you do, could barely, I am convinced, even now tie his own shoes." She crossed her bony arms, closed her eyes, and opened her mouth in a tense grin, as if she wanted Milt to spare extra work not only for Artie Spivak, but also the undertaker.

And so Milt clipped a bib across her age-flattened chest and went about his business—the excavator, the drill, the amalgam and mercury, pack, shape, all done, only a few sharp breaths from Generva Sink to remind him that this was a living woman on whom he worked. She was ninety-three years old, and she would die and take with her all her knowledge of mathematics, as Milt himself would die and take with him all the learning, intuition, and dexterity he had acquired in four decades as a dentist. That was a man's life. He devised his own technique for fabricating an anterior crown, taught himself the best way to remove an impacted lower wisdom tooth, then he went to his grave and whoever took his place started over from scratch. Artie Spivak could buy Milt's instruments and his record cards. But he couldn't buy Milt's brain. Or his hands. Just as well. The human mouth was only so complex. If Artie were able to inherit Milt's knowledge, he would have nowhere to progress to.

Milt plucked the last wad of gauze from Generva Sink's cheek, which collapsed in a hollow way that frightened him. "That ought to do it," he said loudly, so she would startle awake. He saw she couldn't rise from the chair and offered her his arm.

"My advice to you, Milton Rothstein, is to keep your mind active."

He thought she was going to assign him math problems to do in his retirement, and he was going to tell her in sharp terms that he had no intention of doing them, but he heard a commotion in the waiting room. The hairs on his neck pricked up.

"No! The doctor is with a patient! You can't go in there!"

Generva Sink, as if she too feared this visitor, untied her purse and handed Milt a check for whatever sum she had determined ought to cover whatever work he might do. She walked as quickly as she could past Olivia Golden and the dark shape she was wrestling.

"*Ver vet zikh farnem mit mir? Blayb! Blayb!*" The man bellowed like a bull granted human speech, but Milt understood what he had said—*Who will care for me? Stay! Stay!*—because Milt had grown up with this bull.

"*Loz op dos meydl!*" Milt ordered. *Leave the girl alone!* And Sonny did as he was told. He let Olivia Golden go. Then he charged Milt, grasping him around the shoulders and laying his shaggy head across Milt's smock. The odors of urine, sardines, and Vitalis nearly gagged him. He thought the heavy body would pull him to the floor.

"*Genug!*" Milt cried. *Enough!* And he meant not only enough of Sonny's carrying on, but enough of Milt's repaying a debt he had never owed. Were they related? No. Well, all right, there was some sort of shirttail connection between Milt's grandfather and Sonny's grandfather, way back in Galicia. But mostly it was an accident of proximity—Sonny's father's farm had been up the road from Milt's and Moose's fathers' farms, and those first two years of school, they'd all walked down the hill together. Back then, in second grade, Milt and Sonny had resembled each other so strongly that their teacher, Mrs. Milhaus, had asked in a puzzled way if the boys were brothers, as if Jews used the suffix "-stein" to show they were related. Then Sonny had that first horrible fit, thrashing in the row between his desk and Milt's. The pencil Mrs. Milhaus jammed between Sonny's teeth snapped, and that was the last anyone at school saw of Sonny Kuppelstein.

Sonny's mother had been bad-mouthing Sonny's father for years. He was, she said, a stupid farmer who was good for nothing but shoveling cow shit, and their son's terrible disease was his fault. The few times Milt went over there on an errand, he found Sonny in the barn, which was where Sonny went to have his fits—fifteen, sometimes twenty fits in one day—in the manure-sodden hay among the cows. Year by year, Sonny had grown more twisted and more distorted, so Milt came to think of Sonny as some ill-fated shadow of himself; all the bad luck Milt should have had visited on him in the normal course of a human life had been visited on Sonny Kuppelstein instead. Sonny had been a handsome boy, but who could tell that now? If Hollywood wanted to make a Yiddish version of *The Hunchback of Notre Dame*, well, here was their star.

And then, miracle of miracles, a drug was invented and Sonny's seizures stopped! That wasn't progress, the hunchback left his barn? Too bad he couldn't read or make his own living—the mother should roast in Hell, Milt thought now, ruining a child's life from her own embarrassment. And the husband giving in to her . . . though at least Mr. K. had made sure Sonny would get a little check each month from the sale of the farm, on top of the disability, enough to pay Milt for the dental work he managed to do for Sonny. Because even miracles have their side effects—the Dilantin swelled Sonny's gums so badly his teeth dropped out, and the poor son of a bitch couldn't sit still long enough to get fitted for dentures, so Milt had to work on Sonny's mouth practically running around the office after him, and the dentures never did sit right, they slipped out and cracked every few months.

Oh, Daddy, they have a name for people like you, his daughter Wendy said. *It's a disease, thinking you have to take care of everyone.* As if his daughter were the authority on taking care of people. She moved every six months—West Coast, East Coast, Ohio, Alabama, she thought it was a big sacrifice she had to take off a few days from the newspaper where she worked when Greta had that lump removed. A lump in the breast, now *that* was a disease. It was *not* a disease that a person should enjoy taking care of other people. Okay, maybe there was a little bargaining involved—*I help him and You help me.* But did that make taking care of people a disease?

"*Ikh vel nisht geyn!*" Sonny bellowed. *I will not go!*

Sonny was still hanging on to Milt, pawing at him, fat tears struggling along the patchy stubble of Sonny's cheeks, and all this so revolted Milt that he found the strength to push him off. That was the trouble with helping a person like Sonny. You reached a point in your life where—it was only the truth—you wished that he were dead.

Sonny slumped against the wall and let his monstrous bulk slide to the floor. He sank his big face in his palms and cried: "*Ikh vel nisht geyn!*"

"So stay!" Milt told him. "Only don't make such a fuss."

Sonny did as he was told, sobbed and rocked softly in the corner through the rest of Milt's morning appointments, all of whom were too busy chiding Milt about his retirement to notice Sonny. How could he desert them? How could they trust another man to do anything in their mouths? Milt grew angrier and angrier, his hands shaking so badly he dropped a scaler, and when he picked it up, it was all he could do not to jab it through Sonny's heart.

Then, mercifully, it was lunchtime. He thought of the bowl of tomato soup and the cheese sandwich and glass of cold pineapple juice waiting on the kitchen table at home, imagined Greta telling him about her ride to Roscoe that morning, how the doctor had said her breasts were fine, she could wait another year before getting them checked again. After lunch, Milt would lie down for a little nap, and Greta would lie down with him.

But when he called home to tell her that he was on the way, there was no answer. He let the phone ring, figuring yet again how long it must have taken her to drive to Roscoe and back. Maybe she had turned off at the Beaverkill River to sketch the covered bridge?

He grew so dizzy from the effort of performing these calculations that he staggered back past Sonny Kuppelstein—a mound of moaning laundry—and slumped into the spare dental-chair in his back room. He must have dropped off to sleep, because he dreamed he was working on himself, dentist and patient both, his hands shaking in his own mouth so badly that he started yelling at himself: *You're a shame to the profession!*, until he jerked awake, hungry and woozy, with Olivia Golden calling him from the door to announce his one-thirty appointment.

How could he go back to work? It was as if he had been laboring with someone in his sleep, a man as large as Sonny—who, thank God, was gone from his corner—and every joint in his body ached. He splashed water on his face, ran his wet fingers through his hair, and then he was all right, he worked the entire afternoon without losing his temper. *This is the last patient you'll ever work on,* he lectured himself, but he couldn't convince himself to care. Only after he had settled the gridded tray of instruments back in the sterilizer and begun unsnapping his smock and lathering his hands did he panic. Without these rituals, these ablutions, what would give his days structure? A mistake. All of it, a big mistake. He had thought he was cutting himself free of the net that entangled him, but it was the safety net he'd gotten rid of.

"Doctor?" Olivia looked in. "Oh, I'm sorry!" She had never seen him in his undershirt. She tried to wipe away her tears, but she couldn't, because she was still carrying that cardboard box. "Doctor, you've been very good to me, and to Hunkie, and if there's anything I can ever do . . ."

Do? For him? A woman whose whole professional life could be contained in a cardboard box?

She stepped forward to hug him, but the box was in her arms, which was just as well, Milt being in his undershirt. "Oh, Doctor, I hate to leave this way, so quick, but I can't hold this box much longer. Good-bye, Doctor! Good-bye!"

When she was gone, Milt buttoned his shirt, went out to the bare desk and rummaged through the drawers. All he found was his appointment book. Pens. A few stamps. He opened the book to see who was coming in the next day, and the empty page startled him.

"Milt? Miltie, are you in there?"

His friend Moose stood by the coat rack, this man Milt had known for sixty-nine years and whom he was now moving away from.

"Milt? You ready?"

Milt stumbled from the shadows and wrapped his arms around his friend.

"You goddamn son of a bitch," Moose said, "it's about time."

"Moose, Moose, I never stopped to think. Why don't you come with us? Give away the business. Do you need the aggravation? All those widows down there, a healthy guy like you . . ."

"Ahh, widows, just what I need." He pushed Milt back. "I'll drive down for a visit. If it's as good as you say, maybe I'll unload the dairy, get what I can for the house."

But Milt knew his friend would never move. It was like some war movie, the guy whose hitch was up making plans to meet his buddy in New York, after the big battle, and both of them knew the buddy would never live to show up.

They walked through Milt's foyer, and Marv was suddenly following them, as if he had been peeking out his office door, waiting until they went by.

"You talk to Spivak yet? About the rent? About the papers?"

Milt didn't bother with a reply. Marv asked for these impossible things only because he didn't know how else to talk to his brother, the way some people never prayed to God except to ask Him favors. Something else was on Milt's mind. Had he unplugged everything? Locked the office door behind him? Well, so what if he hadn't. The thief would be stealing from Artie Spivak.

Still, it was as if someone were following them. Milt looked back, expecting to see Sonny Kuppelstein lurching along the walk, but Sonny wasn't there.

Oh, who wanted to sit in a smoky restaurant eating fatty meat with a bunch of old farts? Let them give their award to the man who'd attended all those meetings in his place. Milt would be home with Greta, who surely must be back from her appointment by now.

He stopped, right there in front of the post office. *Fool!* he thought. She had been home all along.

89

Moose and Marv kept walking.

"I'll see you later," Milt cried out, and he started running up the hill to his house, up and up through air that was the same butterscotch gold as those candies Olivia Golden liked to eat, past the maples with their quivering yellow leaves. *Lucky. Too lucky. Got away from the farm, made it through all that fighting, through dent school—thank the GI Bill for that. Then Greta—you didn't deserve her. A daughter, then a son, both healthy normal kids.*

He passed the boarding house where Sonny Kuppelstein lived, and Milt saw in his mind's eye Sonny's father, a big sloppy man, though a kind-hearted one, lowering his suspenders and unbuttoning his pants and walking glumly to the bedroom he shared with that *yachne* Sonny's mother, and Milt wondered if he had in fact ever seen Sonny's father unbuttoning himself that way. Some boyhood glimpse? But how could Milt have known that Sonny's mother would be waiting in that bed, yellow slip pulled grotesquely above her thighs, scolding her husband as if he already had failed to please her? And why should Milt be thinking about this *now*, for God's sake?

Gasping, he hurried past the maple on his own lawn, noticing the spot where Wendy's cat had scratched the trunk, the claw marks now two feet long and as widely spread as if a saber-toothed tiger had raged there, and Milt felt as if that same sabertooth might be crouching behind his own front door.

Not a light was on inside, although Greta's keys were on the metal-and-glass table beside the door, with a glossy brochure such as a doctor might give you to explain a diagnosis so terrible he couldn't bear to explain it to you himself.

Greta herself was in the living room, staring out the back window, not out the kitchen window in front, as she usually did, so it was as if she had chosen to look backward, at their past, instead of at their future. She wore a dress so dark the only luminous thing in the room was her neck. *Long hair*, he thought, then *no hair*, and he slammed his fist so hard against the glass table that Greta screamed and jerked around to face him. The silence was hissing at him already, and he muttered back, indistinctly, so maybe Greta thought he was cursing *her* instead of God.

"You son of a bitch!" he said. "You couldn't have waited a little longer? All these good years, and now *this*?"

Milk

How many nurses cared for her needs? The first dressed Bea's wound, a puckered red mouth silenced with staples. A second nurse brought her a cup of chilled juice to wash away the sour taste in her mouth. A third nurse, a man, massaged her sore back.

Then a fourth nurse came in, a small dark-haired woman with a pen in her curls. She knelt beside Bea's bed and covered her feet with paper slippers, then helped Bea to stand and shuffle to the bathroom. Bea's bladder was bursting, but everything below her waist was so numb that nothing came out. When she finally gave up, the toilet bowl was gory with blood and clots of tissue. Had a mess like this really come from her body? Even as she stood there, blood dripped to the floor. She bent to wipe it up and nearly passed out. Too embarrassed to ask the nurse to do this for her, she left the blood on the tiles. The nurse handed her a belt and a sanitary napkin as thick as a book, then helped Bea lie down.

"If you need anything at all pull that cord by your bed and ask for Patrice." The nurse tapped a pill into Bea's palm. "Do you want your baby?" she said.

She was asking, of course, if Bea wanted to see him. But the question Bea heard was: Do you want to keep the baby you've given birth to?

She hadn't conceived him on purpose. She had slept with a man without taking precautions, like any ignorant schoolgirl. But she had decided to keep him. She had worked with abstractions for so many years that she'd forgotten it was possible to catch a glimpse of the thing in itself. When she'd realized that a fetus was growing in the universe deep inside her womb, she couldn't bear to abort it. She had talked to it for months, asking it questions. She had looked forward to meeting it as she would have looked forward to meeting an alien who could tell her what life on another planet was like.

But for now she was tired. She swallowed the pill, then slept like a woman who has been up for three days and has just given birth to an eleven-pound child.

* * *

She awoke to a gong. Cheering. Applause. A floor-length blue curtain surrounded her bed. From beyond it came the sounds of a television turned up to full volume.

An orderly brought her soup. The warm salty broth tasted so delicious that Bea savored each sip. Then she turned to watch the sun set above the river; the buildings dissolved until only the lights in their windows were visible. A distant observer would have guessed that the city was nothing more substantial than a few panes of glass with light bulbs behind them, as earthly astronomers had assumed for so long that the universe was composed of comets and stars, of things they could see. Instead, it turned out that all but a fraction of the cosmos was dark, invisible matter—black holes, some new gas, giant cold planets.

Bea looked around, as if someone could see her thinking about invisible matter instead of about her child. She heard her roommate say: "Lie still, stop your wiggling." Bea was certain that if only she could watch another mother diaper her baby, she would learn to do this herself, but the heavy blue curtain blocked her roommate from view.

* * *

In fact, Bea didn't see her roommate until late that afternoon, though the woman's TV was on the whole time—soap operas, game shows, even cartoons. Every so often, the woman groaned. Then, about four, the curtain rings squealed, and Bea's roommate emerged. She was short, but so broad that her johnny wouldn't close, exposing a long dark swatch of buttocks and spine. She was thirty, maybe older, her hair shapeless and short. Crooked in one arm was a half-naked child; in the other hand, a diaper. She scuffed to the bathroom in her blue paper slippers without glancing at Bea. After ten or fifteen minutes, she opened the door and scuffed back beyond the curtain.

When Bea hobbled to the bathroom to use the toilet, she saw a mustardy smear on the lid of the trashcan. Why hadn't the woman wiped up her baby's feces? Well, some people just weren't clean. Then she chided herself for thinking that. Wasn't it more logical that her roommate hadn't noticed the dirt? Or she still was too weak to juggle a baby and a wet paper towel? She probably had left the smear where it was in the confidence that the janitor would wipe it away. Though the next time he came, he left the smear on the can . . . and the stain of Bea's blood on the tiles beside the bowl.

* * *

The nurse rolled a Plexiglas crib through the curtain. The baby inside the crib was swaddled in blankets. His eyes were screwed tight, but his mouth was wide open, like the mouth of a pitcher waiting for someone to fill it with milk.

"He's hungry," Patrice said. She laid the child in Bea's lap, across her incision.

This is my son, Bea repeated to herself, but the fact seemed unreal. He was heavy and round, with a triple chin and jowls; she was gaunt, with high cheekbones. (Did he look like his father? She could barely recall.)

"What's his name?" Patrice asked.

"Isaac," Bea told her, and, as she named him, he suddenly seemed real.

"Isaac," Patrice repeated. "Biblical names are so full of meaning."

Bea didn't bother to explain that she had named her son after Isaac Newton.

"Time to get started," Patrice said. "Your milk won't come in until tomorrow, at least, but you both need the practice."

Bea weighed a breast in one palm: it felt like a Baggie with a spoonful of milk in the bottom. She lifted her son. He was crying from hunger but wouldn't turn his head to suck.

"Here's the trick," Patrice said. Gripping Bea's nipple, she rubbed it across the baby's cheek.

As if by arrangement, Isaac turned toward the nipple and

opened his mouth. But when he clamped down his gums, the pain was so intense that Bea cried out and jerked back. He was wailing more shrilly. She let him latch on again, steeling herself not to push him away. The pain abated slowly. Still, as he sucked, she felt a vague irritation, as if a street-corner beggar kept pulling at her arm.

"That's enough," Patrice said, just as Bea started to feel more at ease. "I'll take him to the nursery. Here's a pamphlet to study." The cover showed a mother in a lacy white nightgown smiling down angelically at the cherubic infant nuzzling her breast. "A bruiser like this will want to eat every hour," Patrice said. "He'll be an eating machine. You've got to relax and let him eat!"

* * *

It was after eleven, but Bea couldn't fall sleep. In another few days she would have to take her child home. She had never been alone with a baby. Her mother lived in Cleveland and was legally blind. Few of her friends or colleagues had children. She had read books about babies, but she sensed that a new kind of knowledge was called for.

Still, she might have been able to fall asleep if only her roommate would turn off her TV. Bea hated to ask, but maybe if she asked politely, pleading the strains of their common ordeal.

She crossed the room, barefoot, and nudged aside the curtain.

The woman sat with her knees drawn up to her chest and her baby propped against her shins. She was watching a talk show whose dapper black host Bea knew she ought to recognize.

He said something about a basketball player named Larry, and the woman snorted through her nose.

"I didn't mean to disturb you. It's just, well, it's late."

The woman seemed to expect Bea would do what she had to do—take her pulse or draw blood—and leave her alone. She stared at the screen with such fierce gravity that no light leaked out.

"Your baby," Bea said, just to make herself known. But then, to determine what to say next, she had to look at the child. It wore a frilly pink dress. Thick auburn hair curled past its ears. Its coppery brown skin was lustrous and smooth. "She's pretty," Bea said.

"Huh. That child ain't no she." The woman seemed to say this without moving her lips; Bea needed to shut her eyes to concentrate to make out what her roommate was saying.

"Oh, I'm sorry. I didn't—"

"Ain't your fault. Didn't I buy all these dresses? How's anyone supposed to know a baby's a boy if he's wearing a dress?"

The thought crossed Bea's mind that only a poor, uneducated woman would predict her baby's sex based on some old wives' tale. "You thought you'd have a girl?"

"'Thought' nothing. Those doctors took a picture with that sound thing, said they couldn't see no Johnson, I had me a girl."

Bea suddenly felt ashamed, as she did when a colleague found a mistake in a paper she had written. The baby started to fuss. Though his mother's huge breasts swelled beneath her johnny and were ringed with wet cloth, she poked a bottle in his mouth. Bea almost believed she did this to spite her. "What's his name?" Bea asked.

"Only name he's got is fit for a girl. Can't think of no new name until I ask his father. Man don't like it, his boy gets some name he ain't said he liked."

Bea couldn't help but think that a man who cared so much about his son's name ought to have attended the baby's birth. "Did you have a cesarean?" She asked this for reasons she didn't like to admit: if the woman said no, she might leave the next day and be replaced by a roommate who wouldn't make Bea self-conscious or watch TV all the time. "Or was it natural?" she said, to mask her suspicion that the woman didn't know what "cesarean" meant.

"'Natural,' huh. Last time I was in here I had me twin girls. Doctors cut my belly open, I went home in two days. This time I had this teensy little boy, came out on his own the minute I got here, no cutting, no drugs, I can barely stand up. Hurts me down there like a sonofabitch."

The woman pushed the buttons on her remote until she found the news. A snowstorm. A plane crash. The mayor of Washington, D.C., had just been arrested for buying cocaine. According to his lawyer, the mayor had been framed by government officials waging a vendetta against powerful blacks.

"Huh." The woman snorted. She turned to face Bea. "What you think? Think he's guilty?"

Did she? Of course. "He's innocent until they prove he isn't," Bea said.

Whatever the test she'd been given, Bea had failed it. The woman rolled toward the curtain, her backside toward Bea and her fleshy black forearm shielding her son. Then she seemed to fall asleep as a movie about Pearl Harbor began to unroll its credits over Bea's head.

* * *

Someone was jiggling Bea's leg.

"I'm sorry," Patrice said, "but you'll have to get used to it."

Patrice handed her Isaac. He was crying again. "I don't want to worry you, but if you can't feed him soon we'll have to give him formula. Then he won't want to suck. And if that happens, well, your milk will never come in."

His mouth worked Bea's nipple. Where was this milk supposed to come from? Bea wondered. Why couldn't she simply will it to be?

The baby sucked at each side for exactly eight minutes; Patrice timed him, eyes trained on the watch on her sharply cocked wrist.

"You don't have to do that," Bea said. She heard an unfamiliar edge in her voice.

The nurse stopped and stood blinking. She picked at the beads trimming her sweater. It occurred to Bea that Patrice was as uncomfortable with people as she was. Unlike the other nurses, she couldn't seem to sense what a patient might want. Bea pitied her for being so poorly suited to the job she had chosen, as she pitied the student who had been her advisee for the past seven years; he thought that *having vision* meant seeing stars clearly through a telescope.

Patrice stopped picking at her sweater. "Never mind. I can be that way sometimes. We'll try again tomorrow." She wheeled the crib toward the door. Beyond the blue curtain she said to Bea's roommate: "Wake up there. Wake up. Don't you know you could crush her? Here, let me take her back to the nursery."

"Uh-uh. You leave that baby right where he is. I don't want my baby in no nursery."

Bea wondered if her roommate actually believed that the nurses would harm her son. She was being . . . what was the word? *Paranoid*, Bea thought as she managed to fall asleep.

* * *

It was just after breakfast. A girl with red hair poked her face through the curtain. "Statistics," she said. She consulted her clipboard. "Are you Beatrice Weller?"

Bea nodded.

"Maiden name?"

"Beatrice Weller."

The girl regarded Bea closely. She asked what Bea "did."

"I'm a cosmologist," Bea said. She started to explain that cosmologists were scientists who studied the universe—how it formed, how it grew. But the girl interrupted.

"You do make-up? And hair?"

Bea surprised herself by saying, "Um. Sure."

"Do you mind if I ask how much you charge for making someone over? Before, you know, and after? Could you maybe do *me?*"

"Oh, no," Bea said. "I couldn't. I don't have my . . . tools."

The girl seemed disappointed. "Are you sure? There's this guy I just met. You'll think I'm silly, but, I don't know, maybe you could give me some beauty tips? I get paid Wednesday." She leaned forward, head cocked, palms pressed together.

"I suppose. I'll be here until Friday." She would think of something later. Already she sensed that, once you started lying, it was easy to say things you didn't mean.

"Oh, thanks!" The girl asked a few last questions: Bea's nationality (U.S.) and her age (thirty-six). "I'm sure you had the sense not to smoke or use drugs while you were pregnant." She made a mark on some form, promised to return for her beauty consultation, then dragged a chair behind the curtain. "Hello? Coreen Jones?"

Since the name was so common, it had the effect of making Bea's roommate seem less real, not more so, as if she weren't a person but a whole class of objects: chair, atom, Jones.

Bea couldn't help but eavesdrop. Coreen mumbled her answers, which the girl asked her to repeat again and again, her voice louder each time.

"You're unemployed?"

"No, I ain't."

"You've got a job?" the girl asked. "Where?"

"At a school."

"You've got a job at a school?"

"Don't worry," Coreen mumbled. "All I do is cook there."

And so on, until the girl asked Coreen for the name of her child.

"Ain't got one."

"Excuse me?"

"I said my baby doesn't have no name."

"She doesn't have a name?"

"It's a he, not a she, and he doesn't have a name."

Tell her, Bea thought. *It isn't your fault. You're not a bad mother.* But Coreen explained nothing.

The girl asked Coreen if her child had a father.

"Think I done it myself?"

"I *meant* are you married."

"Man never needed no piece of paper to make him a father."

The girl asked for his name. Coreen mumbled an answer. "Can you spell that?" the girl asked.

"Always make sure I can spell a man's name before I have his baby." Coreen spelled the letters slowly: "N . . . A . . . T . . . E." This ordeal over, the girl asked Coreen for her "ethnic category."

"American," Coreen said.

"Oh, no," said the girl, "I mean, where were you born?"

"America," Coreen said.

"Well, what country do you come from?"

"Come from? Way back? Guess you could say Sierra Leone."

"That's not a country. It's a mountain. In Mexico."

"Sure it's a country. Sierra Leone."

"All right then, where is it?"

"West Africa," Coreen said.

"But that's not a country! You mean South Africa."

Bea heard Coreen grunt. "You so smart, put down whatever country you want. You got any more questions?"

"Only one," the girl said. "Now, think hard. Did you use alcohol, or smoke cigarettes, or take any drugs at all—heroin, or cocaine, or even marijuana—while your baby was inside you?"

A pause. Then Bea was startled to hear Coreen laugh.

"Girl, if I done all that awful shit to my baby, he wouldn't have turned out so perfect, now would he."

* * *

Bea had just spent another fruitless half-hour nursing her son when a woman's voice barked over the intercom that the photographer was there to take pictures of their babies, but they had to line up outside the door to Room 3 within the next fifteen minutes or they would forfeit their chance. She usually considered taking pictures to be vulgar and vain. But if something were to happen to Isaac, she wouldn't have a picture to remember what he looked like.

From behind the blue curtain came the sounds of her

roommate preparing her child. Bea took Isaac as he was, in a hospital T-shirt stamped BETH ZION BETH ZION, as if that were his name. The two women wheeled their babies' cribs down the hall. Every few steps, Coreen clutched her belly. Her forehead was wet, her face ashen.

"Are you all right?" Bea asked. "If you want, I could take him—" She was suddenly afraid that Coreen would react with the same paranoia she had shown toward Patrice.

Coreen mumbled what sounded like "tell me I'm fine" and kept pushing the crib.

They lined up behind a dozen other mothers, most of them black women half Coreen's age, their hair elegantly done up in beads and braids. Their babies, like Coreen's, were dressed in fancy outfits; one of the boys wore suspenders and a bow tie. A middle-aged white woman in a pink linen suit handed out brochures. Bea saw the cheapest price—for a five-by-seven photo—and nearly turned back. But when would Isaac be a newborn again? She wiped the spittle from his mouth. He gnawed at her finger with his sharply ridged gums.

"Huh," Coreen said. "How come they never tell you what things like this cost until you're standing in line?"

Bea expected her roommate to wheel her baby's crib back to their room. How could she afford twenty dollars for a picture? Bad enough that she was spending an extra five dollars a day for that TV, an expense Bea herself, from years of living on a stipend, had elected to forego.

But Coreen stayed in line. She filled out the form, holding it against the back of the woman in front of her. Then she let the photographer perch her baby on a pillow and snap a light in his face.

"I'm not buying it right now," she told the woman in pink. "But you better take good care of it. This boy's bound to be famous. Reporters need his picture, you just might get rich."

* * *

Bea hadn't wanted anyone to see her until she had gotten the hang of taking care of her son. She disconnected the phone, but in the middle of the week a boy in a Mohawk brought her a basket of fruit. "Congratulations on your own Little Bang!" read the card, which was signed "from the crew." Her friend Modhumita, who worked in a lab not far from the hospital, stopped by every day. Bea caught herself hoping that her roommate would see Mita's dusky skin and think she was black.

Coreen's phone rang often, but no one came to visit. From what Bea could tell, none of Coreen's friends could get the time off from work, or they couldn't leave their children without a sitter. As the TV set blared, Coreen told someone on the phone what she hadn't told Bea.

Her "pains" had begun on the subway to work. "Know what scared is?" she said. "Scared's thinking you're gonna drop your baby right there on that nasty old floor, all those white boys looking up your nookie." Instead of getting off at the T stop near the school, Coreen had taken the train to her clinic. "Time I get inside, I can't hardly walk, they say I'm still closed, I got a month to go, it's only false pains. I say, 'You ain't careful, you gonna have yourself a false little baby right there in your lap,' but they don't want to hear it. I go out and call Lena and ask can she keep the twins a while. Then I call me an ambulance. Time it pulls up, the driver says, 'How come you

105

people always waiting 'til the last minute? You like giving birth to your babies outdoors?'"

Her friend must have asked a question.

"Nate?" Coreen said. "He's away on some haul, he don't even know." She complained she still felt terrible—she was all hot and cold and she hurt something awful. Then she shushed whoever was on the line because the announcer was saying that the police had a videotape of Marion Barry smoking cocaine in that Washington hotel room, and not with his wife.

"Huh," Coreen said. "They got his black ass by the balls. Just let him try to lie now!"

* * *

After dinner that night, Patrice brought in Isaac. He worked Bea's nipples so hard he raised a welt on his lip, but still no milk came.

"He's losing weight," Patrice told her. "You'll have to calm down. Just look at his face and think loving thoughts."

But the baby kept crying. His face was red as lava; his mouth might have been a volcano into which Bea had been ordered to leap. According to Patrice, if Bea's milk didn't come in within twenty-four hours, they would have to give him formula.

"Hey!" Coreen called. "I need me a doctor."

Patrice shot Bea a glance, then she flung aside the curtain. "You're just engorged," she said. "That means your breasts are too full. We'll have to dry you up. Then you'll feel better."

Bea wondered why her roommate wasn't nursing her child. Didn't she know it was healthier and cheaper to breastfeed? Maybe she disliked the feel of a mouth tugging at her nipple as much as Bea disliked it. Or she couldn't afford to stay at home with her baby. Bea stared at the curtain. Why could she imagine what was going on at the other end of the universe but not beyond that drape?

* * *

In the middle of the night, Bea heard Coreen moaning, "Help me. Lord, help me. I'm freezing. I'm burning up."

Bea stood from bed, wobbling, and pushed aside the curtain. Coreen lay with her head thrown back on her pillow and her johnny pulled low as if she had clawed at the neck. Her breasts were exposed, hard and full and rippling with veins; they looked like twin hemispheres carved from mahogany, the North and South Pole rising from each.

"I'm freezing. I'm dying." She was shaking so violently the bed squeaked beneath her. Her blanket lay on the floor.

Slowly, Bea bent and picked it up, then tried to draw the cloth over her thrashing roommate. Her wrist brushed Coreen's arm and Bea flinched away, scorched.

She pulled the cord to call the nurse, then tugged the blanket from her own bed and spread it over Coreen, whose shaking wouldn't stop.

Patrice came. "What's the matter? What's wrong?"

"She's freezing," Bea said. "She feels like she's dying."

Patrice took Bea's arm and led her back behind the curtain. "She's just being melodramatic. The state gives them formula. They can't bear to turn down something for free. I'll get her an ice pack. She'll be fine, don't you worry."

Bea glanced at the curtain. "I'll get a doctor myself."

Patrice stalked out of the room. Bea pushed through the drape. She didn't know what to do, so she stood there and waited. Without the window, this side of the room was so gloomy she almost reached up to turn on the TV.

"Don't."

Her heart jumped.

"Don't let them take him." It seemed to cost Coreen a great deal to speak. "Don't," she repeated.

"I promise," Bea said. But already Coreen had started thrashing again and she didn't seem to hear.

The baby was sleeping face-down in his crib. When Bea lifted him, he hung limply from her hands, surprisingly light compared to her own child. She carried him the way one might carry a puppy, then sat with him on her bed. Was he breathing? He hadn't stirred. She stroked his curls and neck, and he turned toward her belly, nestling against her thigh. He moved his lips. Her breasts tingled.

A doctor came in. Bea huddled closer to the child, partly for warmth and partly to protect him.

The doctor asked Coreen this or that question; he called her "Miss Jones" and murmured "I see" after each of her answers. Then he slowly explained that she had developed an infection called en-do-me-tri-tis. "It's really quite rare for a natural birth, but sometimes it happens." He sounded offhand, but Bea knew this was a disease women used to die from. "We'll put in an IV—that's an intravenous line—and you'll feel better very soon."

The baby in Bea's lap looked up but didn't cry, as if he understood that it was in his best interest to lie still. His smooth copper skin reminded Bea of the telescope her father had bought her as a gift for her tenth or eleventh birthday. She had cradled it for hours, unable to wait until the sun set and, she was sure, the telescope would bring her the power to *see*. The child in her lap held this same promise. Unlike her own son, he appeared to want nothing. But how could that be true? How could a baby not want anything?

A sweet-faced young woman—Korean? Japanese?—wheeled an IV pole next to Bea's bed. She must have been a medical student—she had that overly serious expression of someone who is hiding how uncertain she feels.

"Here," the student said, "let me take . . . Is that your baby?"

Bea held the boy closer, hiding his face. "You want my roommate, Coreen Jones."

"Oh," the student said. She still seemed confused, but she wheeled the pole through the curtain. "Hello," she said. "Don't worry, I'll be done in a minute. It won't hurt one bit."

Bea could hear her roommate mutter, "You ain't got it in."

"Just a minute . . . right there . . ."

"Missed by a mile, girl. Might as well of stuck that thing in my ear." Coreen mumbled these words; if Bea hadn't grown accustomed to hearing her voice, she wouldn't have known what Coreen had said.

The student kept up her patter—"See, that didn't hurt"— and Coreen stopped complaining. When Bea carried the baby back to his crib, his mother lay snoring, the blanket Bea had given her pulled up to her chin.

* * *

The statistician returned. "I got paid!" She waved a check. "We've got twenty-four hours to create a new me."

Bea was changing Isaac's diaper—she was holding his ankles in the air with one hand and swabbing yellow stool from his bottom with the other. She hadn't washed her hair since coming to the hospital. She wore tortoiseshell glasses she had picked out in seventh grade. "I'm really very tired."

"Just one little beauty tip?"

Bea stared at the girl. What was the name of that stuff on her eyes? Liner? Mascara? "Maybe you could use less shadow," she said. As she taped Isaac's diaper and wiped his feces from her hands, she searched for a phrase from the glamour magazines her mother used to buy. "Let the real you come through."

"The real me?" The girl seemed baffled. "Well, my friends always say I'm a typical redhead."

Bea could hear Coreen groan. "I mean your *best self.* Let your best self shine through."

"But how?"

Bea shrugged. "That's the same advice I give to all my clients."

The girl nodded gravely. "I'll try it." She waved the check. "How much do I owe you?"

Bea flapped her hand, a gesture that made her feel both generous and mean.

"Thanks!" the girl said. "I'll let you know how it goes." On her way to the hall, she stopped to chat with Coreen. "How *are* you?" she asked. "I looked in an atlas, and Sierra Leone was right there in West Africa, just like you said!"

* * *

Coreen got a visit from a tired-sounding woman who seemed to run the clinic where Coreen had received her prenatal care.

"What's this? Who put in this IV?" The doctor summoned Patrice. "Just look at this arm, the way it's all blown up! My patient's IV has been draining into everything *but* her vein— for how long? Ten, fifteen hours? Where do you think all that fluid's been going?"

The doctor couldn't stay—another of her patients was about to deliver—but she gave Patrice instructions as to what to do next.

"I didn't put this in," Patrice grumbled when the doctor had left. "I would never do a job as sloppy as this."

"Huh," Coreen said. "If I treated hamburger meat as sloppy as you treat the folks in these beds, they would fire my ass."

* * *

Coreen was feeling better, but her baby was still sick. "He shits all the time," she told the pediatrician.

"Oh, all newborn babies have frequent bowel movements," he said. He sounded like the same well-meaning young intern who had given Isaac his checkup. ("The nurse tells me you and your baby aren't bonding," he'd said to Bea. "Is there anything I can do?," as shy as a boy whose mother has asked him to unhook her brassiere.)

"Ain't just frequent," Coreen told him. "And the color ain't right." The pediatrician started to say that all newborn babies had odd-colored "movements," but Coreen stopped him. "Don't you think I know what a baby's shit looks like? Ain't I raised myself twins?"

His voice tensed. "I'll look into it. But I'm sure if the nurses had seen anything amiss, I would have been notified."

Bea assumed that he was right, until she remembered that even at Coreen's sickest, she had changed her baby's diapers herself.

* * *

Coreen's boyfriend came to visit. Bea saw nothing but his running shoes, caked with dry mud, as they moved back and forth beneath the curtain. She could hear when he kissed his son. Then he must have kissed Coreen.

"Go on," Coreen said. "I'm too sore for that stuff."

The boyfriend drove a moving van or a truck. He had been away on a trip to some city out west. How could he have known that Coreen would give birth to their child five weeks early? When no one had answered at home, he'd called the hospital from a pay phone, but someone at the switchboard kept cutting him off. He drove without stopping until he reached Boston, but he couldn't find a place to park his truck and worried because he'd left it in a spot from which it might get towed.

They talked about names. The man suggested Mitchell, after a younger brother who recently had died. But Coreen vetoed that idea. "This boy isn't lucky as it is." She spoke softly but didn't mumble. "I can feel it in my bones." Bea heard something in Coreen's voice she hadn't heard before. Or maybe she was hearing Coreen's voice as it really was.

"Never mind your bones," the boyfriend said, laughing. "All you women, nothing you like better than worrying. Hell, we got us a son! Come to Daddy, little Mitchell! First thing's gonna happen now your daddy's back home, he's gonna buy you some pants!"

* * *

Coreen's fever returned, no one knew why. The doctors spoke to her kindly, but they said she couldn't leave the hospital. She told them that her twins were only three years old, and she might lose her job if she stayed away too long. Precisely, they said. What she needed was rest, which she wouldn't get at home.

In the middle of the night, Coreen changed her baby's diaper for the third or fourth time. Then she rang for the nurse.

"Look at these diapers! You tell me his shit's supposed to be red!"

"Oh! Oh my!" Patrice said, startled. Bea heard the nurse's shoes slap the linoleum as she ran down the hall. She returned with a doctor whose voice Bea didn't recognize. He had a rich soothing accent—English, or Australian. He paused between phrases as if to gauge the responses of someone whose reactions might be different from his.

He was . . . concerned, he told Coreen. Her son probably had acquired an infection in the bowel. This was not so rare, really, especially for babies like hers, who had been born so premature. They were taking him to Children's Hospital, just down the street. She could see him as soon as she was feeling "more perky." In the meantime, he said, they would send her word how he was doing.

An orderly wheeled the child out the door. Bea thought of pushing through the curtain to comfort Coreen, but what could she say? That the doctors at Children's Hospital were the best in the world? That she hadn't broken her promise not to let anyone take him?

* * *

Early the next morning, Bea dressed herself, then dressed her son. Bundled in the snowsuit Bea's mother had sent, Isaac seemed thoughtful, as if he were contemplating this latest change in his life. Bea took a deep breath and pushed aside the curtain, holding the gift her colleagues had sent; she had eaten only one pear, and the rest of the pyramid of fruit remained intact. She waited for her roommate to say *Keep your damn apples*. But Coreen didn't remove her gaze from the woman in shiny sequins spinning a wheel on TV.

Bea set the fruit on Coreen's nightstand. "I hope you feel better soon. I hope your baby is all right." She tried not to wish that her roommate would thank her. "Is there anything I can do?"

Coreen swiveled on her side to face her. For some reason, Bea thought she was going to tell her to pray. But Coreen shook her head, then turned back to watch the wheel spinning on the game show.

* * *

From the moment Bea got home she had no trouble nursing. She locked the doors and pulled down the shades. She peeled off Isaac's diaper, then his T-shirt and his hat, and she settled him in his tub. Seeing him naked and whole the first time, she felt a catch in her throat, a pressure in her chest. She assumed this was love, but the word seemed too weak, as if she had grown up calling pink "red," and then, in her thirties, seen a crimson or scarlet cloth and had no words to describe the sight.

Isaac slept with her in her bed. Whenever he was hungry, she gave him a swollen breast and milk spurted into his mouth so quickly it choked him; she needed to pump out the excess, which sprayed from each nipple like water from a shower. He would have sucked for hours, if she had let him. How could she watch his face for so long and not grow bored? Her elation, she knew, had to be hormonal. But who would have thought that a chemical substance could produce such a strong effect? If vials of oxytocin could be bought at a store, who would drink alcohol or use drugs? She hadn't suspected that of all the emotions a person could feel, this . . . what would you call it . . . *tenderness* . . . was the one she craved the most, the one she could no longer do without.

* * *

After a good night's sleep, Bea phoned the hospital and asked a nurse in obstetrics if Coreen Jones had gone home. "Yes," the nurse said. And her baby? Bea asked. The nurse asked Bea to wait, then got back on the line and said the baby had been transferred to Children's Hospital. That was all the information she could release at that time.

When Bea called Children's Hospital, she introduced herself as Dr. Beatrice Weller, which technically she was, and learned that a patient listed as "male infant Jones" had died the night before. She said, "Yes," then hung up.

That afternoon, she borrowed a pouch from the woman next door, strapped Isaac inside it, and walked to the T. As she stood beside the turnstile, struggling to get some change from her pocket, a woman behind her said, "Honey, don't rush. What a mother needs isn't a pouch, it's an extra pair of hands."

The woman who'd said this was six feet tall, with soft sculpted hair and perfect brown skin. She wore a cashmere suit and enormous brass earrings. Bea wondered if she was one of the anchors on the Boston evening news, then decided such a celebrity wouldn't be taking the T. The woman dropped a token in the box for Bea, then pushed through the gate and, briefcase to chest, ran to catch her train.

When Bea got to the hospital she went straight to Room 3. She said she'd come to buy a picture for a friend who was ill, wrote a check for twenty dollars, and was handed a portrait in a flimsy pink folder with bears along the edge. Clipped to the front was the form Coreen had filled out: MOTHER'S NAME . . . ADDRESS . . . Coreen's writing was shaky; Bea remembered her leaning on the woman in front.

She opened the folder. Yellow pinafore. Curls. Full lips. She thought of mailing the portrait to Coreen but decided to follow through with her plan. To hand a person an envelope and offer your condolences for the death of her child seemed a minimum requirement for living on the planet.

She took the subway to a neighborhood she'd never been to before. The three-decker houses weren't all that much different from the ones where Bea lived, but the smallest details—a pair of red sneakers dangling from a telephone wire, an unopened pack of gum lying in the gutter—seemed mysterious and enlarged. Most of the houses were enclosed by steel fences. German shepherds and Dobermans strained at their leashes and barked as Bea passed. Isaac stirred inside his pouch; with her cheek to the soft spot in his skull, she could feel his brain pulse.

She found the right address. Three rusty mailboxes hung askew on the porch: HERRERO, GREEN, JONES. Had Bea really believed she could simply ring Coreen's doorbell and explain why she'd come? When Coreen saw the photo of her dead baby, she would scream. Maybe she would faint. Besides, Bea was holding a healthy child, and that, more than anything, would make Coreen hate her.

A light flickered behind a window. Bea pictured Coreen lying on her bed, stone mute with grief. Her boyfriend came in. *Don't worry, sweetheart, we'll have us another baby. It wasn't your fault.* Bea wondered where the twins were. And Lena? Coreen's mother? What about Coreen's job? Would her supervisor at the school allow her time off to recuperate? How useless the eye without the imagination to inform it, to make sense of all that darkness surrounding the light.

A child started crying across the street. Bea's breasts began to tingle. She slid the folder in the mailbox. Milk flowed from her nipples, soaking her blouse. She hurried to the subway station, where she zippered her parka around the pouch so that only Isaac's head poked out from the top. During her last night in the hospital, Bea had lain with her hands pressed against her ears as Coreen had changed her baby's diaper again and again. By then, Bea herself had come down with a fever. Every joint ached. Her breasts had swollen grossly. They were lumpy and rock hard, as if someone had pumped them full of concrete. Another few drops of milk and they would burst.

And yet they kept filling. Every time Coreen's baby whimpered, milk surged into Bea's breasts, pushing through ducts that felt tiny and clogged, like irrigation ditches silted with clay. In another few minutes, she would be forced to get up and stagger down the hall and try to stop Patrice from feeding Isaac the formula she had warned that she would give him. Bea longed to feel her baby's mouth sucking at her nipples, sucking and sucking, easing her pain. In the meantime, she lay there, palms against her ears, her breasts filling with milk for another woman's child.

Uno

THE FIRST TIME HELOISE SAW MITCH, he was standing beside the vending machines in the hospital cafeteria, angular and fresh in his puckery clean white scrubs. She had come in for a Coke and chips, not that she wanted either, only the excuse to escape her rounds with the hospital chaplain and her classmates from the Divinity School. It freaked her out how much she was attracted by the misery of the people in those rooms. The stumps. The scars. The pins. Unlike her classmates, she couldn't force herself to ask a patient's name, sit beside a bed, and hold a hand. All she wanted to do was stand by the door and stare.

She fled to the cafeteria and stood sipping her Coke, trying to remember why she had wanted a degree in religion in the first place. As an undergrad, she had taken courses in paintings of the Renaissance, the poetry of Donne and Blake. The next thing she knew, she was a student at Harvard Div, tagging along behind a stocky Congregationalist minister and a bunch of sincerely devoted ministers-to-be, all of whom wanted to offer dying people the comforting words of Christ.

She looked up and saw Mitch. He twisted apart an Oreo, scraped the icing with his teeth, and studied her as if he were diagnosing some disease. Absently, he curled his wrist to stroke the shiny head of the stethoscope around his neck. She suspected he could put that instrument to her chest and discover things about her that she didn't know herself. Like maybe she had a better heart than she thought.

"So you really believe in God?"

She must have looked startled.

"Upstairs," he said. "I saw you with the other student ministers."

She knew that the accepted way to eat an Oreo was to split the layers and lick the icing, but she always had preferred biting the entire cookie. Not that she had eaten an Oreo since she was five.

"So, do you?" Mitch asked again. "I've never met anyone our age who believes in God."

"I'm trying," Heloise said. "But sometimes I have to wonder if God believes in me."

Opposites attract. Everyone said it. Mitch was tall and she was short. He was fair and she was unfair. Mitch had never had a girlfriend, while Heloise had been having tortured romances since her senior year in high school, when she had instigated an affair with the witty bisexual black man who taught history in her town. She tended to earn good grades, but each success came hard. Mitch was healthy, handsome, smart. He had grown up in a loving family and won scholarships to MIT and Harvard Med. He was a non-believing Jew who put his trust in antibiotics and NMRs; she was a half-assed Unitarian trying to justify her faith in a supposedly loving God.

So yes, opposites did attract. The question no one ever asked was: How long can opposites *stay* attracted? What were people, magnets? That was why so many marriages fell apart. For a few years, in your twenties, you thought you could be your opposite. People who were weary of their madness married people who promised peace. People bored with their own stability married spouses who were sure to shake things up. But souls could only stretch so far, for so long.

Still, their marriage might have worked. She admired Mitch. She loved him. She hoped his goodness might rub off on her. Really, there was nothing wrong with the man except that he had never suffered, and what kind of flaw was that? She might have survived forever as a sort of Persephone in reverse, tolerating three seasons a year with Mitch in his cheery sunlit world, if only she had been allowed an occasional brief fling in Hades. But she depended on Mitch for everything. They moved when he got his fellowship, and later when he got his first job, and still later when he became chief of anesthesiology at the largest hospital in Troy, New York. She finally found the time to work on her dissertation, an overly ambitious attempt to understand the appeal of martyrdom in Judeo-Christian art. But this meant she stayed at home mired in confused ideas about sex, despair, and strange deaths, while Mitch spent his days and nights in an unambiguously bright OR, where everything was clean and measured—the rise and fall of a patient's chest, the unwavering needle on a clear-faced dial.

They moved so many times that she misplaced her friends along the way, like the measuring spoons she had inherited from her aunt and the tablecloth her mother had embroidered before she died. With no friends of her own, Heloise was forced to borrow Mitch's. Like Mitch, they loved to hike. All that greenery and dirt made up for their sterile days in the hospital's harsh blank corridors. Most of Mitch's friends had been Boy Scouts in their youth, and even in their thirties they still radiated the boyish confidence and sincerity Heloise associated with that group. Camping or not, Mitch acted as if nothing could go wrong so long as he made sure to carry the right equipment and keep a clear head. At least once a month, the surgeons and dieticians planned some sort of trek, and Mitch and Heloise trekked along with them. On regular weekend nights, everyone got together for potluck dinners, although the two-doctor couples could have afforded to cook—it drove Heloise nuts, the way Mitch's friends pretended they weren't rich. Still, she always prepared a dish and went. And when everyone else got pregnant, Heloise and Mitch got pregnant, too.

* * *

A year after Eunice was born, Heloise and Mitch planned a trip with another couple. The other mother, Deb, showed them a brochure that had been printed on recycled paper. "It's called Sunshine Lodge," she explained. "It's on a mountain up north. Everything's solar powered. The owners keep llamas, goats, and sheep. There's a playroom for the kids, a sauna and hot tub for us, and an orchard with miles and miles of cross-country trails."

Later, Heloise scolded herself for not knowing better than to spend her vacation at a petting zoo. She hated cross-country skiing. Why make a sport of the exhausting horizontal slog a downhill skier was forced to endure from the parking lot to the lift? But Mitch was too deliberate to enjoy skiing downhill. He loved getting out in the woods, pouring cups of cocoa, and watching the snow sift prettily through the trees. Oh well. You couldn't crash down a black-diamond slope with a toddler on your back.

"We have an extra kiddie-pack you can borrow," Deb offered. "That way, you can ski with Eunice, and Hank can carry Inga."

Deb and her husband, Hank, were a warm good-natured couple. Heloise didn't dislike them. They signed petitions. They volunteered. They were just a little too earnest. It wasn't as if their lives were untroubled. Deb's father was in the late stages of Alzheimer's and Hank's parents were dead. Deb was a neurologist; Hank specialized in eyes. They saw heartbreak every day. But these troubles didn't seem to trouble them. It was as if they were standing in the rain, talking about how wet they were getting, but you could see the water rolling right off their Gore-Tex shells.

It was five in the afternoon before they left. An hour north of Albany, Hank steered the Volvo off the highway and maneuvered it past a shabby snowmobile-showroom and a general store and bait shop that sat clustered around the exit like hoboes around a fire. Hank drove for another hour up a narrow gravel road that ought to have brought them somewhere more worthwhile—San Francisco, say, or Heaven—than the remains of a barn and silo and a sign that said SUNSHINE LODGE with a smiling sunflower-face below.

The buildings were squat and dull. A ski lodge ought to be quaint, oughtn't it? Oughtn't it have a gable or two? Some gingerbread? The man behind the desk was as round and timid as a friar; he even had a tonsure like a monk's, although it turned out he had struck it rich with a computer start-up, then left the whole technology rat-race and gone back to simpler things.

"Greetings, wayfarers," he mumbled, then inked their names with a quill pen in a ledger. Showing them their rooms, he barely said a word, but later, when he took them on a tour, he couldn't seem to shut up—organic this, self-composting that, vegetables kept warm and lush beneath their Plexiglas pods, a hot-tub kept hot with power from the sun. Index cards in lavender calligraphy were tacked beside each fixture, detailing what a person should or shouldn't throw in, the proper way to stoke a stove, what lotions and perfumes mustn't pollute the tub.

Heloise and Deb carried their children to the game room while Mitch and Hank lugged in the duffel bags and portacribs, the collapsible highchairs, the diaper bags, wipes, and diapers, the juice boxes, bottles, snacks, and pacifiers. A mother, Heloise decided, was a woman who remembered to bring her daughter's six favorite stuffed toys but neglected to pack underwear for herself.

"Isn't this place just perfect?" Deb said, tugging off the hiking boots she wore whenever she wasn't at the hospital. She settled on the rug, swirling her skirts around her. Heloise tried not to hold it against her that she still styled her hair in a pageboy and never tweezed her brows. Inga, a chunky blonde toddler nearly twice Eunice's size, although both girls were eighteen months, grabbed a wood spindle and began setting one hand-carved ring atop the next, from the largest to the smallest. It amazed Heloise, the way Inga always seemed to know what a toddler was supposed to do. Eunice clumsily grabbed the smallest ring and jammed it in her mouth. To avoid suffering further damage to her illusion that her daughter wasn't developmentally delayed, Heloise wandered to a table where a guest had pieced together a puzzle of a busy New England town. Heloise fingered the centermost piece, which bore the image of a parson. When Inga began to wail, Heloise slipped the parson in her vest pocket before turning to convince her daughter to give up the smallest ring.

Another child came in. She was eight or nine, with a pasty face and lank brown hair. "Hello," she said, "I'm Alice," and began to tell the new arrivals about her sisters. "They're twins," she said. "But they're *special* twins. Everyone who meets them loves them." Something in her voice brought to Heloise's mind a carnival barker, or God help her, a pimp.

The door to the game room opened and Alice's sisters tumbled in. They wore identical purple stretch-pants and yellow shirts. They were hugging, Heloise thought. Then she realized their connection was more intimate than that. They were joined by a thick band of flesh from their navels to their necks; they held their inner arms draped around each other, with the rest of their bodies opening outward like a book. The sister on the left seemed flush with life and strong, but the other sister's skin was as transparent as tracing paper and her head lolled to one side.

Alice ran across the room and threw both arms around both girls. "Here they are! This one is Sarah"—she indicated the stronger of the twins—"and this one's Meribeth."

"Yesterday was our birthday," they said together. Or maybe not together. Meribeth spoke first and Sarah echoed, although sometimes Sarah spoke first and Meribeth chimed in. At other times, one girl pronounced the first few words of a sentence and her twin sister completed the idea.

"We're having a party when we get back home."

"We've got so many friends—"

"We can't hold it at our house."

"We had to rent a restaurant."

"But we like to play in the snow."

"And go sledding."

"We can't do that in Boston."

"So our parents brought us here."

"They have a special sled," Alice explained. "They can sit on it side by side."

"We have a special tricycle, too."

"One of us pedals."

"And the other one rides for free."

Mitch and Hank came in, smelling of snow and smoke. With his curly pale hair, delicate face, and silver glasses, Hank wasn't a bad-looking man, just surprisingly insubstantial; even at forty-two, he seemed to delight in his gawky innocence. He was followed by a boy whom Alice introduced as Jarred, the innkeeper's son. Mitch leaned against the door and studied Sarah and Meribeth the way he had studied Heloise the day they met. The four children started playing a card game called Uno. It didn't seem fair to Heloise, as if one sister might guess the other's strategy. Of course this made no sense; the sisters didn't share a head. Yet weren't their cells patterned by identical DNA? Hadn't they shared the same experiences from the moment they were born? What was an individual if not a single set of experiences bound inside a skin?

"It's so upsetting," Deb whispered behind a hand. "I see sick kids all the time. But usually there's something I can do to help. This just goes to remind us all how lucky we are."

Heloise nodded. How could she not feel blessed by her daughter's brutish good health? But Deb's view of the twins seemed limited. It was as if she thought that Sarah and Meribeth existed solely to make the rest of humankind feel blessed. But the girls weren't symbols of misfortune; they were people in their own right. If Eunice, Inga, and Jarred were to grow up with the twins as their only playmates, they would assume that some kids came in ones while other kids came in twos. They might even be jealous that their own bodies were so plain. Besides, the twins seemed happy. It was Alice who seemed forlorn, which was probably why Heloise's attention was drawn to her.

A bell chimed. "That means dinner is ready," Alice informed them. "The food here is good, so long as you don't want hot dogs." She led the parade of guests down the stairs to the dining room, where the innkeeper's wife, Eleanor, was ladling out the food.

Eleanor was small and neatly made but even shyer than her husband. "Hello," she said in a voice as thin as a wisp of steam. Then she ducked back in the kitchen. Heloise got the sense that Eleanor and her husband would have preferred to run the lodge for the theoretical beauty of the self-composting toilets and manure-heated pods, as God might have preferred to run Heaven for Himself.

But the woman could cook. Heloise had never seen such food. She didn't even recognize the ingredients. Nuts, but what kind? Exotic forms of grain. Rich velvety pools of cheese. Mushrooms nestled in flaky crusts, as sweet as pecan pie. No additives, no funny colors. This was food you needed a spiritual license to be allowed to eat. Probably, if you ate it long enough, it endowed you with eternal life.

The dining room was arranged in two long tables, with benches on either side. Heloise, Mitch, Deb, Hank, Inga, and Eunice took up one end of one table, with a pair of tall gaunt lesbians named Carol and Kim in the center, and Alice, Sarah, Meribeth, and their mother holding down the other end. The twins' mother turned out to be a soft pear-shaped woman with flowing brown hair and a face that bespoke great patience. Gently, she laid a hand on Alice's arm and cautioned her not to eat so fast—it occurred to Heloise that Alice felt the need to eat twice as much as normal to make up for being an only child, or rather, for being only one child.

After everyone finished eating, Alice, Sarah, and Meribeth came over to pat the toddlers and admire Inga's dress. Alice gestured toward their mom. "She sews my sisters' clothes."

Now that Alice mentioned it, Heloise noticed that Sarah and Meribeth's shirts were cleverly designed with a sort of cloth tunnel where their bond of flesh connected them.

"She used to be a teacher," Alice said, "but now she stays at home and takes care of my sisters and me. But I don't really need much taking care of."

Deb and Hank could only nod. But Mitch, bless his heart, pointed at the sliding glass doors and sang out: "Look, everyone, snow!"

Sure enough, the flakes were battering the glass like weary travelers trying to get inside.

"Snow!" Alice shouted.

"Our mom worries when we go sledding," Sarah said.

"She thinks we'll die sooner," Meribeth added.

"But we'd rather go sledding now than live a long time later."

"Girls?" their mother called. "Don't make nuisances of yourselves. Come over here and eat your tofu pudding."

Heloise desperately wanted a drink, but the lodge served no liquor. Instead, Eleanor lectured the new arrivals on the importance of sorting the remains of their dinner into color-coded bins for compost and recyclables. After the twins' family had left, Mitch, Deb, and Hank reached the opinion that Sarah and Meribeth shared a single heart and Meribeth was not getting enough oxygen, which was why her lips and skin looked blue. Eventually, Meribeth's lungs would fail and she would die, and, not long after that, Sarah would die as well.

Heloise wondered if the twins' parents knew this. They must. But did the twins?

Everyone migrated to the game room, except the twins' father, who, despite the girls' plot to sneak up to his bed, tickle his feet, and wake him, didn't appear that night. Alice, Sarah, Meribeth, and Jarred played Uno while Deb and Hank traded the task of keeping Inga occupied. Mitch rarely minded Eunice, not because he didn't want to, but because Heloise spent so much more time with the baby that she knew Eunice's needs better than Mitch did. Mitch was fine when Eunice was happy, but he seemed unable to understand her discontent or imagine a remedy. A vicious cycle, Heloise thought. A vicious cycle that kept producing vicious wives.

Deb, Hank, and Mitch stood whispering in the corner. Their plan, it turned out, was to put the girls to sleep and get naked in the hot tub. Heloise could see by Mitch's face that he wanted her to say she would go with them. But it gave Heloise the creeps the way Deb and Hank liked to take off their clothes. Whenever they went hiking, Deb and Hank would plan the day's adventure to include a pond. *Oh, just look at that pond!* they liked to giggle. *Don't you feel like taking off your clothes and jumping right in?*

They loved their naked selves and wanted Inga to do the same. How could Heloise object? But she did. "I object!" she felt like shouting every time they tried to shame her into taking off her clothes. Hank owned a guidebook that listed every nude beach in America. Heloise had nothing against swimming nude, as long as it was done at night in a forbidden place with someone you hoped to fuck. But how could she explain such reasons?

She lied and said she was reluctant to leave Eunice by herself.

129

What could happen? Deb insisted. We'll be a few yards out the door.

Well, what if the inn caught fire? Heloise would be outside while Eunice would be sizzling in her portacrib.

Come on, Hank said. What were the chances the building would catch fire during the hour they were in the hot tub?

Heloise looked to Mitch. Wasn't he Mr. Logic? Hadn't every parent who had ever watched a baby go up in flames thought nothing bad could happen in just the one hour they had left the kid alone? But Mitch wore the defenseless pleading face that Heloise always found impossible to refuse.

She changed tactics. What if the girls started crying?

Deb had already thought of that. They could ask the lesbians to come and get them.

The lesbians? If the lesbians wanted to be minding kids, they would have brought some of their own.

"Please?" Mitch said. "For me?"

But she was angry at how many times he had come home late and fended off her advances. He consented to sex infrequently, as a form of recreation, like a hike or a bad TV show. And it bothered her that he thought he could fix their marriage so easily, with a trip to Sunshine Lodge and a midnight dip in a hot tub.

"I can't," Heloise said. "I've got my period." This wasn't technically true, but she expected it at any time. And she hadn't packed protection. This truth hit her like a punishment. She hadn't packed tampons, and the nearest store that sold them was thirty miles away.

She put Eunice to sleep while Mitch took a towel and slumped off to the hot tub. Heloise sat on a chair outside their room, considering whether to ask Eleanor for some tampons. No, a woman like that probably used some weird environmentally friendly product like peat-moss napkins or reusable rubber cups. Heloise might have tried Carol and Kim, but they passed in the hall just then, so entwined about each other that Heloise didn't have the heart to interrupt.

"It's spooky," Kim said to Carol.

"Don't worry," Carol said, "I'll protect you."

"That's what I'm afraid of."

The two women quickly kissed and clattered down the stairs. From the second-story window, Heloise saw them heading off. Both were dressed in thick blue parkas, identical striped wool hats, and jeans. Did lesbians still do that thing where one pretended to be butch while the other was more femme? Was it kinkier to make love to someone like yourself, or to someone very different?

The two women vanished down the path, at which Heloise discovered that the view from the window allowed her to glimpse the hot tub; it was surrounded by a fence, but, looking down from that angle, she could just make out three heads. She heard Mitch's laugh, then Deb's. Oh, why not go down and join them?

She peeked in the room and saw that Eunice was asleep. But instead of going out, Heloise put on a nightshirt and crawled beneath the scratchy blanket. Sometime later, Mitch came in, but by the time Heloise had struggled up to consciousness, his eyes were already closed and his breathing was as regular as if he had given himself a whiff of whatever anesthesia he used to knock out patients.

She slipped on Mitch's boots and hobbled down the stairs and out the door. The air was so frigid it made the hair on the back of her neck stand up, or maybe that was the effect of seeing who was in the hot tub.

He was swarthy, with broad flat cheeks and a prominent crooked nose—he might have been an Indian, or an Arab, or maybe a Jew like Mitch. Even though his nipples cleared the water by several inches, the ends of his long black hair floated on the surface like some sensual ooze.

"Hi," he said. "Join me?"

Her plan had been to yank off her nightshirt, simmer herself back to some semblance of relaxation, then slither back to bed. "I didn't think anyone would be here."

His shoulders lifted. "I'm not anyone. Anyone was here before. I'm nobody. Who are you?"

How could it matter if a stranger whose name she didn't know, in a town whose name she also didn't know, saw her with no clothes on? As she unbuttoned her nightshirt, he made no effort to look away. She stepped out of Mitch's boots and tossed them over the fence so they wouldn't be standing there tapping in disgust while she sat naked with another man. Without looking, she climbed in the tub. It was like lowering her body into a roiling tub of sex. She could sense the stranger's cock twitch. Even his armpit hair turned her on. Women! Men got turned on by women's breasts, which everyone knew were beautiful, and women got turned on by armpit hair. Or maybe only Heloise did.

"Are those your girls?" she asked. "Sarah and Meribeth? And Alice?" She could sense his cock deflate. Did he expect her to say something thoughtless? "They're beautiful," she said, then winced. Using a man's twin daughters to get his cock to stand back up!

"That they are. They are beautiful. All three of my girls are beauties." He let his head drop backward to expose a vulnerable throat; with his arms along the rim of the tub, he seemed to be waiting for someone to shoot him full of arrows. Like St. Sebastian, Heloise thought. St. Sebastian of the Hot Tub.

"So, this is your first time at Sunshine Lodge?"

Heloise said it was.

"Like it?"

"It's all right."

"Just 'all right'? I don't think you're allowed to say it's just all right."

"No?"

"You have to say it's perfect."

She laughed. "Okay. It's perfect."

He ducked beneath the surface, then reappeared and shook his head, wringing water from his hair. "Don't all the little signs and compost bins and all that healthy food make you feel like shooting up?"

"Well," she said, "now that you mention it."

"I have some heroin in my jeans. But you have to supply your own needle."

"Oh," she said, "I always bring my own needle."

As they laughed and talked, they kept inching around the tub until they were sitting side by side. She needed to remind herself this was someone else's husband. She had a toddler named Eunice. The naked man beside her was father to a girl named Alice and twins named Sarah and Meribeth. He loved all three of them, he said. "I love all three of my daughters." He said the sentence twice. He was just tired of being good. "People think just because you have disabled kids, you somehow become a saint."

Under normal conditions, she doubted he would have been the self-pitying kind of man. But the hot tub brought it out, like some torture pit from Dante, broiling him until he confessed his sins. It broke his heart, he said. How could it not break his heart that his girls would die young? But every now and then he caught himself looking forward to not having to spend every waking moment worrying about their pain.

Before the twins were born, he had been planning to leave his wife. But how could a man leave a woman who had given birth to Siamese twins? Not that she wasn't strong enough. She was stronger than he was. The twins had given her life a purpose. But it had robbed him of his. If a sacrifice was given grudgingly, in his wife's book, it didn't count. He taught music in the public schools. Squeaks and squawks. Lost tempers. The constant abuse of strings. Before the girls were born, he had been planning to make it as a jazz clarinetist. But with all the extra bills and the need for someone to stay home with the twins . . .

Heloise shifted around and stroked his knee. He put his hand a few inches below her breast, which was more arousing than if he had put it *on* her breast. Their nakedness, thank God, was anything but wholesome.

"I'd better go," she said, although really, she didn't want to go. She got out and found Mitch's boots, clutched her nightshirt to her chest, and darted to her room. Eunice was still asleep. Mitch lay curled to the wall. She got in and sniffed his neck, which smelled like bubblegum and vanilla icing. "If I ever run away, come after me," she whispered. She had said this to him many times when he was awake, but she didn't trust that he would come. She would run away, remembering everything he'd ever taught her about blazing signs along her trail. But Mitch would be too proud and hurt to follow.

* * *

The next morning, she awoke to the sore breasts, bloated stomach, and intense pressure to commit multiple gory homicides that indicated her period was about to come. She sucked down her pride and asked Eleanor if she had some tampons. Without a word, Eleanor pulled a cardboard box from

beneath the sink. Sifting through a litter of sunglasses, con-
doms, deodorants, and mismatched boots, the innkeeper's
wife lifted out a single linty tampon, the old-fashioned kind
that came in a cardboard tube. Heloise only hoped it didn't
date from the Age of Toxic Shock. Well, one tampon was
better than no tampon. She would horde it until she absolutely
needed to borrow the Volvo and drive the sixty miles to the
general store and back.

After breakfast, the twins' mother bundled them in a snowsuit she must have designed and sewn. Packed in its padded
double womb, the twins went out to play. With Alice's help,
they built a snow mother, a snow father, and, thank God,
instead of a set of Siamese snow-twins, a lopsided snow-dog.
Then they instigated a war against Jarred; the twins windmilled
snowballs at the boy while Alice packed ammunition. Heloise
was so incensed at the way the twins took advantage of their
Siameseness she almost enlisted on Jarred's side. They rushed
him, tore off his hat, packed it full of snow, put it back on his
head and pulled it down, at which Jarred lunged their knees
and Sarah and Meribeth went over backward.

Heloise screamed.

"Do angels!" Alice cried, and the girls lifted their arms and
lowered them, then struggled to their feet, leaving the indentation of a two-headed angel when they went inside.

* * *

At lunch, Heloise overheard the twins' family argue about
their plans for the afternoon. The twins wanted to go sledding,
but their mother insisted they were too tired. "We can do it if
Dad carries us," they said. "Like that last time, in Vermont."
Their mother shook her head; she had promised their father

135

he could take the afternoon off to ski. But the twins' father assured their mother that he would enjoy nothing more than carrying his daughters up the hill; while their mother zipped the girls inside their snowsuit, he turned to Heloise and shrugged.

The six of them—Mitch and Heloise, with Eunice on her back, and Deb and Hank with Inga—spent the next few hours skiing. Heloise enjoyed the way Eunice caught her breath and screeched and grabbed Heloise's ears whenever they skied downhill. And something about the melancholy landscape— the bare apple-trees, as hunched as old women, surrounded by rows of firs like pinheaded guards just waiting, waiting, waiting, their hands behind their backs, for someone to escape—moved her more deeply than the magnificence of a vista from a mountain might have done.

Around and around she skied, and each time she and Eunice circled back, Heloise saw Vincent carrying his girls uphill, hugging them awkwardly to his chest like bags of gro- ceries. Up and up, like Sisyphus. Alice pulled her own sled, looking wistfully at her sisters, and if Mitch could extrapolate from Meribeth's blue lips to the twins' future, or rather, their lack of a future, Heloise could look at Alice's expression and imagine the story she would one day tell her therapist: *I once had twin sisters. They weren't ordinary twins. They were conjoined twins. I loved them. I really did. It was just that I was jealous of the attention and love they got. The grace they had that I didn't have.*

The irony, Heloise thought later, was that she and Mitch had one of their best afternoons ever. Mitch plodded around the trail, and whenever Heloise and Eunice lapped him, he would lift his fist and curse. "You miserable rutabagas! You bungee jumpers! You foghorn leghorns!" He took to weaving among the apple trees, and every time their paths crossed,

Mitch would snowplow around Heloise's skis, kiss her, then kiss Eunice, who bounced happily in her backpack.

When they stopped for hot chocolate, Mitch leaned against a stump and poured two steaming cups. Just as Heloise took hold of hers, Eunice began to whimper. "Mumma, dog!" Heloise turned and saw a fox quivering at the forest's edge. It lifted one paw daintily and sniffed, like a society queen uncertain if the party she was about to enter was beneath her pride, then flicked its tail and trotted off.

"It's good luck to see a fox," Mitch said.

"Really?"

"Aren't fox's feet lucky?"

He was so pleased with himself that Heloise didn't have the heart to say he meant rabbits.

"Why don't you go for one last run, without us slowing you down?" Mitch said.

She felt as if he were sending her off to sleep with another man. "You don't mind?"

No, no, go on, Mitch said. He took Eunice from the pack—getting the baby out of that backpack required more effort than the doctors had required to extricate Eunice from Heloise's womb. She kissed Mitch and took off, legs pumping as strenuously as if, even without the aid of gravity, she might yet achieve the blind happiness of flight.

Near the woods she stepped off the trail to catch her breath—literally, her breath was curling past her face and she snatched at it with her glove. The sun was watery pink and blue, like the colors in a nursery. Vincent passed her hiding spot, skiing backwards, encouraging someone to try to reach him. Alice plodded around the bend, red faced and out of breath. "You can do it," he kept repeating. "Slide those skis. *Skate.*"

Heloise waited to give Vincent and Alice a decent length of time to ski back to the lodge, but she came upon them not a hundred yards down the trail, Alice frozen at the top of a tiny incline, her father at the bottom.

"I can't, Dad. I can't! I'll give you fifty dollars if you don't make me ski down this hill!"

"Damn it. Why can't you be as brave as Sarah and Meribeth?"

He might as well have shot her, that's how quickly Alice crumpled. She must have been crying, but Heloise didn't hear a sob; the child was crying in that way that goes beyond mere sound.

Vincent sidestepped up the hill, took off his skis, and held his daughter in the snow. At first she writhed away, but then she let him comfort her. He helped her take off her skis, then carried the skis downhill and went back for Alice. He helped her put the skis back on, then towed her by her poles, bent double, like a horse. His suffering wrenched Heloise's heart. But it also turned her on. And what did that say about *her?* If you fell in love with a person's suffering, you would never try to cure it. Deb, Hank, and Mitch weren't nearly as shaken as she was by suffering, but neither were they attracted to it, and that allowed them to get on with the business of easing people's pain.

No wonder she couldn't bring herself to finish her degree. If she had ever found the courage to state her thesis clearly, it would have been this: Suffering is erotic. That was at the heart of her attraction to Christianity. Maybe it was true of most people's attraction to Christianity. Why build an entire religion around Christ's suffering on the cross, instead of, say, His miracles? Why the whips and thorns, the punctured ribs and palms, not to mention all the martyrs His suffering had inspired, all those men with pierced chests, the women with hacked-off breasts, the smiling, genderless innocents, flayed alive or burnt?

She shook her head to clear the images. Wasn't that a howl she heard? It couldn't have been. But the woods' shadowy darkness filled her soul with dread. She forced herself to give Vincent and Alice a while longer. Even so, when she reached the lodge, he was still hauling Alice, trudge by laborious trudge, up that final hill.

* * *

By the time Heloise and Mitch had showered and dressed, everyone but the twins and Alice was downstairs waiting for dinner. Heloise and Mitch had just settled beside Deb and Hank, with the kids on their mothers' laps, when the door at the top of the stairs opened and Alice and the twins came in.

"Watch what we can do!" they cried. With a little help from Alice, the twins ended up on the banister, not straddling the rail but side by side. Their mother shouted "No!" but Alice gave them a push. The twins slid a few feet down the rail. Then one twin tottered backward and the other twin slid forward, arms and legs flailing.

Their father leapt the stairs three at a time, scooped the twins in his arms, then sat cradling them on the step while Alice threw herself across her sisters' backs, crying, "I didn't mean to! I didn't mean to!"

Everyone tried to get back to normal, but the mood was too subdued. Deb suggested charades. Carol and Kim declined so they could take their turn in the hot tub, but the twins and Alice were all for it. The problem was that Sarah and Meribeth performed their clues in unsettling synchronicity, and when it was their team's turn to guess, they shouted "'Over the Rainbow'!" and "'Cinderella'!" in such eerie unison that the game ended after only a few rounds and each family went up to its room far earlier than was normal even for parents with children that young.

* * *

Heloise liked to think she fell asleep that night with the intention of staying asleep until morning and it was only a case of nerves that made her startle awake at two and led her outside to the steaming tub. But when she saw that no one was in the water, she admitted that her nerves had been crying out for more than relaxation. She passed the indentation in the snow where the twins had made their angel. "Baa," called a sheep, or maybe it was a goat. How odd that the two creatures sounded so much alike in the dark.

She slid down the hill on the soles of Mitch's boots, then headed toward the woods. Not twenty yards in, she saw Vincent against a tree, wrapped in one of the heavy striped wool blankets the innkeeper kept beside the hot tub. With his raven-black hair and the wings the blanket gave him, he looked more than a little vampirish.

She walked over and leaned against him. He moaned, then wrapped Heloise in his blanketed arms and held her. She rested that way, breathing the horsey odor of the wool, the sandalwood of his skin. Then her mouth found his chest, and—she hadn't planned this—she slid to her knees in the snow. The cold seeped through her leggings, but the pain was almost pleasure. A few minutes later, as Vincent lifted his arms above his head and cried out, Heloise turned and saw the fox's eyes glittering in the moonlight not fifteen yards away. She gasped and struggled up. Vincent remained against the tree, eyes closed, arms lifted as if someone had pinned his wrists to the trunk.

The fox shook itself like a dog and trotted off. Panting, Heloise looked down and saw a steaming clot of her menstrual blood. Had the fox scented it? Was that why it had come? She was tempted to reach down and taste her menses. Instead, she lifted her chin and howled.

* * *

The marriage didn't end that winter. After they left Sunshine Lodge, Heloise never saw Vincent again. But once she started hurting Mitch, she couldn't seem to stop. A year after their divorce, she read about the twins in the local paper. As Mitch and Deb had said, the girls had shared a single heart—a defective heart at that; it had only three chambers. Meribeth died first. Sarah survived another hour. Most conjoined twins died at birth, the reporter wrote. The luckiest lived a year. But Sarah and Meribeth had celebrated their eighth birthday a few weeks earlier.

"They had the sunniest disposition," their mother was quoted as saying. "I don't think it bothered them a bit. On alternate days, Sarah or Meribeth got to make decisions. They argued, but they made up. If you're attached to a person, you have to figure out a way to get along. You can't just stay mad."

The girls died at home, surrounded by their parents, Kathleen and Vincent Black, various grandparents, aunts, and uncles, and their older sister, Alice. They were buried in a single casket. Donations could be sent to build a playground for disabled children in a park near where they lived.

After reading the obit twice, Heloise picked up the phone to call Mitch. Then she remembered that Mitch had asked her never to engage him in conversation unless it concerned their daughter. If Heloise tried to talk about that weekend at Sunshine Lodge, Mitch would hang up. Her infidelities had made him suffer, and his suffering had turned him into a person she could love. But Mitch couldn't forgive her disloyalty. He refused to take her back.

She put Eunice to bed, patted her on the arm until she closed her eyes, then went into the study to write a homily for that week's service. Since finishing her degree and taking her first assignment—as chaplain at a women's college outside Schenectady—Heloise had fallen into the easy routine of using an incident from the news or her personal life to serve as a guiding metaphor for a larger spiritual truth to be explored in that week's sermon. She wanted to compose a tribute to the twins. But what kind of metaphor could Meribeth and Sarah provide if not, as Deb had said, a reminder of everyone else's sublime good luck at not being them? Maybe what they symbolized was the beauty of suffering gracefully. But the twins hadn't suffered. Not until the end. Their father and sister had suffered, but not in ways that seemed particularly enlightening.

No, the twins stood for nothing. Maybe nothing stood for anything. Pain was what it was. The pieces of people's lives fit together to make a pattern like the puzzle of that town, the central piece of which Heloise now discovered in that long-neglected vest. But there was nothing beneath the surface. No deeper, third dimension. She was left with nothing from Sunshine Lodge except a lost-and-found of images: a two-headed angel; a fox's glowing eyes; a dark red clot of blood steaming in the snow. And she knew it would be a sin to stand before her congregation and try to weave these images into a symbol for the perversity of a woman who, for no reason, would destroy her marriage to the man she loved and, in the process, condemn herself to spend the remainder of her life with the corpse of her better self joined to her like the angelic twin sister with whom she once had shared a single three-chambered heart.

Beached in Boca

EVEN BEFORE THEY LEFT THE BAGGAGE AREA, Wendy knew her father was dying. The flaps above the luggage chute, those frayed canvas vulva, gave birth to her suitcase. "That one's mine," she said, and was stunned when he allowed the bag to circle past. They watched it complete a lifetime around the belt and disappear into the windswept nothingness beyond. He might as well have watched Wendy herself struggle past him, drowning.

The bag reappeared and made its way toward them. She waited to be sure her father wasn't going to lift it, then hefted it herself. She was strong, in good shape, but the suitcase seemed weighted with foreboding. She dragged it through the terminal. Blue pipes, red wires, and silver-coated heating ducts dangled from the ceiling like the arteries and veins of a heart patient who has been split open and abandoned. Wendy followed her father outside and the bag grew heavier yet, sucking gluey moisture from the air. Halfway across the lot she had to

145

stop. Luckily, they weren't far from her father's car. He thumbed his key ring and the big silver Grand Marquis yapped, winked, and popped its trunk. That eased Wendy's heart, as if they were being greeted by the family pet. But when her father made no motion to lift her bag into the trunk, she stifled her grief and yanked it up and in.

"Dad? Dad, what is it?"

He was staring up at a jet whose belly was so low it was like the palm of God descending. Even in his seventies, he was as slender as those ibises you spotted along the road here, alabaster birds too elegant and rare to be standing in a gutter, yet there they were, lording it over the shredded tires and crumpled cups. Except for the curve in his upper spine from so many years peering down at patients, her father's back was stiff and straight. His hands shook, but it wasn't Parkinson's, just some hereditary tremor passed on from his father (her own hands, thank God, were steady as rocks). Her father never smoked. At most, he drank a thimbleful of Cherry Heering to calm his nerves after a tough day's extractions, or a whiskey sour at a party. He walked miles around the development's fake lagoon and played golf in daily foursomes. But men in their seventies got diseases of organs women didn't have. And organs they did have. Was he going blind from glaucoma? Would he soon forget her name?

"Nothing you need to bother about," he said. But that didn't suppress her fear, knowing as she did that the emphasis was on "you" rather than "nothing" or "bother." A man like Milt Rothstein no more allowed his problems to upset his child than he allowed her to support him—physically or financially. And so, when he tossed the car keys across the roof, Wendy nearly tossed them back. The last time her father had permitted her to drive a car in which he had been a passenger had been twenty-seven years earlier, when he was teaching her to drive, and even then he kept trying to snatch back the wheel.

She took the keys and slid in. Despite the giant cardboard sunglasses above the dash, the car was furnace hot. The cardboard glasses made Wendy feel as though she were suffocating inside someone else's head. All the retirees' cars had them. Caddies and Grand Marquises sprawled across the lots of southern Florida like has-been actors on a beach turning their wide metallic faces to the sun. Her parents had bought this car the week they moved to Florida. Every couple did that, traded their ten-year-old Impala or Skylark for the larger and fancier car they would drive until they died. Wendy's mother had gone to Wal-Mart and bought this cardboard shield. Her feet had touched these pedals. Her thighs had sweated against the beaded wood contraption that protected the driver's skin from the scalding leather.

Wendy adjusted the seat to fit her legs, but the car seemed to resist her driving it, the way her lover's horse stiffened when she tried to mount it. She had gone from being the daughter of a man who drove a Grand Marquis that resisted her driving it to being the fiancée of a man who rode a stallion named Rapscallion—Harrison called him "Rap" for short, which, in his Montana drawl, sounded more like *Rape*—that didn't like her riding it. Her own dented blue Corolla liked Wendy just fine, but she couldn't keep driving a Corolla if she moved to Harry's ranch. The image of her squat little Corolla bottoming out on the rutted road or getting stranded in a snowdrift brought to mind the many times her father had carried their beagle, Bing, outside to find a spot where the snow was shallow enough so Bing could do her business. After the dog was done, Wendy's father would scoop Bing in his gangly arms and

147

nuzzle the dog's belly with his head, the memory of which nearly set Wendy sobbing.

Dad, she wanted to say, *I'm getting married.* Except that she wasn't officially engaged. *Don't you dare go pulling that stunt again,* she told herself. She had been so upset by her mother's first lumpectomy that she had blurted out the news that she and Sam were getting married, although Sam, in Sacramento, knew nothing of this engagement and, when Wendy related the anecdote that night, hoping to jolt him into saying, "Well, why don't we make the news true?," told her that she had no right to use his life for her own nefarious purposes, at which Wendy said, "Nefarious? What is nefarious about wanting to make your mother happy?," which led to more words, an avalanche of *words* that swept them away from each other and led to Wendy's move to Alabama, so by the time her mother's breast was removed, Wendy was inspired to make the same sort of declaration about Andrew, in Anniston, who, until then, hadn't been aware that she expected him to leave his wife, which, it turned out, he had no intention of doing.

It occurred to her now that she had lived in so many cities and loved so many men and worked for so many newspapers— couriers, eagles, bees, telegraphs, messengers, even a beaver, there had been a beaver in there somewhere—that her life sounded like a rhyme children might skip rope to: *A, I lived with Andrew in Anniston, Alabama, and was an arts reporter for the Star; B, I lived in Bloomington with that baker named Zack and covered business for the Herald.* By her mother's third operation, Wendy could sense that her mother didn't believe that Wendy truly intended to marry Arick, the poet she had met while writing features in Kentucky. Although they did move in together. Arick even flew with Wendy to the funeral. He was a big, deep-hearted Irishman, and events like a mother's death moved him in ways that American men rarely seemed moved by anything except the deaths of their athletic heroes. Wendy and Arick didn't break up until the following year, when Arick published his book of poems, got a decent job teaching, began working out at Wendy's health club, drinking organic carrot-juice, and blathering on and on about how "the body is a text" and "the Irish are the perpetual European Other," which drove Wendy nuts in ways that his getting drunk and pissing in potted plants had never done. Her mother must have guessed that she would never marry Arick, and it tormented her that her mother had been buried with this lie lodged insidiously in her chest like another malignant tumor.

But Harry *had* proposed. It had started as a joke. Everything serious with Harry started as a joke, which only made the mood darker once it turned. He had been down on his knees, smoothing the cement floor of the shed he was rebuilding. Wendy waited for him to finish, watching his long, hardened fingers smooth the trowel back and forth, leveling the wet cement. He looked up at her and grinned. "As long as I'm down here, where it isn't so easy for a man my age to be, I might as well propose." He clasped his hands in fake prayer. "Will you marry me, my darling Wendy?" Then he got up—slowly, even for a man of sixty, as if some change were over-taking him—and brushed a cap of wet cement from each knee. He rubbed the grit between his fingertips in a gesture that reminded Wendy of her father rubbing mercury amalgam between his palms (maybe *that* was why he was dying, all the toxic metal seeping through his skin). Then Harry took her by her elbows, and she was seized by the premonition that he would swing her around and bury her feet in the wet cement.

But he had something else in mind. What Harry did to her in the shed that day made Wendy tell him that she didn't ever want to see him again. She was going away, she said. Her father had offered to pay her fare to Florida. He was lonely, he had said. He needed her. She hadn't intended to accept his invitation. Who would want to spend a week in Florida in July? But after what happened with Harry, she decided she ought to go.

Now, she powered down the window and placed the parking ticket in the attendant's disembodied hand. "$12.00," the meter read. Which meant that her father must have gotten to the airport three hours early. Was he that eager for her company? Or that afraid of getting lost? Either way, his newborn vulnerability scared her. When her mother had been alive, she and Wendy's father planned their arrivals to the minute. Her mother would begin monitoring the weather channel days before Wendy was due to fly in. She called the airline to make sure that Wendy's flight was on time, then plotted the quickest route from Boca to West Palm, scouted the most convenient parking spot, and ran interference for Wendy's father so they would be standing at the gate ten minutes before Wendy got there.

Like most retirees, her parents expended a Herculean effort attending to the minutiae of their lives—charting the shortest distance between the condo and the club, the restaurant and the mall, the barber shop and the grocery store, with the fewest left turns and the least chance of getting stuck in traffic. They kept themselves apprised of which roads were being fixed, which stores carried which brands. For God's sake, they knew how long it would take a given stoplight to change. They seemed to believe that in dissecting every act into the smallest intervals, some stasis might be achieved. It was the Zeno's Paradox of aging: halve the distance between the starting point and the finish line, halve and halve again, and the destination could not be reached, the arrow would be arrested in mid-flight.

Except that Wendy's mother had indeed reached the end of her flight. Wendy knew she was naive to admit this, but she had been astonished when her mother died. Until then, Wendy had believed that everyone survived every kind of cancer except the really bad ones—lung, stomach, liver. If you took whatever tests the doctors recommended and caught the tumor early, if you didn't give in to vanity and let the surgeons hack off whatever they wanted to hack off, you could live a long life. Thinking as she did—or rather, not thinking— Wendy hadn't visited her mother often enough. It wasn't that she was self-centered. All right, maybe she was. But only with the same goofy optimism as the rest of her generation: she couldn't believe that anyone she loved would really die.

Well, she wasn't going to make that same mistake with her father. Whatever disease he had, she would take it seriously. She would demand long leaves from work, buy tickets to come and see him. She would help him fight whatever battle he had to fight, and, if he lost, sit by his bed and help him die.

"Do you miss her?" she asked as the parking gate swung up.

"Who?" her father said, and instead of rolling up the driver's window, Wendy hit the wrong button and powered down the other three.

"Mom. There's someone else?"

"There was," he said. "Not now."

The idea of her father mourning anyone but her mother was as disturbing as if he had installed a statue of the Virgin Mary on the dash. Her parents' marriage had been as close to ideal as the institution ever came. They never tired of each other's company. Neither made the smallest joke at the other's expense. If they fought, they made up. And both of them liked sex. According to a family story, the day before their wedding, Wendy's aunt Mae had advised Wendy's

151

mother to just close her eyes, take a deep breath, and "try to get through that part." Wendy's mother, being bookish, had gone to the library and ascertained that a woman might indeed enjoy "that part" if she and her husband *thought* she might enjoy it and took appropriate steps toward that end, which Wendy's father did. "If you don't enjoy it, there's something wrong," her mother had once said, although, being who she was, she felt obliged to add, "Of course, it can only be enjoyed with someone you truly love and know will stick around." The best testament Wendy could give her parents was that even as a teenager she hadn't been upset to imagine them having sex, and how many kids can say that?

Her parents' love had cast an invisible globe around them. No one else could get inside, except her father's friend, Moose, and Moose's wife, Cynthia, because Cynthia and Moose had the same kind of marriage. Cynthia died first, and her death pricked a hole in the fragile globe they lived in. (Wendy was thinking here of the souvenirs she and her brother used to buy when they visited their grandparents in Miami Beach, those cunning glass globes with flamingos and snow inside. Cynthia's death had started the water leaking, and when Wendy's mother died, Moose and Wendy's father were left gasping, high and dry.) Moose had given up his dairy business and retired to the same development as Wendy's father. Talk about friendship. But six months later, he had keeled over from a heart attack while helping some new arrivals unload their valises from the car. Wendy's father held no brief with self-pity, but he had just been recovering from his wife's death and Moose's death knocked him down again.

"You broke up with someone?" Wendy asked.

"Get in the left lane," he ordered. "You want the next exit."

She figured he would use this as an excuse to ignore her question, but after they were off the highway, he said, "Yes. And I'm also sick."

Her heart pounded so hard she thought the Grand Marquis had sprung a flat. "What are you sick with?" she said, trying not to sound as panicked as she felt.

"It isn't important," he said, and she forced herself to keep driving, although what she felt like doing was pulling off the road and forcing him to tell her what was wrong. The avenue down which they drove was lined with miniature palm-trees like the plastic decorations in the habitats for turtles Wendy had kept when she was young, an impression reinforced by the heavy smell, like the odor of rotting hamburger meat and wilted lettuce she used to feed those same pets.

They reached the turnoff for her father's pod—that's what the occupants down here called the sections of their developments, *pods*. On her first visit, Wendy had dubbed her parents' pod "Boco Loco," nestled as it was amid Boca This and Lago That. Now, she stopped before the security booth, where the guard, who looked like an elderly version of the steward on *The Love Boat*, sat on a high stool stitching a plastic wallet. Even in his distress, her father took visible pleasure in raising one arm in a casual salute, the guard nodding at Mr. Rothstein in his big silver Grand Marquis and pushing a button to raise the gate.

Ninety-nine percent of the couples who lived here were Jewish, the remaining one percent being an Indian family who'd moved in because an unscrupulous agent had neglected to inform them that they would be the only non-Jews, the only couple under sixty, and the only family with kids. The only other dark-skinned people inside the gate were the Jamaican gardeners kneeling around the flowerbeds and the Hispanic cleaning-women who lugged pails and mops from condo to condo. Wendy would have been more disapproving, but she knew that her parents had moved here less from prejudice than a desire to relax among people like themselves after years of discomfort among the gentiles they feared.

Her parents' generation had been able to control so few things about their lives. Their own parents had washed up as teeming refuse at Ellis Island. They'd worked their eyes to blindness sewing buttons on ladies' coats or cutting and pressing pants, and just when they were getting somewhere, they got flattened by the Great Depression. If not for World War II, Wendy's father could never have become a dentist. But who wanted to go to war? Her soft, good-natured father had been forced to claw his way across the coral islands of the South Pacific, taking back a bunch of worthless reefs from the Japanese. And her mother's generation . . . raising their kids in their parents' back parlors while working swing shift at a plant that made bombs or ammunition, not knowing if their husbands would ever come back alive.

The fifties were the high point. The reunited couples bought ranches in the suburbs, or, in Wendy's case, in the small dairy-town upstate where her father had grown up. They nurtured their dental practices, their optometry practices, their podiatry practices, their plumbing-supply concerns. They pruned their willows and edged their walks. They ironed their children's sheets and dressed them in tweeds or crinolines even to go to school. They made sure the toilet-paper roll was installed with the sheets coming down from the bottom, the butter was in the butter bin, and the individually wrapped slices of American cheese were sealed tightly inside the Tupperware container for American cheese. But after the fifties came the sixties, and the children despised their parents for devoting so much energy to optometry and weeds. They moved to ashrams in California, did cocaine, and got divorced. And so, when Wendy's parents and their friends retired, she forgave them for buying condos in communities where at least they could control who was permitted inside, the color of the plants, and what attire could be worn.

What her parents and their friends didn't understand was that they had brought up their children to seek the very life that frightened them—not safety but risk, not a small controllable existence, but a huge volcanic life that nothing could contain. Wendy's parents had told her over and over to pursue what made her happy, which gave her the impression that it was *possible* to be happy, it was her *business* to be happy, it was her *duty*—to herself and them—to pursue what made her happy. She belonged to the first generation in human history whose members had been raised to think they could and should be happy. They could live anywhere they wished, be anything they wanted to be, marry anyone who thrilled them, and, if the thrill fizzled, marry someone else.

But it was impossible to discover the best place to live unless you kept moving. You couldn't settle for any one job, or any one partner, because settling might mean *settling*. In Wendy's case, the only part of her life she had been able to commit to was being a reporter. She could, for an afternoon, sky dive or dowse for water or ride in an ambulance with the EMTs without having to become any of these things herself. And finally, after all that moving, she had found the ideal place to live. Certainly, everyone who lived in Helena, Montana, thought it was ideal. Where else could you climb a mountain without leaving downtown?

And for a while, Wendy had thought she had found the ideal man. She could marry Harry Yates without worrying that she was settling. He had grown up on his parents' ranch in a

155

village so remote it was where the Unabomber lived before his brother turned him in. Harry had gotten his degree at Harvard—his specialty was William Blake—then returned to Missoula to teach. By the time he had retired, not only was he the chair of the English Department, he was the most popular, charismatic professor on campus. He moved back to his parents' ranch forty miles from Helena, but forty miles in Montana wasn't far.

Wendy had met him while she was interviewing people who had befriended Ted Kaczynski before they knew who Ted Kaczynski was. Harry had provided her with a few eccentric quotes, then invited her back to the ranch to ride. She had accepted and driven out there, not knowing what to expect except that her host resembled an aging Clint Eastwood. He was a cowboy, of sorts, with the exaggerated chivalry and manly roughness that stereotype implied. But he was a gracious well-traveled cowboy, and he seemed to be the only man in Montana who, on a daily basis, read anything besides the pages of her newspaper devoted to beef and wheat.

She hadn't ridden a horse in years, but she managed to climb on Harry's favorite mare and remain in the saddle through a grueling two-hour ride. Somewhere in the mountains, after a particularly skull-rattling gallop, he looked over at her and said, "Ma'am, you have what in the old days used to be called a good seat." And she'd looked back at him and smiled and avoided saying the expected: *You have a pretty good seat yourself.* The attraction was near miraculous. The very horses on which they rode couldn't help but try to mate, with their riders still on them.

Wendy tried to imagine bringing Harry here to meet her dad. In her mind's eye she saw a fifty-foot cowboy step down from a Marlboro billboard, crush the security gate beneath his boot, then bend to pick up a handful of the Jewish pygmies swarming around his feet. *You're the cowboy of Boco Loco,* she would whisper when they made love on the fold-out bed in her father's guest room.

Except that she had vowed never to let Harry make love to her again. You couldn't even call what they had done that last time making love. But then, why had she enjoyed it? If she had ordered him to stop, Harry would have stopped. It wasn't as if what they'd done had come out of nowhere. Maybe she should forgive him. If he wanted to be forgiven. Maybe she should call and see what he had to say.

Except the technology didn't exist that could connect Harry's world to this. Her father couldn't possibly understand the relief that washed over her when Harry ordered her to lie still and let him do what he pleased. She didn't need to make a choice. She could give herself to a man pinning her arms above her head, biting her breasts, then flipping her over and pulling up her hips and striking her with a riding crop.

Wendy glanced across the seat and was sickened to realize that her father resembled Harry. Frailer. More distracted. Not as muscular or tan. But both of them were tall rangy men with melancholy faces. And there was something about their eyes. Despair. Or maybe lust. Harry had left his first wife; the other two had left him. Her father had remained faithful to Wendy's mother for forty-seven years. Yet there was something the same about them. Something to do with sex. Neither man could live without it, the difference being that Wendy's father had found it with his wife, and Harry still was looking.

Until now, Wendy had assumed that in dating so many men she was trying to please her mother. But it was her father to whom she kept returning, like a child who's found a shell and wants to be reassured it's the best shell on the beach. Wendy couldn't help but think her father would approve, if not of the way she and Harry made love (say "bondage" to her dad and he would think of the Pharaoh forcing his Hebrew slaves to make bricks without straw), then of the way she couldn't stop thinking about having sex with Harry and her intention to marry him because of it.

She maneuvered the Grand Marquis into her father's lot. Each of the twenty buildings in the pod looked like all the others; she could pick out her parents' condo only by the brass sculpture of the naked girl half-hidden in the hibiscus. Wendy's mother had fashioned that sculpture the year before she died. It was better than her other pieces—not cute so much as coy, even a bit seductive. Yet the board of trustees had engaged in endless wrangling before they had approved the sculpture's placement in that bush. For which Wendy couldn't forgive them. They'd known her mother was dying. What would have been the harm if their worst prediction had come to pass and all the development's residents began sculpting naked girls and setting them around the pod?

"Son of a bitch!" her father yelled, and Wendy tried to figure out what she could possibly have done wrong. He liked to park the Grand Marquis so it was centered between the lines, but she hadn't even pulled in yet.

"That schmuck!" her father shouted. "All these other spaces and he has to take mine?" Her father leapt from the car and started pounding on the door of the condo opposite his own. "You son of a bitch, get out here and move that damn Kraut-car before I do it for you." He climbed back in his Grand Marquis, and he and Wendy watched as Morrie Ashkenazi, a retired jeweler from Cherry Hill, New Jersey, scuffed out in orange thongs and moved his BMW, and then, on his way back inside, gave her father the finger as only one old Jewish man can give another old Jewish man the finger, looking up to God and ordering Him to correct the unforgivable mistake of having created Milt Rothstein in the first place.

Wendy pulled into her father's spot, so shaken she almost scratched the brand-new steel-blue Grand Marquis to her left. What could be going on inside her usually placid father that he could rage so furiously at a fellow Jew? Maybe Morrie Ashkenazi's wife had been her father's lover. No, things of that sort didn't go on here. These men liked to *think* about sex. They liked to *joke* about sex. (What was the story Moose used to tell? The sexy Boca widow motions her neighbor to park his Caddie and come inside. He succumbs to temptation and goes in and finds the woman in bed in a skimpy negligee. The widow beckons him closer, but when the poor man takes off his trousers, she slaps him. "What was that for?" he says. "Didn't I see you in the window, motioning me to come inside?" "*Nu*," she says, "I invited you to come inside. I didn't say nothing about parking in my spot.") But the men in Boco Loco didn't let their passions overwhelm them. The possibility of another man diddling your wife seemed to arouse less anger than the possibility of that same man inserting his BMW where your own car ought to be.

The interior of the Grand Marquis began to steam up, but her father laid his bony hand on her arm and wouldn't let her open the door. "It's AIDS," he said. "I have AIDS. That's what I'm sick with."

Wendy had been sweaty and chilled before, but now she started shivering. AIDS? Her father couldn't have AIDS. He wasn't gay. A drug abuser? Right. He'd made it through some of the worst combat in World War II only to pass out cold on the day of his discharge when a medic drew some blood. To Wendy's knowledge, he'd never required a transfusion. Then

159

she thought: *Idiot, he worked with blood all day.* He'd refused to wear gloves because they interfered with his dexterity. "That's for the new guys," he used to claim, as if he were too old to catch some newfangled disease that hadn't been invented until decades after he'd finished dental school.

"You got infected from a patient?" she asked.

He could have avoided the active lie and merely not denied it. But her father said no, he had gotten it from "a friend." He had been lonely, he said. So very, very lonely. And being so lonely, he had done things he wouldn't have done if Wendy's mother were still alive. "I met someone in Miami." That's how he put it. "I met a woman named Rosina." He gave no indication how long her mother had been dead by then, or who this Rosina was. All he said was, "Rosina and I kept company. We had a lot of good times. Then I started to feel rundown."

"Rundown?"

"I lacked strength. What little I ate, I couldn't keep down. I began to get sores."

She didn't dare ask what sores. The idea of her father having sores from anything, let alone AIDS . . . She couldn't be hearing this. She couldn't. Her father had gotten AIDS from some woman he'd slept with after her mother died? He might as well have told her that he had been leading a secret life for fifty years. Not to mention that he would die. He would have died eventually from something. But dying now, from AIDS?

She gasped and gave a cry, but her father didn't seem to hear. On he went, describing the vitamin pills, iron supplements, and Geritol he'd started taking, although he suspected all along his weakness wasn't caused by poor nutrition. Rosina, he said, was a very good cook. Being from South America, she liked preparing dishes that were tastier than Wendy's mother's. (Wendy flinched at this treachery. It was almost as upsetting as if he were discussing her mother's timidity in bed. Not that her mother had been timid in bed.)

No, the cause of his fatigue wasn't a lack of vitamins. He had been so sure that he had leukemia, he almost hadn't bothered to consult a doctor. Still, being a medical man himself, he couldn't condone such ignorance. The internist he finally consulted also assumed leukemia—the sores on his legs, the bruises that refused to heal. But the doctor did some tests— here, her father turned away—and the results surprised them both.

That was it. End of story. Wendy sat shivering and sweating and trying to assimilate the news that her father had gotten AIDS from some woman he had picked up in Miami. She was getting up the nerve to ask if he had informed Rosina of his diagnosis when he laid his head against the window on the passenger side and beat it against the glass. Nothing in Wendy's life had frightened her this badly, not even the time she'd been held at gunpoint by a sex offender in Alabama who'd demanded her "understanding" of what he was going through in trying to start a new life after she had alerted his neighbors to his crime. She wanted to reach across the seat and take her father in her arms, but the space between them seemed too clotted with heat and pain.

"What are you doing?" her father moaned. "Look at what you've done!"

What *she* had done? She hadn't gotten AIDS. She wasn't the one beating her head against the glass. Then she saw. She must have started to reach out to hold her father, then let her hand drop and, in her distress, worked the car key through the seat. She stared at the puncture, which was edged with yellow foam like the fat beneath an animal's hide. She expected blood to flow, but nothing seeped out except a sigh of stale air like the final exhalation of a giant dying beast.

* * *

Milt left his daughter puttering in the guest room and wandered to the screened-in porch. The Florida room, they called it, which had always struck Milt as odd. If you lived up north, you might call a screened-in porch a "Florida room," the way in Florida you called pizza or bagels "New York style." But if you lived in Florida, calling it a "Florida room" made no sense.

Well, whatever it was called, he hadn't been out here in a while. The condo backed onto the fairway of a golf course that nearly every other couple in the development belonged to. He and Greta hadn't joined because it seemed ridiculous to pay $40,000 in equity to join the club, then shell out another twenty bucks every time you played because the rules required that you rent an electric cart. Where was the exercise in that? If he and Greta wanted to play nine holes, they got in the car and drove a few miles to the public course. Otherwise, they found their entertainment sitting on the porch and watching the other couples play.

He rarely came out now. A foursome of old men didn't upset him. But a couple such as this, a nicely dressed pair of senior citizens, twisted Milt's heart like a dishrag. The husband took his shot, then bent and set his wife's ball on a tee. The wife walked up to the tee and drove, shading her eyes to see how far the ball had gone and laughing the way Greta might have laughed. Milt tried to turn away, but he couldn't avoid the sight of the man cupping his wife's elbow and helping her up and in the cart. When the man put the cart in gear, steering expertly with one hand and dangling his free arm around his wife's sweatered shoulders, tears sprang to Milt's eyes.

The cart puttered out of sight, and the next cart, when it drove up, held two older men. But Milt knew that another couple would drive by soon. Idly, he pressed his fingers in the dirt that held the rubber tree plant. A week after Greta's death, he had begun to notice that several ferns were shriveling and turning brown, while other plants remained eerily fresh. Shuffling from room to room, he had been stunned to discover that some of the plants were fake. The reason the six-foot ficus hadn't grown through the ceiling was the damn thing was made of silk. It bothered Milt to learn this, not because the plants' artificiality made Greta guilty of some deception, but because his ignorance made him wonder what else he hadn't known. Making a circuit of the condo, he stuck his hand in every pot to see if the dirt was real, and that upset him, too, that he couldn't distinguish living things from fake and couldn't remember from week to week which plants were which.

Now, on the porch, he made a mental note to water the ferns and rubber tree, then tried to bring to mind what else he had meant to do. Put sheets on the bed in the guest room? No, better if he didn't. Not that touching his daughter's linens would infect her. He was a medical man. He knew all there was to know about infections, saliva, germs. For that matter, Wendy was an educated girl. She had to be aware that the virus could be transmitted only by secretions. But the fewer things Milt touched, the fewer things would remind his daughter of what disease he had and how he had come to get it.

To pass the time, Milt rifled the magazines in the wicker rack, pushing aside the yellowing copy of *Vogue* he hadn't been able to discard and the last three issues of *Consumer Reports*, to which he might as well cancel his subscription. Half the pleasure used to come from comparing notes with Greta, debating the relative merits of a Sunbeam or an Amana, engaging in the harmless but thrilling risk of a disagreement. But Milt already had purchased all the appliances he would ever buy. The washer he owned, even that last gallon of detergent he had bought the week before, undoubtedly would outlast him.

Snatching up the *ADA Journal*, Milt settled in to read. For a while, the ads for high-speed drills, the case studies, and the editorials about government regulations brought a familiar joy. Once, Milt had derived a comforting satisfaction from the mere feel of the magazine. The entire publication was designed for a man like him—a man with a wife and kids, a profession, and a practice. And now? He tried to focus on the lead article about the crisis in dental health insurance, but it was more economics than dentistry and he had little patience for the terminology. Still, he kept the journal as a decoy in case Wendy came in to talk. Because that's what she would want to do. As if talking had ever cured a thing.

Then again, there had been no point in inviting her down to Florida if he meant to avoid her. If he didn't set her straight, she would assume he had driven to Miami and cruised Collins Avenue with the specifically thought-out purpose of picking up a tramp. It hadn't been like that at all. He had signed up for a tour of the Deco District, more for the company than any interest he had in architecture, although once he was standing in the District he'd become so fascinated with a certain rococo theater that he'd wandered off to inspect it, thinking this might be the very same theater to which his father had brought him fifty years earlier, the first time they'd driven down to Florida and rented a room on Lincoln Road.

Milt had gotten so involved in his memories that the bus

had left without him. Stopping for a glass of cold seltzer and a chance to rest his feet, he met a nice-looking older woman. Respectable. Well dressed. She'd come up to his table and stood tapping her cheek with a polished nail.

"Excuthe me," she said, as if her tongue got in the way, an accent or affectation Milt found irresistible, making him think as it did of her lips, teeth, and tongue. "Do you have maybe the time?" He thought at first she was asking if he had the time to spend with her. "My girlfriend, I think, is not coming. We planned she would meet me here at four, but I am thinking it already must be five."

She wore shiny high-heeled shoes not even Greta could have walked on, and shimmery pink-red pants. A little too bright, but what the hell, Spanish women liked to wear bright clothes. Her top was composed of a filmy white material that Greta might have worn as a scarf but not a blouse. Although such a light material must have felt comfortable in all that heat.

"I'm sorry your friend disappointed you," Milt heard himself say. It was the first time he had spoken that afternoon. Even on the bus ride down, he hadn't talked to the man in the seat beside him, who kept yanking out his hearing aid, then plugging it back in and tapping it. Come to think of it, Milt hadn't talked to anyone in days. "Perhaps you would allow me to buy you a beverage?" he asked, noting that the woman's clumsiness with the language was rubbing off on him. Or maybe it was the situation. He couldn't remember the last time he had tried to pick up a woman.

"No, no, you mustn't do that." The woman shook her finger at Milt as if he had said something out of line. "You mustn't feel sorry. This friend of mine, she is always, what is it called, standing up on me?" ·

165

At which Milt himself stood up. "Please, feeling sorry for you had nothing to do with my offer."

The woman smiled and allowed Milt to pull out the metal chair and guide her into it. "I am Rosina Alvarez," she said and held out her small white hand—awkwardly, Milt thought, like a woman who wasn't brought up to shake hands. And so, when he took Rosina's hand in his own and introduced himself as Milton Rothstein—he almost added "DDS"—he turned the hand sideways and raised it to his lips as if he might kiss Rosina's wrist, although never in his life had he kissed a woman's wrist.

Then he called over the waitress and asked Rosina what she wanted. "What will you have, Rosina?" He said her name—*Ro-si-na*—as if tasting a delicious new fruit. And Rosina did in fact order the juice of some exotic pinkish fruit Milt had never heard of. She offered him a sip, and merely putting his mouth to the glass beside the print of her lips aroused him so strongly that he was glad he had the table to hide his lap. "Delicious," he said. *"Deliciosa!,"* and he laughed happily, because already he could see that new experiences lay in store. A new language. New fruits. As embarrassed as he had been at having missed his ride home, he was able to confide this to Rosina, at which she told him that she had "always liked the mens who aren't following like the sheeps." Milt found her difficulty with the idiom beguiling, like some problem with her teeth—a gap, perhaps, a chip—that could easily be fixed but was more charming the way it was.

Rosina finished her drink and Milt called for the check and paid. Thankfully, she seemed as reluctant to end their date as he was. She offered to guide him on her own tour of the Deco District, and after a perfunctory protest, Milt gave in. How she managed to walk so many blocks in those high heels he couldn't comprehend. First, she showed him the District's most notable architectural features. Then, her favorite shops, eccentric boutiques that sold women's clothes and shoes and what Rosina called "cha-chas"—Milt needed a while to realize that Rosina mean *tchatchkes*, and he found this charming, too.

They promenaded down to First Street, then sat along the walkway and watched the sun set, after which Rosina startled Milt by offering to drive him back to Boca. "I couldn't trouble you to do that," he said, but really, he had no other way to get home. He followed her the few blocks to her building and down the stairs to her garage. She drove a boxy and out-of-date light blue Continental, a gift, she confessed, from the gentleman who'd been her friend when she'd first arrived in Florida. "I should not be taking such expensive gifts from the mens," she said. She adjusted the rearview mirror. "But there is, in those days, a lot of difficult to pay."

Milt couldn't make out whether the man's profession had had to do with "eyes" or "ice," but the combination of possibilities provoked him to imagine corpses on ice, diamonds smuggled into Florida in various distasteful ways, and gangsters stabbing ice picks in each other's eyes. Whatever the man's profession, the jealous bastard had accused Rosina of carrying on affairs with other men. Discounting her denials, he had hired thugs to tail her. "Maybe they scratch my face, they throw acid," Rosina said. "I know these mens are capable of very many bad thing."

On the hour drive to Boca, Rosina told Milt about her life as a young woman in Argentina. "Are very many Jewitsh person living there, from getting away from Hitler. I have so many Jewitsh friend, I am thinking I maybe have Jewitsh blood myself." Here she tapped Milt's knee, which sent his own Jewitsh blood coursing to parts it hadn't coursed to since Greta's death. Rosina's perfume smelled the same as that delicious juice he'd

167

sipped. He didn't want to stop smelling it. He couldn't bear to return to his dark apartment and get in bed alone. Besides, he couldn't very well allow Rosina to drive all the way back to Miami without thanking her with a meal.

And the dinner, thank God, went well. They talked for so many hours it was too late to send her home. Milt coughed and cleared his throat and said he didn't mean to be inappropriate, but he wouldn't hear of Rosina driving back to Miami, especially since she had drunk a glass of wine. He offered to sleep on the fold-out couch, and Rosina laughed and said, Yes, well, come to think of it, she was a little-little bit too tired to drive. Yawning and laughing, she helped Milt take the cushions off the couch in the guest room. "Oh, is so much trouble over nothing," Rosina said.

And though she never did suggest that they sleep in his bed instead, that was where they ended up. All it seemed to take was Rosina reaching up and putting her long cool fingers to his neck. On their first date, they slept together! And the next morning, when Milt woke up, he was so happy he couldn't keep from crying, which made him feel ancient and incontinent, unable to perform, when in fact he had performed like a much younger man. Twice. He had done it twice. It had been years since he had done it twice, even with Greta.

Greta. When he thought of Greta, he almost sent Rosina home. But Rosina chose that moment to pick up Greta's photo from the nightstand, holding the sheet demurely against her throat. "She is a beautiful woman, your wife," Rosina said, and even though Milt knew it was Rosina's limited control of English that made her use the present tense, he was grateful that she had. "She is a lovely, lovely lady," Rosina said. "You are lucky man to have her." Then she picked up the dental journal that was also beside the bed. "You are *dentista?*" she asked, biting her tongue in that way that made Milt feel like kissing her.

Which he did. They made love an unbelievable third time, and Milt got out of bed and nearly floated to the kitchen, where he fixed Rosina breakfast and brought it back on one of Greta's silver trays.

"Lovely man, I will eat. But then I must go. I have this little-little job. Not for money, but, how they say, for passing time. I care for these sweet little babies." She shrugged her beautiful bare white shoulders. "What else can I do? In Argentina, a girl like me is raised only to be a mother. I never am blessed with my own babies, but I know how to do for these."

She shooed Milt from his own bedroom so she could dress. Then he walked her to the door. "Will I see you again?" he asked.

Rosina laughed. "Is no law against seeing me. I am very free woman." And she got in her boxy car and backed out, waving as she turned, and Milt sat on the porch for hours, then went in to take his shower, where he found himself so excited by the idea of taking a shower with Rosina that he had to do to himself what he hadn't done in years, not since he married Greta. He could barely restrain himself from calling Rosina until that night. What a relief to dial her number and hear her voice! They went out a few days later, Milt driving down to Miami and taking Rosina to a club where they danced and drank cocktails made with an overly sweet liqueur distilled from the juice she loved. There was nothing cheap about her. Not that Milt Rothstein was such an expert on class. But he knew good manners when he saw them.

Then why was he so sure that Rosina had come up to him in

that café with the express purpose of starting an affair so she could milk a lonely retired dentist for everything he was worth? Milt had no cause to doubt that she had been a respectable married lady before her husband died and she learned that he had been involved in various shady activities that caused her to pack and flee. After arriving in Miami, she'd had that "gentleman friend." She'd admitted as much to Milt. He certainly had no cause to assume that she'd had a long string of gentleman friends before she'd met him, or that she'd given her favors to these friends in return for monthly checks.

But his assumptions, it turned out, were true. When Milt received his diagnosis, the wool dropped from his eyes. (Wool? Or was it scales? What kind of scales would cover someone's eyes? What was he, a fish?) To be completely honest, he had known what Rosina was from the moment he saw her. If he hadn't known, he wouldn't have needed to keep denying it. But he did know. Of course he knew. He knew it from the way she'd come up to him so readily, from her ease and lack of shyness and her familiarity with the world. Greta was no wilting flower, but if Milt had been the first one to go, Greta wouldn't have been cha-chaing around Miami Beach on such a regular basis that at least half a dozen maître d's knew her name. So yes, Milt knew from the start what this Rosina Alvarez was, but he pretended not to know so he could continue to enjoy her affections. Which made him as much to blame as she was.

* * *

Wendy and her brother, Joel, used to make fun of their parents' fondness for habit. "Why do we do things the way we do?" Joel would start the chant, and Wendy would chime the chorus: "Because that's the way we do things!" But now, in her father's condo, she saw that habit allowed you to keep living when you were too stupid and dazed by grief to come up with something new. You did what always came next. What you always did in Boca.

She dragged her suitcase to the bureau. If her mother had been alive, the bottom drawer would have been empty, but her father hadn't cleared it. Colorful wooden tees and stubby pencils skittered like palmetto bugs beneath the cardboard scorecards from countless rounds of golf. She saw a withered blue corsage, a napkin from "Club Azul" emblazoned with the print of a woman's lips, and a bottle of Zoloft, the aluminum seal intact even though the prescription was two weeks old. Not knowing where to move these things, Wendy laid her underwear across the top and shut the drawer. Her father had neglected to set out fresh linens, but she found these on her own. She removed the cushions from the fold-out bed but couldn't bring herself to open it. Everything in Boca reminded her of a coffin.

She carried her cosmetics case to the bathroom. She never brought floss; her father still had crates of it stockpiled beneath the sink. For that matter, she rarely brought her own toothpaste or nail clippers. Sometimes, if she forgot to bring her razor, she shaved her legs with her father's blade. Well, time to grow up. She would have to get through the week with stubbly shins and ragged nails. She needn't worry about getting sick from mooching a little dental floss or taking a shower in his stall. But the mere consideration of these possibilities led her to remember that her father was ill and face the enormity of the loneliness that must have spurred him to take up with this Rosina, not to mention his humiliation at having to reveal his sex life to his daughter.

She set the cosmetics case on the sink and walked to the

screened-in porch, intending to offer the consolation she should have offered him in the car. But her father was sitting calmly in his chair reading the latest issue of the dental journal to which he had been subscribing for the past half a century. Beyond the patio, a trio of older women rattled past in a golf cart. Even if her father hadn't just revealed he had AIDS, she would have found it strange that he was sitting there reading a dental journal. What reason could he possibly have to keep up with the latest bonding techniques or the studies as to how much fluoride was enough to keep a child's teeth from rotting? How could anyone love dentistry for its own sake rather than merely tolerate it as a means to earn a living?

To stave off the nearly ungovernable impulse to throw her arms around his neck, Wendy picked up the newspaper and scanned the bylines. The paper's columnist, a Latina named Sherí, had roomed with Wendy's best friend Monica when all three of them were interns at the *Anniston Star*. Wendy also knew the *Sun-Sentinel*'s sports reporter, an inhumanly good-looking man named Quaid, who had been Wendy's boyfriend in Seattle until she'd dumped him because he was too polite in bed. Neither of Wendy's friends had a story in the paper that day, but the article above the fold gave her a pang of fear:

SENIOR SHOOTS SELF
TO AVOID CONSEQUENCES
OF HIDDEN LIFE.

A man her father's age had driven to the beach, put a rifle between his legs, and pulled the trigger with his toe. According to the police, this man had once owned a house in Englewood, New Jersey. After he'd retired, he'd deeded the house to his son, who had lived there fifteen years before putting it up for sale to settle a divorce. A couple made an offer, contingent on the owner removing a metal drum from the crawl space beneath the porch. The son hired two employees from his import-export warehouse—or rather, from the warehouse his father still owned—and hauled the barrel to the dump, where the supervisor wouldn't accept it without proof that it was empty. The employees hacked off the lid, only to watch a shriveled hand and a lady's purse flop out.

The cops in Englewood had phoned the son's father in Boca to inquire if he knew anything about the young Chinese woman in the drum. "I do," the man said, but his wife was in the room and he couldn't discuss it now. He promised to drive to the police station and tell the officers everything he knew. Instead, he'd bought a gun, driven to the beach, and taken his life.

"Did you know this guy?" Wendy held out the paper. "It says he lived in this development."

Her father shook his head.

"It says he's been living in Florida for fifteen years."

"He lived in Florida that long, but he and his wife kept changing developments. They've only lived here about a year. Over there in Pod Six."

Pod Six lay on the other side of the hedge behind the pool. An elderly Jewish man who had killed a Chinese girl and buried her beneath his porch had, for the past year, lived across the hedge from her father's pool. Wendy wondered if she'd ever met the man or passed him on the street.

"He was a queer duck," her father said. "Didn't socialize much. Never picked up a golf club. The fellas say he played a mean game of tennis, but he was, you know, too moody. He yelled if he missed a shot. Threw the racquet. The fellas finally had to ask him to find somewhere else to play." Her father scratched his leg; despite the heat, he was wearing pants. Just as well. If Wendy ever saw those sores, her heart would explode with grief.

"Why would you care about a man like that?" her father asked. "If you want a good story for your paper, you should talk to Mrs. Braun. Now there's someone to write about, a woman like that, surviving the camps, losing two husbands, and still she volunteers. She teaches those children to read. Black, Hispanic, she doesn't care, she pays for the taxi, buys the books out of her own pocket."

Wendy started to say she had no interest in writing a story about Mrs. Braun—whose first name, amazingly enough, was Eva—or the murderer across the hedge. Montana had its own share of sociopaths. Her readers didn't need to know about some Jew in New Jersey who'd stuffed some Chinese woman in a drum. If they did, an editor could pull the story from the AP wire. Her father's comment, Wendy guessed, had more to do with his worry that she might connect the story in the paper with his own calamity. And in a way he was right. Not that she equated her father's dalliance with murder. But she saw the similarities.

She read the story a second time, trying to figure out which disturbed her more—that a man her father's age, the founder of a company that imported the kinds of little toys her father used to give his youngest patients, would stuff a woman in a drum and hide it beneath his house, or that an elderly Jewish man would kill himself rather than face the consequences of such an act. Surely her father would be incapable of putting a woman in a drum. Then again, she hadn't thought him capable of sleeping with a hooker. He wouldn't kill himself, would he? Her father hated guns. After that terrible war, who wouldn't? When she and Joel were young, their father had kept his service revolver in pieces around the house so they couldn't turn it on each other. But no one could have assembled that gun in time to shoot an intruder. Maybe that had been the point. The only person her father would ever be angry enough to shoot was himself.

"There are treatments now," she blurted. "It isn't hopeless, the way it was."

He rolled his journal and smacked the stucco wall. "Don't talk to me about treatments. Hundreds of thousands of dollars to keep a worthless old fart alive."

"You're not worthless!" Wendy said this so vociferously the golfer teeing off looked her way. "You got lonely. Why punish yourself for being human?"

"I only told you so you'd know." He got to his feet unsteadily. "I signed a living will. I don't want anyone to keep me going by artificial means. If I can't make the decision, you'll need to make it for me. And you'll need to know where to find my papers. Joel will expect to be the executor, with all his jobs in 'finance.' But I would rather it be you."

The golfer dubbed his shot, which skidded to a stop in the tall grass beside the porch.

"What you have is HIV," she said. "If you take the drugs, you might never get full-blown AIDS. You're just being stubborn. And selfish. Don't you think it's worth it to keep living for Joel and me? To see his kids graduate? To dance at my wedding?"

"For your sakes, I should linger in pain? I should suffer?"

"You wouldn't suffer if you took the treatment." The duffer addressed his ball; Wendy could see the age spots mottling his skinny calves. "Does anyone else know?"

"No. And there's no need to."

"I understand how you must feel," she said. "But you don't need to be embarrassed. You need someone you can talk to.

175

You shouldn't have to go through this alone." And, what she really meant: *I need someone I can talk to. I shouldn't have to go through this alone.*

"Stop!" He waved the journal. "Stop with all this. Go back to Wyoming or Montana or wherever the hell you live."

The golfer swung awkwardly, the head of his iron swishing inches past their screen. He turned to face them, his silhouette overlaid in wire mesh, then lifted his hands in a demonstration of regret, whether for the way he had hit the shot, or the intrusion, or whatever was causing her father's grief. Finally, he walked off to find his ball, which had careened across the fairway into the rough on the other side.

"I don't get it," Wendy said. She realized she was crying. "Why are you so mad at me?"

Her father's gaze lingered on the golfer, who addressed his ball carefully, then flubbed another shot. The ball skidded twenty yards before lodging beside the cart path. The man walked up to the ball and kicked it, then followed it out of sight.

Her father turned to face her. His eyes were moist. "Oh, pussycat. You keep saying you understand. But what do you understand? You, who never got close enough to anyone to feel the way I felt about your mother. You might be an expert on all those things you write about in the paper. But that doesn't mean you know the first thing about what's important in an actual human life."

* * *

Well, Milt thought, he wasn't dead yet. And as long as he had the strength, he could put a decent lunch on the table for his daughter. An onion bialy—Wendy's favorite. A few slices of

176

lox, a knish, some Muenster and cottage cheese. He took a can of tuna from the cabinet, held it to the little magnet, and let the opener do its job. Thumbs pressing the lid, he tipped the fishy water down the sink. Until Greta died, he hadn't known how to use the can opener, let alone mix dressing with the fish, shave the threads from a stalk of celery, dice onion and mix it in. There was a bitter satisfaction to acquiring this new proficiency, even at his age. And he wasn't a bad cook. He had a flair for adding a key ingredient—horseradish, say, or relish—to give the tuna or egg some zing. He wasn't about to stand on his feet all day making blintzes from scratch, the way Greta used to do. But neither was he reduced to the helplessness of those widowers who wandered the grocery stores and bakeries making a meal by noshing samples.

He unfolded the waxy packet to reveal the small neat whitefish he had picked up the day before. He peeled back the delicate golden skin as tenderly as if he were removing a lady's coat, an impression reinforced by the feminine regard of the fish's dark wet eye. With the tip of a knife, Milt loosened the little bones and lifted out the spine. He touched the oily meat and applied his finger to his tongue. "Not salty enough," he said, "but better than too salty." And the fact that Greta wasn't in the kitchen to hear this assessment nearly made him weep. Sure, they'd discussed the same insignificant topics—the price of lox, how salty, the latest complaints from Joel—but what they actually said wasn't of much importance. All that really mattered was that the other was there to hear.

He lifted the tomato and sniffed its earthy scent, then set it on Greta's cutting board and used her serrated knife to pierce the slick taut skin. Milt had always taken pleasure in common things—the prospect, when walking home, of his wife in her bright blue apron slicing a tomato; the way she fanned the

177

opulent red slices across a bed of heart-shaped lettuce leaves and topped everything off with the perfect purple rounds of a sweet Bermuda onion; the hour after dinner when he finally got to sink into his favorite chair and read the paper; the bedtime glass of Cherry Heering and the chunk of Velveeta cheese on soft fresh challah; the delicious sensation of climbing into bed, the heady Jergens scent of Greta's neck, and the satisfaction in her sigh as she snuggled her back against him. Such moments had become exceedingly rare since Greta's death, but now and then he still had them, and, as infrequent as these moments had become, they made Milt want to keep on living, and, since he knew that he had to die, made him curse the life he'd blessed.

"Dad, really, you shouldn't have. I could have made us lunch."

His daughter stood in the doorway shaking her head as if the exertion of setting a plate of whitefish on the table might send him to his grave. (Or maybe she was worried that eating food from her father's hand might send her to *her* grave.) What had he been thinking to invite her to come and see him? What would they do to pass the time? Usually, Greta took Wendy to the flea market, shopping. They talked. Or rather, Wendy talked and Greta listened—the latest job, the latest boyfriend. A woman in her forties, and she still referred to them as "boyfriends"! The only effort Milt ever made to entertain his daughter was to take her out to play a late-morning round of golf.

Well, he thought, why not. When he had first been diagnosed, he hadn't had the strength or spirit to think about playing golf. He'd made excuses to the fellas. *Pulled a muscle in the groin. Ate some sturgeon the other night and it didn't agree with me.* Lately, though, he had been itching to pick up a club. He had been playing golf since he was a kid, knocking a torn-up ball from one pile of cow shit to the next in his father's back pasture, and the last time he'd played, before he'd heard the news, he'd shot a lousy fifty-nine. Christ, leaving the game with a fifty-nine would be like making fumbling love to Greta and not knowing it was the last time they were making love. He and Greta, thank God, had been able to make love one last time before he'd taken her to the hospital. Gently. With desperation. He hated to admit it, but that desperation had made it one of the most arousing times they'd ever had, as if she were already beyond the grave and God had allowed them this one reprieve. Granted, playing a last round of golf was far less important than making love to your dying wife. But he wanted to be able to play a sweet last nine and make his exit like a gentleman.

That was all he'd ever asked, wasn't it? To go out like a gentleman? And God was saying no. God was saying that he, Milt Rothstein, must exit this earth as emaciated as those poor Japs Milt and his buddies had found hiding in those caves, legs oozing pus, too weak to take a piss, blind and ranting nonsense.

Well, he still had the strength to play a round of golf. It was something he and his daughter always did. Something he looked forward to. That daughter of his had the best swing of any woman he'd ever seen. When she smacked a drive, the sight of this strong graceful woman who happened to be his daughter made Milt's heart whip up in the air and soar above the fairway with the ball. A natural, that's what Wendy was. And she didn't even bother to pick up a club from one visit to the next. He doubted she even owned a set; down here, she played with Greta's. Instead of choosing one sport and getting good at it, she fooled around with every sport there was. Tennis. Both kinds of skiing. Those new roller-skates for

179

grown-ups. Bikes you rode up and down mountains. She even went through a phase of jumping out of airplanes—some sport, just try jumping out of a plane over a nest of Japs taking target practice on you and your buddies coming down. And now, riding horses with this professor she kept talking about. As if Milt didn't know what she was saying—namely, that this "professor" of hers was taking her horseback riding so he could *shtup* her in the great outdoors, which made Wendy think she knew something about love and sex he and Greta didn't know, just because they'd had the decency to confine it to their bedroom, at least after the kids were born.

Never mind. No one was tying Wendy up and forcing her to do anything she didn't want to do. It was her loss if she'd never experienced the satisfaction of making love to the same person for so many years that you knew every secret spot, every unspoken want, how fast or how slow. That was where passion came from, choosing one person and getting good at pleasing her. And she at pleasing you. Although maybe—something tore at Milt's chest, as if one of the alligators from the lagoon had snapped a gash from one lung—maybe it was a good thing his daughter had never known that kind of love, because she would never know the agony of missing it.

"Agony." Unbelievable that he, Milt Rothstein, should apply such a word to his condition. Until now, he would have thought any man using such a word was being, what was it called, hyperdramatic. No, that wasn't the right word. Wendy would know the word he meant. She had always been good with words. Too bad she didn't have a clue what those words meant. "I understand," she kept saying. Better she should admit what she *didn't* understand. *That* would indicate she understood a little. Besides, he didn't *want* her understanding. First would come her understanding, and next, God forbid, her forgiveness. "You're just *depressed,* Daddy, you've been a *caretaker* all your life, you're *co-dependent,* you're not used to letting other people take care of you." Hadn't she said similar words when Greta died, and again at Moose's funeral? She understood nothing. To betray the woman you loved for a prostitute with a disease . . . "You goddamn bastard!" she should have shouted. "How could you have done this to my mother, fucking around with some whore you met in Miami Beach!" Instead: "I understand." What did she understand? That he couldn't keep his pecker in his trousers? That he would take up with a woman he barely knew because she seemed kind and well mannered and obliging enough to do for him what so few women her age would do for any man? "Understanding" wasn't what you gave a man who had defiled his wife's memory by having sex with a common whore, getting a filthy disease, and besmirching the family name.

Amazing that he, Milt Rothstein, would even need to use such words—"whore," "disease," "besmirch"—to describe his life. But that was how God maneuvered things. He gave you a wife you loved as much as any husband could love a wife. Then He took her away and said: "Okay, buddy, see if you can remain faithful to her now."

Still, the God in whom Milt Rothstein had always believed would never dole out such a punishment for an infraction that, bad as it was, didn't demand its perpetrator die a miserable, shameful death. Why *shouldn't* they have slept together? Neither of them was married. It wouldn't have occurred to any man what Rosina was. Surely she wasn't doing with other men what she was doing with Milt *while* she was doing it with Milt. If he knew anything, he knew that much.

No, it didn't seem fair that a man could spend so many years trying to do right, then slip and commit one sin and be so unjustly punished. Even in that goddamn filthy war he'd tried not to do any more harm than he absolutely had to do. And later, in his practice, he'd used his wit and skill to ease his patients' pain. He had helped persuade the citizens of his hometown to fluoridate their water, although this meant incurring the accusation that he was poisoning the village well. Why else would a dentist advocate a plan to make his patients' teeth stronger? It must be a Commie Jew plot. Hadn't anyone noticed that the Rothsteins didn't drink water from the city well but trucked in crates of that Jewish seltzer?

The memory of those accusations almost made Milt glad to be leaving a world in which such idiocy could reign. But he also felt pride that the children of Fern Glen, New York, had grown up with healthier teeth than would have been the case if Milt Rothstein had never lived. He kept meaning to curse his life, but, like that fellow in the Bible, the one with the rebellious ass, all he did was bless it. The mere prospect of pouring himself a nice cold glass of seltzer seemed a reason to stay alive. After they'd finished lunch, he and Wendy would play a last round of golf.

Milt looked over to tell her and was swept with the miraculous reality that this serious grown-up woman was the same little girl who used to wait at the kitchen window until he walked home from work, then run out on those chubby *pulkes* to greet him, so that he, Milt Rothstein, a soldier who'd survived a war, could go skipping up the sidewalk to his house with his daughter's hand in his.

He reached out and squeezed that hand. He would die for her this instant, and not because he was dying anyway. She was a good big-hearted girl. A beauty. Tall, like Greta, with Greta's high color and reddish hair, although he couldn't understand why she'd clipped such beautiful hair so short. And those muscles! Not to his taste, but he could imagine a younger man going in for that sort of thing, a woman strong like that, giving herself to you. Sure she was tough. She had to be tough to do that job. But she was soft, too, underneath. She let those "boyfriends" take advantage. Of course he wanted to see her married! If he was reluctant to stay alive, it wasn't because he didn't want to keep living for her.

Milt took the last banana, twisted the stem, and peeled it, unable to keep from thinking how good the fruit would taste cut up in a bowl with sugar and sour cream. "So, doll," he said, "you want to go out later and play a round of golf?"

* * *

None of this was happening. She couldn't be pulling on a pair of peds and tying on her sneakers, on her way to play a round of golf with her father not three hours after he'd revealed he had AIDS.

But yes, here she was, slathering sunscreen on her legs and following him out the door. If that wasn't odd enough, she noticed that a front and rear tire on the steel-blue Grand Marquis parked beside their gray one were so flat the car listed.

"That putz," her father said. "He couldn't even get the right car."

She needed a while to realize that Morrie Ashkenazi had exacted his revenge on the wrong Grand Marquis.

Her father opened the driver's door of his own car and slid in.

"Don't you think you ought to tell someone?" Wendy asked.

"It wasn't my doing."

She looked around to see if Morrie Ashkenazi was watching from his house. The two middle slats of his Venetian blinds sprang apart, then back in place. Wendy pointed to the car with two flat tires. "Shouldn't we tell the owner?"

Her father stuck his key in the ignition, adjusted the seat, then tapped the gas pedal once or twice so the engine raced. Once, in Atlantic City, he had accidentally scratched the bumper of a rusty VW bus and insisted they wait until he could offer the owner his address and a face-to-face apology. What was in the water down here that all these old Jewish men lost their sense of right and wrong? They got close to death and thought they could get away with anything. They no longer saw the point in playing by the rules. But if there wasn't any point in playing by the rules at seventy or eighty, why play by the rules at all?

Well, she wasn't about to convince her father to sic the police on Morrie Ashkenazi. "Maybe I should drive," she said. After all, if he had been too exhausted to drive before, he would be more exhausted now. But he refused to slide over, as if he were so disappointed by her response to his being ill that he no longer saw the point. He seemed to expect her to berate him, but if the positions had been reversed, he wouldn't have berated her. He might have accused her of being careless. But his paramount concern would have been her health.

She got in and let him drive. The whole situation was out of hand. She had to be the only member of her generation whose father had gotten AIDS. With *her* sexual history, her father had been the one to come down with AIDS! She would need to guard against saying this to her friends to get a laugh. The reality of his illness hadn't yet struck. When it did, she wouldn't need anyone's laughter. She couldn't imagine telling Harry. She knew how he would take it—one eyebrow cocked at her insistence that her father wasn't the sort of man to sleep with whores. *Every man is the sort of man who sleeps with whores, my dear, if you give him half a chance.*

Harry was the one who should have gotten AIDS, what with all the students he had slept with and all the women he'd picked up in Missoula bars. Although if she truly did love him, she wouldn't be wishing that he had AIDS in her father's place. It was as if she wanted to punish Harry for making love to all those women who weren't her, although Wendy had slept with nearly as many men.

* * *

Milt glanced over and saw that Wendy was fingering the wound in the car seat. He was about to tell her to cut it out, the damage was bad enough, but he had yelled too much already. She was upset, he could see that. What was he worried about, the trade-in value? No, he was frightened of letting go. All those years of keeping his life on track—taxes, tuition, wills, life insurance, homeowner's insurance, car insurance . . . Milt had even kept his brother's life on track—Marv, who reminded Milt of the locomotive in a book Wendy used to read about a little red engine that preferred zooming around the meadow to staying on its rails. Milt had ministered to his patients in a manner that had exceeded mere concern for their dental hygiene. He had looked out for the tenants who lived in the apartment above his office, and the epileptic kid who'd been his neighbor when they were boys and who, for forty years thereafter, had depended on Milt for his dental work, groceries, daily visits, and conversation. There were the children's lives to oversee, especially poor Joel's before he'd straightened out, if you could call the life Joel lived now straightened out, a grown man quitting job after job because his duties wouldn't permit him enough time to play the drums.

Ever since Milt's boyhood, he had known that the key to a

185

successful life lay in thwarting the normal human impulse to let things go. If you neglected the milking for a single morning, if you let the mucking slide, the small corner of the world you had been trying to keep in order would erupt in disarray. The rest of his life confirmed this. Those few malignant cells in Greta's breast had run amuck, which had led to his own infection, which might yet lead to other horrors—Wendy's death, or Joel's. The wound in the leather seat seemed a manifestation of whatever small scratch had allowed the poison from Rosina's blood to infiltrate Milt's own.

For the first time, he *felt* infected. All those filthy viruses in his blood made him think of the times he had been working at his chair and gradually become conscious of an insistent clicking from his supply closet, which baffled him until he remembered that Wendy liked to order those damn Mexican jumping beans from the toy supply catalogue. He hated those fucking jumping beans, all those invisible caterpillars writhing in their shells, clicking inside those beans. Thousands of voracious worms eating blindly in the dark.

* * *

As they rattled up the pot-holed drive to the public golf-course, Wendy felt such an overwhelming affection for her father she drew her fist to her mouth and bit it. Here was a man who would prefer to play at a public course rather than belong to the expensive club in which he owned a condo. Despite what Joel thought, their father wasn't cheap. He just considered it sinful that any human being, even if he had the money, would shell out tens of thousands of dollars to join a golf club.

Not that Wendy could understand anyone paying anything to play golf. She preferred vigorous games that allowed her to work off her energy without requiring that she concentrate on perfecting subtle moves. She didn't consider golf to be a sport as much as a way of spending time with her father, talking current events and politics, the cost of real estate in whatever city she was living in that year, her sleazy insider's knowledge of whatever beat she was covering. She wondered, if he died, if she would ever play golf again. What would be the point, except to conjure her father's spirit dragging his cart along the fairway as thoughtfully as if he were leading a blind friend by the arm, or replacing a divot with the care a plastic surgeon might bestow on repairing a young girl's face. There was magic in such rituals. She hadn't realized that before. A man spent his life traveling the same circumscribed route, and after he was dead, his survivors knew where to find his ghost.

She watched her father remove the hand-drawn cart from the trunk of his car, straighten the legs and wheels, then lift out his bag and set it on the frame and fasten the strap around it. He did the same for Wendy's cart and bag; the head of each club was still protected by the multicolored yarn cover that her mother had crocheted, with a pompom on the top. Balancing against the rear bumper of the Grand Marquis, Milt unlaced one brown street-shoe and pulled it off, tugged on a beige golf-shoe and double laced it, then did the same for the other foot. They wheeled their carts across the lot, the black rubber wheels grating against the gravel. Her father went inside the clubhouse to pay their fees, then emerged with a scorecard and a pencil. Each of them bent low to the fountain and gulped long cold draughts of sweet water. Then they headed to the first tee.

Everything glowed in the brilliant light—the red plastic pail with its clever brush-and-well contraption for cleaning balls; the carved wood portrait of the course; that bird with the tufted tail, twittering like some overexcited spectator on the bench beside the tee. Wendy removed her mother's glove from the zippered pouch. When she reached inside the pouch again to get a ball, she felt her mother's collapsible plastic rain-hat, and she knew that she would never remove the hat from the bag, but would encounter it each time with genuine surprise and the need to resist the impulse to unfold the plastic hat and snap it beneath her chin, as if, in so doing, she could invoke her mother's blessing like a halo.

"Milt! Hey, Milt! Milt Rothstein!"

Two hand-carts rattled up behind them, pulled by a pair of men, one short, one tall, each with a bulbous nose, a scalloped white mustache, and a tuft of unruly hair sprouting from his otherwise bald pate. Each wore a pastel polo shirt, plaid shorts, and brown and white golf-shoes.

"Hesh!" Her father seemed genuinely glad to see the tall man, who turned out to be the owner of the plumbing service that maintained the sinks and toilets of Boco Loco. The other man was Hesh's brother, Lou, who also was a plumber, although his business was still up north.

"Just figured we'd fit in nine holes before Lou here has to fly home. Mind if we pair up?"

The three men turned to Wendy. If she and her father teamed up with the Sunshine brothers, they wouldn't get a chance to talk. That appealed to her, and it didn't. She glanced at her father, who shrugged and asked the brothers if they planned to rent an electric cart.

"Nah. Me and Lou prefer to walk. Closer to nature. You ride in a cart, it's like making love with a rubber."

Wendy's father waved a palm to erase his friend's vulgarity. He was anything but prudish, but her presence made him shy. Wendy, on the other hand, was far more concerned how her father might react to this mention of a condom. Obviously, he hadn't worn one. He must have assumed that Rosina had no chance of getting pregnant. It would never have occurred to him that a woman of his generation might infect him with HIV. For the life of her, Wendy couldn't figure out why she was so sure this woman was a hooker. Who knew, maybe Rosina was the one who had gotten the disease from a transfusion.

Suddenly, she regretted having agreed to play with these two men. She really did need to ask her father if he had informed Rosina of his diagnosis. Then again, they might have played for days and she wouldn't have found the courage to ask.

"Hey, Milt," Lou said, "ever heard this one?" They were waiting for the foursome ahead of them to tee off. "This widower, see? He has eyes on this widow . . ."

Wendy had heard the joke a million times. What shocked her was that Lou, as he told the story, kept stroking the shaft of his driver in a vague unconscious way. Such unconcealed desire was so endearing it made her smile. For all their crude jokes, her father and his friends retained an innocence that touched her.

"So anyway"—Lou hurried to complete his joke—"the woman asks, 'What's that black ribbon tied around your putz?' And the man says, he tells her . . ."

Wendy tried to guess what her father must be thinking, hearing this joke about an elderly man trying so hard to get laid. As far as she could tell, he showed no signs of distress. But she'd given up the illusion that she could read her father's thoughts.

The foursome ahead was putting. "She could take her drive," Hesh suggested, inclining his head toward Wendy. "She can't hit the green from here."

189

"Yeah?" her father challenged. "You watch, this girl has some swing."

So of course she flubbed the shot. Inflated by her father's bragging, she swung too hard and sliced the ball into a clump of palms.

Lou shook his head. "Quite a wallop. But the name of the game is control. It's all in the wrists. Here, let me show you." He stepped behind Wendy and wrapped his arms around her, pressing against her back and legs in a position that reminded her of what Harry liked to do, although she guessed that Lou Sunshine would be scandalized to know that any man would actually do to any woman what Harry had done to her. All Lou wanted was to hold her. Most of her father's friends gave Wendy effusive hugs, patting her on the back and holding on a few moments too long. It wasn't sex they wanted. They just wanted to feel young flesh. The least she could do was let them.

What bothered her was that Lou Sunshine assumed he had the right to administer a golf lesson. In no other sport were you required to take a shot with three people watching, dissecting your every move, advising you on which club to use next, where to aim, how far apart to place your feet. *The game is all in the wrists.* She and Joel used to rib their dad that they would engrave this adage on his headstone, but the joke didn't seem funny now. If anything, Lou Sunshine's impromptu golf lesson took Wendy back to those summer evenings when she was forced to endure the unendurable wait until her father finished dinner, then read the entire *New York Times* and the local *Fern Glen News* (this must have been where she got the notion that being a reporter, even for a local paper, was a vitally important job). Then, if he wasn't too worn out, and if he judged the light sufficient, he would take her to play a round.

She loved everything about that course—the ambrosial scent of the fairways giving up their heat, the fireflies dancing in the woods, the crazy muttering of the brook that ran beneath the bridge you crossed to reach the first tee, the clatter of her father's cleats and the slap of her own white sneakers as she and her father crossed the arched wood bridge, which, her father teased, housed a family of trolls beneath. What Wendy didn't love was how fiercely she tried to please him. The first drive she ever hit sailed a hundred and fifty yards straight down the fairway, which, for a ten-year-old girl, was superb.

After that, she tried so hard to repeat the accomplishment that she swung savagely, blindly, and smacked the club with shuddering violence a foot behind the ball. On her third shot, she swung while watching her father and so missed the ball entirely, spiraling on one leg like a cartoon ostrich. The worse she did the more he coached. Finally, she grew so angry she hurled a club, which brought a lecture from her father on the importance of never letting anything or anyone cause you to lose your temper. Only later, in her teens, when she temporarily ceased to love him, was she able to hit the ball with that grace born of dispassion, and the ball soared above the fairway and made her father proud.

And that was what happened now. She was so indifferent about her score that she cracked the ball and followed through, iron and ball connecting—there really was no better feeling than the head of a golf club connecting with a ball—and reached the green in two. She would always hate the little shots around the green, but she putted reasonably well today and scored her best game ever.

Her father, on the other hand, seemed barely able to lift his club. Once, on the seventh tee, he remained seated on a bench so long that Hesh went over and sat beside him. "You okay there, Miltie? Something getting you a little down? I played with you that last time, you hit such amazing shots I felt like giving up the game. But this time, you don't look so good. There's no color in your face. You want we should call it quits? There isn't any shame in calling it quits." Hesh cleared his throat. "This might be a little presumptuous, but maybe you got something the matter with you?"

Wendy's father squirmed from his friend's embrace. "Sunshine, you get paid to diagnose toilets. My daughter doesn't need your instructions on her golf swing, and I don't need your opinions on my health."

With that, Milt teed up his ball, drove a reasonable distance, jammed his club in his bag, and stalked off. For the next seven holes, Wendy's father didn't say a word, and Wendy didn't press him. As for the Sunshine brothers, they were so full of praise for Wendy's shots that she almost forgot she wasn't one of them, one more old Jewish man in a foursome of Jewish men, and the brothers must have forgotten, too, because they began to discuss the guy who'd buried that young Chinese woman in the drum beneath his house, filling in details they wouldn't have mentioned if they had stopped to recall that Milt's daughter was among them.

According to Hesh, whose work gave him access to information the papers wouldn't print, and Lou, who knew people in Englewood who knew the father, the woman had been eight or nine weeks pregnant when she died. Crammed in that airtight drum, surrounded by some kind of chemical pellets used by shipping companies to protect their wares, the woman's corpse had been so well-preserved that the police had little trouble figuring out who she was or testing the fetus's DNA to see if it matched Stu Haber's.

According to Lou, the girl had been a Chinese alien who worked at Haber's warehouse. She must have threatened to tell his wife. Lou's cousin, who was a cop, had seen photos of the corpse. "Imagine if I took this driver to a cantaloupe." Lou cocked the business end of his driver above an imaginary melon. "That's what the bastard did to that woman's head." This gave the men pause. Lou's hypothesis made sense. What other weapon would a Jewish man keep around the house? But the injury didn't trouble them as badly as Lou's revelation that the murderer had wrapped his victim in his prayer shawl.

"His *tallis*?" Wendy's father echoed. "He buried her in his *tallis*?"

This time, Wendy knew what he was thinking. Any man who could bludgeon to death a woman he loved, or, for that matter, a woman he didn't love, especially a woman who was pregnant with his child, had to be a monster. Except that this monster had done something Milt himself would have done: he had wrapped her in his prayer shawl and buried her beneath his living room, as if to care for them both, mother and unborn child, the only way he could.

"*Tallis* or not, the guy was wacko," Hesh insisted. "I mean, a man might think about *shtupping* some beautiful Chinese girl who works at his warehouse. But to actually *shtup* her? From what I hear, Haber's wife is a witch. But there's such a thing as divorce. The girlfriend tells the wife, the marriage is over, there's a big disgrace, the children find out and hate you. But that's better than committing murder."

193

Wendy was relieved to hear this. She wanted to keep believing that her father and his friends were decent, moral men who had gone off to fight a war, then slaved to raise their families, gotten married, and never strayed. But really, it made no sense that these particular men should be immune to passion. Her generation liked to think it had invented sex, but human nature probably hadn't changed all that radically in the past several thousand years. Only the week before, Wendy had started work on a story about a system of tunnels that used to run beneath the streets of Helena from a brothel to the lobby of a fancy hotel that provided lodging for the ranchers and politicians who came to the capital to do business. When a prominent man checked in, he was given a key to a room upstairs and a numbered tag to a stall in the tunnels. At first, Wendy thought her editor was making this up. But the tunnels still were down there. According to the press release, the city was thinking of restoring them as a tourist attraction.

Wendy looked more closely at her dad, who stood holding the pin so Lou Sunshine could putt. The breeze lifted his soft white hair, ruffling it in the back where her mother, if she still had been alive, would have told him to get a haircut. His face was keen and thin. With the flag fluttering on its pole, he resembled Don Quixote at attention with his lance. But maybe she granted him this nobility only because she was his daughter. If her father had checked into that hotel in Helena and been handed a tag for a stall in which a woman waited to do whatever pleased him, he would have used the tag.

No. A sudden warmth spread over her. Her father would feel sorry for any girl condemned to spend her days and nights underground, opening her legs to any man who pulled back the curtains and waved a tag. Wendy had never met Stuart

Haber, but she knew—somehow, she knew—that if Stu Haber had been presented with such a tag, he would have used it.

* * *

As Milt held the pin for Hesh's idiot brother Lou, he tried to imagine what would possess a man to talk about such a grisly crime while a young woman was listening. Obviously, Hesh had to put up with the same sort of *mishegoss* from Lou that Milt endured from Marv. Look at the schmuck, making the rest of them wait while he measured the roll of the green, the direction of the wind, the moisture in the air. "Christ, Lou," Milt said, "why don't you just get down on all fours and lick the grass?"

Lou looked up from where he squatted and eyed Milt as if nothing in the universe would make him rush. Jesus, Milt thought, the guy was a plumber, he was used to squatting, he could stay down there all day.

"Is something eating at you, Miltie?" Lou asked. "You've got an objection to a man taking a little time lining up his shot?"

Milt felt like tipping the bastard on his ass, but he had no patience for an argument, and there was little point in alienating Hesh, who held a monopoly on the plumbing in the pod. Milt signaled that Lou should take his time, at which Lou shut one eye, held a finger along his nose, and tried to ascertain the exact alignment of ball and hole.

Milt, meanwhile, fumed. He should have insisted that he and Wendy play alone, but the habit of sociability was hard to break. His last chance for a round of golf and he had to share it with a jackass like Lou Sunshine. There was nothing sweet about this game; if anything, he was playing worse than the last

195

time. And his state of mind hadn't been improved by Lou bringing up Stu Haber. Not that he, Milt, would ever sink so low as to get a helpless girl pregnant, bash in her head, and try to hide his crime by forcing his own son to live in a house with the body underneath. No wonder the boy's marriage had fallen apart. But Milt wasn't much better. Committing a crime was one thing, but what you did after to cover up, that also was a crime. Fine if Milt didn't want the treatment for himself, Rosina should get the chance. She was young. She might have a good twenty years ahead of her. She couldn't afford the medicine. He should pay, for Chrissake. All right, he hadn't been the one to get her sick. But if he truly did love her, he would go to see her. He would pay.

Not to mention that he needed to keep Rosina from passing her disease to other men. Milt knew what he had to do, but he hadn't been able to do it. He writhed even now, remembering that late-night drive to Miami Beach and how he'd hoped he might get lost in a dangerous neighborhood, get pulled from his car and shot, although even in his daze he'd managed to find Rosina's building without a single wrong turn. He'd sat at the curb for hours before finding the nerve to go in, then walked slowly down her corridor—it was a nicely appointed hall, with a kind of flocked pink wallpaper that reminded Milt of a coral reef, not that he had such pleasant associations with coral reefs. He stood before her door trying to convince himself that no woman of ill repute could live in such a building. Only respectable people lived here. He would have lived here himself, if he had lived in Miami. But he couldn't bring himself to knock. How could he insinuate to a woman with whom he'd had relations for a year that he thought she was a prostitute? Maybe she hadn't really used him for those minimal checks he'd sent her each month. Certainly, there were richer old farts in Miami Beach than Milt Rothstein. Rosina couldn't have done what she'd done if she hadn't had genuine feelings for him, any more than Milt could have done what he'd done for her if he hadn't cared.

But if he'd cared, he wouldn't have chickened out and driven home. All right, he'd written her a note. But only a chicken-shit coward would write a note to break up with a woman. And what a chicken-shit note it was! In forty years, Milt had written little more than dunning letters to his patients, prescriptions for antibiotics, and a brief roast for a fellow dentist, none of which had provided the experience he needed to write to Rosina. He'd sweated and cursed, using up Greta's last pad of stationery. Christ, he'd needed twenty minutes just to figure out the salutation he ought to use! "Dear Rosina" had seemed too intimate, but "Dear Mrs. Alvarez" had seemed too cold. Eventually, he'd settled on "Dear Rosina Alvarez," followed by a message whose wording made Milt shudder even now. "I am sorry but under the circumstances I must end our acquaintanceship. You are a nice woman but my advice to you is that you should get your health checked by a medical professional." He got that far, only to ruin the letter by adding that Rosina should "refrain from further contact with the opposite sex," a sentence he'd omitted from succeeding drafts, praying she could guess what he meant without his saying it.

In all, he'd spent six hours composing that little note and another hour signing it. "Yours truly," he'd finally penned, although his heart ached at not signing the note with "Love." Because he did love Rosina. He loved her, and she would die, and the thought of his delicious sweet Rosina dying by herself in some crappy apartment—because how could she afford the rent on that fancy condo if she no longer had a sucker like Milt Rothstein sending her monthly checks?—made him twist his head and cry, "Dear God, no."

197

"Milt. What's the matter? Look at what you've done."

He wasn't even sure where he was, let alone what he'd done. Oh, he saw now. He'd been holding the pin for Lou to putt. He followed Hesh's gaze to his feet and saw that he had gored a hole in the perfect grass. This reminded him of the hole Wendy had slashed in the leather seat. His prophecy was coming true. Let one portion of your life get out of hand and everything went to hell. Staring at that hole, Milt wouldn't have been surprised if steam and lava had spurted up, rising and overflowing to engulf the entire wicked world.

* * *

As the Sunshine brothers took turns rubbing Wendy's back and congratulating her on her fine, fine game, she couldn't help but think that her father was right and if she had devoted herself to golf from early age, she would be a pro by now.

Then again, this might be the best she would ever do. She could have practiced for thirty years and ended up giving lessons at low-rent clubs, coming in fifth at penny-ante tournaments. No matter what life you picked, you never knew if you'd been right or wrong. If she married Harry, would they last? Maybe she had picked a man in his sixties because he would die soon and she would be free to try again. Or she'd waited to marry someone so old that he already had proved he would be a success and she needn't risk marrying a guy who turned out to be a flop. She shook her head. Where was the love in that? By that reasoning, everyone ought to wait until her fifties to get married, by which time it would be too late to have a child.

"Miltie, you take care of yourself, you hear?" Hesh Sunshine shook his putter at Wendy's dad. "And you sign up that daughter of yours for the PGA." He grinned and winked at

Wendy. "Bye, doll! Don't take any wooden nickels! Don't get scalped!" He chuckled in a theatrical way. "Although it looks as if I'm too late on that one!"

Without so much as a wave good-bye, Wendy's father turned and pulled his cart across the lot. She pulled her cart behind him, then watched him perform his ritual in reverse, folding each cart, trading golf shoes for street shoes, with the added detail that before he put anything in the trunk, he whisked away the grass with a sawed-off broom he kept beneath the spare tire expressly for this purpose. He wiped each cart wheel with a rag and rubbed the clotted mud from each cleat. He kept his trunk cleaner than most people kept their mouths. After an outing to the beach, her father whisked sand from their umbrellas, coolers, chairs, and bags with a procedure more fastidious than NASA employed to make sure nothing got infected with dust from Mars. What was he afraid of? So what if a few grains of sand got in the trunk?

Then again, who was she to criticize? Reduce the dimensions of your world to the size of a trunk or mouth and maybe you could manage it. She used to think a successful life was composed of a few bold strokes. But maybe, as was true of her mother's needlepoint, an impressive life could be created from many small, meticulous stitches. If Wendy had been a reporter for a newspaper in southern Florida, she would have interviewed hundreds of senior citizens, asking them how they'd lived their lives and whether that way of living had made them happy.

Hey, she thought, *why not?* She could get a job at the *Sun-Sentinel* or the *Miami Herald* and cover the old-people beat. It wouldn't be a bad life. She could go swimming every day. Rollerblade along the beach. Play eighteen holes of golf.

No, that was crazy. She had no business imagining herself playing golf in Miami when she ought to be looking forward to riding horses on Harry's ranch. Unless she was just being practical. Even if she persuaded her father to accept the latest treatment for HIV, he might need her help for years. God willing, he would live a long life. But in the meantime, she could write a column for the *Herald*, go to the beach, and play golf.

They drove past the pool in her father's pod. If she went inside the condo and sat across from him all afternoon with nothing else to say, she would spring this new idea about moving to Miami, and she didn't want to get his hopes up. "How about a swim?" she asked instead.

"No, thanks." He kneaded his temples. "The sun is too bright. I need to go in and lie down."

"Are you okay?" She wondered if he wanted to take a dip in the pool but was reluctant to expose his sores. If only he would confide in her. What had Hesh said that was so terrible? Anyone could see her father wasn't well. At least her own generation wasn't cursed with this outlandish reticence when it came to talking about their problems.

"Don't be ridiculous," her father said. "Go ahead, swim, have a good time."

As if she could possibly have a good time swimming in the pool while her father was in his house taking a nap because he had AIDS.

They went inside and her father stretched out on the porch with the newspaper across his face. But after he'd fallen asleep she figured, *Why not take a swim?* She changed into the sleek red suit she had bought from Victoria's Secret when she still was dating Sam. Then she padded to her mother's closet to borrow a cover-up—the rules in the development forbade walking around outside in a suit. Damn, she had forgotten, her father had given away her mother's clothes. Instead, she borrowed a paisley shirt that she and Joel had given their father

for his birthday years before; she could tell he had never worn
it. Then she put on thongs—the rules prohibited going barefoot—and scuffed across the melting macadam parking-lot
between rows of enormous cars that reminded her of cows or
pigs grazing languidly at their troughs.

Shit. Someone was at the pool. Usually no one used it
except a cadre of elderly women marching in slow motion
goose-step, lacquered heads held high as they jazzercised to a
boombox. Over Christmas break, hundreds of families came
to this development to visit their elderly relatives. Most of
them swam at the big pool at the club. A few harried parents
brought their kids to splash here for the restless few hours
while Nanny and Pop took their naps. But this was July, not
December, and the man beside the pool didn't have a wedding
band on his finger, let alone any kids. He was sitting where the
diving board would have been, if diving had been allowed. He
wore dark pleated trousers, a patent-leather belt, and a long-
sleeve striped shirt that would have been more appropriate for
an office up north. He seemed to be in his mid to late forties,
with that superficial youthfulness of a middle-aged adult who
refuses to admit he is one. His vague, perplexed expression
and the purple moons beneath his eyes, not to mention his
posture, chin cupped in upturned palm as he stared across the
pool, gave him the aura of a nymph, if nymphs were ever male.

Yet he also seemed familiar. He had a sharp distinguished
nose, generous lips, and full black curls. A Jewish man. A handsome Jewish man. So handsome and so Jewish she felt a rush of
pride. There was something biblical about him, like the face
on a Roman coin struck to honor Judea. Not that she normally
found Jewish men unattractive. Only too familiar. And, in her
experience, familiarity and sexual attraction rarely went hand
in hand.

201

She unbuttoned her father's shirt, jumped in the pool, and started swimming. She touched the wall directly beneath the man's feet and continued swimming laps, her long muscled arms rising in fluid arcs.

Finally, she needed to rest. Clinging to the edge, she peered up. The man was still there. Obviously, he wanted to be left in peace. Except that she'd had the sense he'd been staring at her the entire time she swam. And she wasn't going to last in Boca another week without someone her age to talk to. She wasn't being disloyal to Harry. Then again, what if she was?

She levered herself from the pool until she was sitting on the ledge beside him. He still didn't seem to see her, so Wendy ran her hand across her spiky scalp, speckling his pants with drops.

"Hi," she said, breathless. "Why don't you put on a suit and come in?"

A long time went by. His upper lip was sweating. There were stains beneath his arms. She liked the way his nose came straight down from his forehead. His ears were nicely shaped.

"I didn't bring a bathing suit," the man said testily.

"Well," she said, trying not to match her tone to his, "if you want, you could borrow one of my father's extra suits. Until you get a chance to go out and buy one of your own. If you're going to be down here any length of time, you'll want to go swimming."

"Listen," he said, "I have more important things on my mind than buying a bathing suit."

It wasn't as if she'd never encountered such resistance. But usually she'd encountered it only from people who had something to hide.

Then she thought: *My God.* She knew who this must be. The reporter from the *Sun-Sentinel* had said he couldn't get a statement from Stuart Haber's wife because the Habers' phone had been disconnected and their son refused to comment. The thrill of seeing Stuart Haber's son was like the excitement she felt whenever she interviewed anyone famous. And maybe, in this case, she felt a deeper connection. Both she and Stuart Haber's son had turned out to have fathers who weren't what their kids had previously assumed they were.

No. That was crazy. Her father hadn't killed anyone. As unlikely as it sounded, the toys were what connected them. The little plastic prizes that Stuart Haber's company imported from Hong Kong and distributed to dentists like her dad, who gave them to his youngest patients if they sat quietly in his chair. Wendy had loved that box of toys, with its promise that every pain brought its own reward. After you'd endured the drill, you got to put your hand in the box and fish out a pair of braided Chinese handcuffs or a magic writing-pad you erased with the yank of a plastic sheet, or—this was Wendy's favorite—a bag of Mexican jumping beans, which you warmed in your palm until they jerked and jumped like eggs that were about to hatch.

She remembered the way she used to wait impatiently for each month's catalogue—if it wasn't from Haber Imports, it was from a company just like it. She pored over the new selections and chose far better toys than her father would have picked—namely, rulers printed with the words I HAVE VIS-ITED MY DENTIST. She checked some items on a form and a factory in China or Japan manufactured those plastic toys, packed them in enormous crates, and shipped them to New Jersey, where the toys were sorted in a warehouse and trucked to Fern Glen, New York, to the offices of Milton Rothstein, DDS, so his daughter could slit the tape and rummage through a box of cellophane bags with barely comprehensible labels ("NO ESCAPE THIS HANDCUF TOY!," "THRILL FREIND WITH FINGER CUTING OFF IN GULITINE!"), keeping the best toys for herself and setting the others in the closet for the kids her father hurt. And now, decades later, to learn that a worker at that warehouse had been Stuart Haber's lover. And this was Stuart Haber's son, sitting by the pool in her father's pod in Florida.

"I'm sorry," she said. "I was just trying to be friendly. But now, well, I can guess who you must be."

Immediately, she regretted what she'd said. The man struggled to his feet and started flailing around the deck. "Who do you think I am? Do you mind telling me just who you think I am?"

Her heart skittered around her chest. "Please, forget I said anything."

"You bring up something like that, then you tell me to forget it?"

"Okay," she said. "It was in the newspaper. About your father."

"You think that's me? That guy in the paper? The one who . . . How do you know that's me?"

Wendy did what she always did when someone she was interviewing got upset: she took a deep breath and told the truth. "I put two and two together."

"Two and two? You put two and two together? Excuse me, but I don't see how my identity could be as obvious as two plus two."

If only he would stop dancing and flailing like a lunatic. Maybe he *was* a lunatic. This was a man whose father had bashed in a woman's head and buried her in a metal drum. It had to mess you up to be raised by a man like that. If nothing else, once it occurred to you that you'd been living with your father's former lover rotting beneath your house, you might become off-balance.

"It wasn't anything about you that tipped me off," Wendy said. "I just figured, who else could you be?"

"Who else. Sure. Who else. Of all the men in Florida, who else could I be except some guy whose father stuffed a woman in a drum."

He slumped back on the deck and cradled his forehead in his hands. Wendy slid closer. "It's not the season for young people to be in Florida. And I read in the paper that your mother lives over there." She gestured toward the hedge that separated Adam's mother's pod from her father's pool. "I'm sure it's hard for her. But it must be hard for you, too." She wanted to offer her father's illness as a sort of consolation, but it wouldn't be an even trade. "I'm going to be staying here for a while. My father is having his own troubles. I took some time off from work. Look, I'm a total stranger, but if you need someone to talk to . . ." In reality, Wendy was the one who needed someone to talk to. She had considered calling Sherí, or even Quaid, but she hadn't spoken to either of them in years. "I'm over there—Pod Three, Condo Seven," although she knew, in the shape he was in, he wouldn't recall those numbers. "It's got the naked girl out front. A bronze sculpture of a dancer. My mother made it before she died." Shit, a naked girl, that's all he needed to be reminded of.

He started rocking on his haunches. So much for knowing what to say to comfort another member of her generation. Anyone in her right mind would have left. But Wendy couldn't bring herself to go. For his sake as much as hers. She didn't want him to think a woman would give up her swim just to get away from him. She also liked the way he looked. And she hated to admit she was fascinated by his being a murderer's son.

Slowly, she lowered herself back in the water. Chilled now, she swam a few more laps, trying to come up with something wise to say to comfort a man who had lost as much as Adam Haber must have lost.

* * *

He kept his face hidden. Sweat cascaded around his vertebrae and pooled between his buttocks. His belt chafed, as did his cuffs. He wanted to watch the woman swim. But another of his nightmares had begun to play itself out in the theater behind his hands. Adam saw his father talking to that girl—and really, at nineteen, that's all she had been, a girl. They stood at the shadowy end of the warehouse, Melinda Sung startled in the midst of sorting a new delivery, his father a few feet off, taking pleasure in the sight of her narrow hips and flat hard breasts, her shiny black hair and pleasant face. She was shy and deferential. An immigrant, insignificant, flattered to be speaking to the president of Haber Imports, laughing at the way he could slide a penny in a box and make it vanish then reappear.

Adam saw his father hold open a door and usher Melinda Sung inside a fancy restaurant—at least, it would be fancy to her, even if it was only the Garden State Steak House—then drive Melinda to Alexander's Department Store to buy a dress and purse, the very purse with which he later would entomb her. Adam saw his father pay for a motel room, remove his shirt and pants, and stand naked above the bed on which Melinda Sung lay on her belly, prone. Then his father, whom everyone said resembled a stockier, more Jewish version of Errol Flynn—a prophecy of sorts, given Errol Flynn's predilection for little girls—climbed on the bed with Melinda Sung and—

No. He forced the scene to end, then cut to Melinda crying to some older Chinese friend about her period being late, then Melinda showing up at Adam's family's house and Adam's father exploding into the same inflamed rage he used to fly into whenever Adam, in his teens, insisted he would rather die than become an importer of plastic junk. He saw his father reach for the heavy black driver he kept beside the porch and bring it down on Melinda's head. Not that anyone could be sure the driver had been the weapon. But Adam knew it was, given the findings of the forensics experts and Adam's own memories of that club standing beside their stoop, then his father suddenly and mysteriously giving up golf, a game he had always loved more than he loved his family, and, years later, Adam preparing for the garage sale, dragging out his father's dusty golf-bag, and wondering why the driver wasn't there.

The Case of the Disappearing Driver. His father had made a woman vanish, then he'd made her reappear, Melinda Sung's pretty little face squinched as a mummy's when she'd flopped from that drum and waved: *You thought I was gone for good but here I am.* For fifteen years, Adam had lived with Melinda Sung wedged beneath his house and his half-Chinese half-sister balled up inside her. He couldn't help it, the set-up reminded him of those knock-off Marushka dolls his father had smuggled in from Romania, each plastic doll inside an ever-smaller plastic doll, vanishing to a point, a plastic egg, a nothingness inside that last plastic womb. His father—his uptight, upright father—had turned out to be a fraud. A charlatan. A magician. And his father's last and best trick: he had turned that rifle on himself and made the magician vanish.

He had no way of knowing if this version of his father's affair with Melinda Sung bore any relation to the truth. He had never seen Melinda Sung alive. But his version of the affair was enough to convince him that he should never have sex again. It was like the kid of an alcoholic noticing in himself his father's taste for booze. If that happened, the kid should pour all his vodka down the sink and take a vow not to drink anything but milk for the rest of his life.

So Adam was more than a little worried to find himself peeking through his hands at this woman in the pool. To be honest, he felt like taking off his clothes and climbing in. There wasn't any rule that prohibited swimming naked. Although that seemed the only activity that *wasn't* banned. Rule One on the clubhouse wall forbade children in diapers from dipping so much as a toe in the shallow end; any parent who broke this rule would be fined $400 to cover the expense of draining the water and refilling it. Other rules prohibited flotation devices (no rafts, no tubes, no wings). No running or diving. No horseplay or profanity. No eating or drinking, especially alcoholic beverages or drinks in glass containers. The pool seemed large enough to hold a hundred and fifty grown-ups, but the limit said fifteen. Every bather must wear a cap. Every bather must take a soap shower before entering the pool. No wounds or open sores. No Band-Aids, barrettes, or gum.

But the sign didn't prohibit swimming naked. The guys Adam had grown up with would have laughed at him for getting ideas about this woman, who looked as if she could've broken him in two. They didn't understand why he liked women who thought it was their God-given right to do whatever the hell they pleased instead of trying to get their husbands to do it for them.

His friends didn't know a damn thing. Which made Adam wonder why he'd spent three of his past four decades in their company. They thought anyone who wanted to be an artist was a fag. They thought having to wait on tables after you got out of art school meant you were a no-talent bum. So what if the male patrons hit on him more often than they hit on the female waitresses. He'd had girlfriends the entire time. So what if his girlfriends looked like dykes. The French word for the kind of girl he liked was a *gamine*. But his friends just laughed and said *gamine* must be the French word for dyke.

All right, so one of them *had* been a dyke. But she was only a dyke temporarily. When Adam was twenty-one, his girlfriend Estelle had left him for a woman, although she'd left that woman for a man, which Adam used as proof that she wasn't technically a dyke. Around that same time, the best paintings he'd ever done were hanging in the café where he worked when a burglar broke in and took out his frustrations about the few dollars in the till by spattering Adam's paintings with coffee. The owner insisted that his insurance wouldn't cover some waiter's lousy artwork, but Adam suspected that the douche bag hadn't even put in a claim.

Well, at that particular moment in his life, Adam had had more on his mind than art. Not only had his girlfriend left him, but his building was going condo and he couldn't afford to buy. Then his father called in tears, begging Adam to move back home and take over the family business, intimating that his health was no longer what it had been and he ought to move somewhere warm with Adam's mother. Adam had found it surprisingly easy to give up his life in New York—what was he but one more guy with a BFA from NYU?—and move back to a furnished house where he would have entire rooms in which to paint while managing a business so well-settled it took little enough time to run.

But something about Jersey drugged him. He fell into the routine of putting on a suit and tie, driving to Haber Imports, managing what needed managing, then driving home, watching some TV, and getting drunk. He painted rarely. Then never. He gave in to his pursuit by a catalogue designer who'd professed her love for art as ardently as she'd professed her love for him, although after they were married she'd never designed another thing, including the house they lived in, spending twenty thousand dollars to hire an interior decorator who looked exactly like Barbara herself and had the same degree from Pratt. Adam had no idea what Barbara did all day except find evidence for her dissatisfaction with him. Maybe it wasn't fair to blame his wife for their inability to conceive a child, but he couldn't help thinking that she lacked the power of imagination required for creating anything. And she refused to adopt. *That* he could blame her for. She claimed she couldn't love anyone to whom she wasn't related by blood.

Most of Adam's friends carried on affairs with girls they met at bars or girls they knew from work, but Adam couldn't see the point in having an affair with a woman just like Barbara. He'd had the same sort of sex with Barbara that his father had had with Adam's mother, in the same house, in the same bed. By which Adam meant that Barbara seemed unwilling to provide or receive anything that required the least imagination. He'd married a woman like his mother, which was to say a woman who didn't like sex. A woman who lacked imagination. At least Adam's father, for all his faults, had been blessed with imagination.

Oh great, now he was admiring his father for having the imagination to fuck an innocent girl and kill her. Besides, Adam wasn't exactly in a position to judge. It didn't take much imagination to live in your father's house, run your father's business, and marry a woman who was like your mother.

No, Adam had traded in whatever imagination he'd ever had for his father's approval. And his father hadn't fulfilled his end of the bargain. Even after Adam had done everything his father asked, his father had continued to treat him like a shipment of defective goods. If Adam called and asked his father's advice on how to handle a conflict at the plant or dry a damp spot in the basement, his father blew up at him. *You're the boss. Make your own mistakes.* Well, now he understood. His father hated for Adam to look up to him because deep inside he knew he was a philandering, duplicitous, psychotic sack of shit.

The woman in the pool had swum thirty or forty laps. The best Adam had ever done was twenty, back in his Mark Spitz phase. He remembered swimming at his parents' club, hoping to impress his father, and all the time his father had been dreaming of Melinda Sung. Not only had his father ruined Adam's present life, he'd robbed Adam of his memories. He would never be able to think back on an event without needing to reinterpret it. In some ways, he was still swimming laps at his parents' club, hoping that his father would tell him what a good job he'd done so he could go on to something else. Like being an adult.

Never mind. If he kept stewing in self-pity, he would lose the rest of his life as well. His mother's loss was worse. She'd lived with Adam's father longer and therefore had more memories to lose. She'd barely been sane before. Now she refused to leave her condo. She would have starved to death if Adam hadn't flown down to do her shopping. He couldn't return home to Jersey and leave her in such distress.

Then again, he didn't have a home to go back to. He'd already sold the house. Mercifully, the deal hadn't fallen through; the buyers had merely seized the opportunity to bargain Adam down another 10K, the apparent loss of value attributed to a house beneath which a corpse had lain for so many years. He couldn't face his employees. If this deal he was negotiating with two Taiwanese sisters who wanted to buy the company didn't come off, he would sell the business to his workers. Hell, he would *give* them the fucking company.

Except that his mother needed the money to live on. His father had been no magician when it came to investments. And the insurance wouldn't pay a dime, considering that the claimant had been a murderer and a suicide. Adam wouldn't accept a penny if it came from his father's business, but that meant he was nearly broke. It made sense to stay with his mother until she got back on her feet.

Unfortunately, the idea of living with his mother made him want to kill himself. If he played his cards right, he would be able to sell Haber Imports for enough money to support them both. He could buy his own condo, find a part-time job, maybe take a few art courses at FAU.

The woman in the pool got out and toweled off, glancing Adam's way before heading toward the gate. He went back to staring at the water, which still bore her image. And something happened that hadn't happened in years: he saw a painting he wanted to paint. His classmates at NYU used to call his paintings surreal, but to Adam they were merely realistic portrayals of the things he'd seen at home—his mother with her hand inside a chicken, yanking out the guts; his father killing weeds by injecting them with poison from a long red pointed tube; a bunch of Adam's friends lighting their fluid-scented breath while their parents chatted at a barbecue. His classmates said, *Yeah, well, if I wanted to see suburbia, I would have stayed there.* But Adam couldn't help seeing what he saw. And what he saw now was that list of prohibitions above a pool in which a beautiful woman with close-cropped red hair swam the Australian crawl, one arm cocked above her head, water dripping from the hand, her face turned sideways so she could breathe through her parted lips, the rosy red tip of one boyish breast barely visible above her ribs, and her long pale rippling back, nicely mounded buttocks, and powerfully muscled legs glowing in the sun.

* * *

Before her mother's death, Wendy and her parents used to commemorate each of her visits by driving to a small nature-preserve just north of Boca, with its shaded promenade that allowed visitors to stroll through the swamp as easily as they might have sauntered down the boardwalk in Atlantic City. Wendy might have preferred to explore the real Everglades farther west. But her parents confronted nature only when it was tamed. With the boardwalk meandering among the trees, the cypresses seemed no more threatening than elderly men and women up to their arthritic knees in muck, trolling for crabs and fish. Her mother liked to ramble along the path, stopping to point out a spot where a glossy black anhinga perched on a rotted log or a shockingly red bromeliad dangled from a branch, thriving rootlessly in the air. When she discovered something she admired, she took out her pad and sketched while Wendy chatted about her love life and her father settled on a bench and took a nap.

Now, with her mother dead, Wendy and her father were so at a loss they made the pilgrimage without her. But the boardwalk was deserted. The brutal midday light had stunned every creature in the swamp into paralysis, driven them into hiding, bleached them into invisibility. Wendy heard a bird shriek but

213

couldn't see it. Not a single bumpy log sprouted eyes and transmuted itself into an alligator. That was the biggest disappointment. She never considered it a fulfilling trip unless she spotted at least one alligator. She loved the unlikely freedom of these beasts, their prehistoric presence among the Home Depots, condominiums, and parks of southern Florida. A golfer wading into a water hazard to retrieve a ball might emerge missing a chunk of leg. Not many months before, a teenage boy had lost two fingers feeding bread to a plaintive baby gator that had come to beg at a bayside deck.

Wendy and her father emerged from the swamp onto a marshy field that usually attracted spoonbills, cranes, and egrets in shimmering profusion, turtles as big as plates, and massive black gators waiting for errant doves to float too near their mouths. But the meadow lay empty except for a flock of crows that feasted on a decaying possum; her father stamped his feet until they reluctantly hopped away. He'd said nothing the entire hike, but now he broke his silence to inform her that the key to his safe-deposit box lay hidden beneath a comb in her mother's drawer.

"The insurance documents are there, too," he said. "And your mother's ring. She wanted you to have that ring." He kicked at a crow that had ventured back to pick at the possum. "It was my mother's ring. Your grandma Sadie's."

"Stop it," Wendy said. "You make it sound as if the minute you die, I get to go to the closet, stick my hand in the box, and pick out a little toy."

Her father regarded her for a moment. He probably didn't understand what closet she was referring to. He looked up at the sun, took his handkerchief from his pocket, and swabbed his brow. A giant blue heron stepped from behind a bush and walked up to him. He considered the bird indifferently, as if it were an elderly Jewish man he knew vaguely from somewhere, or a bum who'd asked the time. The bird blinked and bobbed its head, then turned and walked off, stooping forward slightly like an elderly philosopher, wings folded behind its back.

Then the bird began to trot. Raising its wings, it flew, elegant as a glider. The resemblance to her father unnerved Wendy. That same stiffness to his walk, the same awkward, hampered stride. And the way, when called to action, something else took over, an unexpected capacity for flight. Wendy had seen this one afternoon as a child when a drunk had chased her around a playground and her father had overtaken the man and thrown him to the ground; years later, at the hospital, a smug intern had refused her mother morphine, and her father had pursued him down the hall and berated him for his arrogant, callous heart.

"Come on." He touched her arm. "I want to go see your mother," which startled Wendy until she remembered that the cemetery was only a few miles beyond the park. While her mother had been alive, they'd often stopped there to pay their respects to Wendy's uncle Julian, her mother's older brother, who, like some pioneer of death, had moved to Florida and died before Wendy's parents got there.

The cemetery lay on a featureless expanse of land on which each grave was marked by a shoe-box-size plaque set flush against the ground among thousands of others like it. Even Wendy's father seemed confused. *Here. No, over there.* She could have sworn that her mother moved between visits, the way she had tended to move in restaurants to avoid the sunlight or the smoke or to gain a better view. Sometimes, she had insisted the family move even after they'd sipped water from their glasses or dirtied their forks and spoons.

215

At last, Wendy saw the granite bench that marked her mother's grave. A massive black alligator lay beside the bench like a suitcase some mourner had left behind. She felt violently cold. She shook. Was the creature guarding her mother's grave or threatening it? Maybe it was some supernatural manifestation of her mother's unquiet ghost.

The beast swung its massive tail and Wendy's knees buckled. Until now, she'd always appreciated the Jewish view of death. You buried your loved one in a simple pine box within twenty-four hours after he or she had died, then you sat *shivah* for a week, lit a candle once a year, and that was it. She couldn't fathom those religions that worshipped death the way the ancient Egyptians did. But as this monster blinked and twitched not far from her mother's grave, Wendy wondered if death might not be too tenacious to be subdued. The dead kept coming back. Maybe it was better to make your peace with their eventual return. Mummify or embalm them. Wrap them in a prayer shawl and slide them beneath a house.

Her father must have seen things differently. He stomped across the graves shouting the same curses he'd hurled at Morrie Ashkenazi and snapping a huge white cloth that must have been his handkerchief. "Go on!" Snap. "Get away from here! Go! Go on!"

All Wendy could do was watch as the monster turned its snout across its shoulder, eyed her father coldly, and, with a malicious smile, waddled back to the marshy park from whence it must have crawled.

* * *

Her father spent the rest of the afternoon lying on the porch watching the duffers golf past. Did he want to play another nine holes? No. Go to the beach? Take a walk? Should she go out and buy him a book at the bookstore?

He shuffled to the kitchen to fix an egg cream, then spat a mouthful in the sink. "Christ, the milk is spoiled."

Wendy's fault. She had been to Publix twice and hadn't thought to buy fresh milk.

He went back to the porch and curled up on the lounge chair. She sat beside him and took his hand.

"Dad." She put his wrist to her lips. "I love you. You know that."

Tears in his eyes, he nodded.

"Please don't give up. For me?" She could see him struggling not to cry. He made a movement that indicated she should go. "Are you sure you'll be—" He waved away her words. "All right. I won't be long. I just need a little air."

Which was true, except that the air outside the condo was too stuffy and hot to breathe. She unlocked the storage closet and wheeled out her father's bike, a cast-off three speed he'd discovered behind a Dumpster. The seat was the right height for her father's legs but far too high for Wendy's; she wobbled as she hadn't wobbled since she'd learned to ride. She'd been five or six, uncharacteristically afraid of falling, and her father, in the way of all fathers, had taken her to the top of their driveway, promised to hold on, then sent her down alone. Wendy had reached the bottom and looked back in disbelief, a memory distorted and intensified by the home movie her mother took, the image jerking back and forth between Wendy's father at the top and Wendy at the bottom, straddling her bike and looking up, her expression in that movie melding now with the emotions she recalled—surprise, of course, and pride, but also anger and humiliation that she'd been duped by this trick every parent knew, and every older kid, even

217

moronic Joel, who stood clutching his belly and laughing in an exaggerated display of mirth, because, just this once, the trick hadn't been on him.

Now, pedaling her father's bike around the flat short streets of Boca, Wendy began to think that her father's deception had been more than a one-time ploy. Parents raised their kids to think they would always be there to help. But eventually you glanced back and saw your mom and dad at the top of the hill behind you, smiling and waving, fading like that last flickering image of a homemade film.

She returned to her father's condo and tried one last time to persuade him to go outside. At which he rose heavily, went inside his room, and shut the door. For a while, she considered calling her father's doctor and demanding that he force her father to accept the regime for AIDS. Maybe he could prescribe an antidepressant. Then again, given the unopened bottle of Zoloft, he already had.

She spent the rest of the afternoon wandering the condo, flicking on the TV, then flicking it off, then on. At one point, she grew so bored that she tried reading her father's dental journal. She went outside for another walk—the clouds were spiraled pink and green like the gaudy all-day suckers she hadn't been allowed to eat as a little girl. A hummingbird jabbed its beak deep in a bright red flower, then darted to the next flower and poked its beak in that, which, for some reason, made Wendy shudder. A woodpecker drummed its spastic rhythm against a pole. She walked to the lagoon and came upon Adam Haber sitting on a bench dedicated to the memory of MY BELOVED WIFE PEARL, A WOMAN OF VALOR, HER PRICE ABOVE RUBIES.

"Hi," she said, wondering if she should apologize for the last time they'd spoken.

He got to his feet and coughed. "Um, I . . . well . . . Mind if I join you? I could use a long walk."

Wendy gestured to the lagoon, which had the bluish-green tint of a toilet with a cake of freshener in the tank. "If you want a long walk, we'll have to go around the lake a million times."

"It doesn't matter." Adam wore the same heavy wool clothes he'd been wearing the day before. His curls were matted to his scalp. He and Wendy circled the lagoon in silence, then toured the mazy streets, which hadn't been designed to go anywhere, only to provide a space on which to build more condos. The streets were named for trees—Cypress Walk, Palmetto Drive— or animals and birds the residents couldn't have identified if these creatures had come up and bitten them. Eventually, they ended up beside the Woman of Valor bench.

"You know," Wendy said, "you don't have to tell me any- thing. But if you want to, well, you can."

A lizard skittered across Adam's shoe. "What's to tell?" He slumped backwards on the bench. "You find a barrel under your family's house, you cut it open, and a body falls out. Your father shoots himself. The cops knock on your door and tell you that he killed himself because he was the one who put the body in the barrel."

A couple taking their evening walk turned and smiled and waved. Something rustled through the stiff dry grass, and, a moment later, Wendy heard something splash heavily into the lagoon.

"So what's wrong with *your* father?" Adam said. "You said something about your father having troubles."

"What? My father? Oh, his troubles aren't nearly—" She stopped before she could categorize Adam's father's crime as so heinous that nothing could compare to it. Then she revealed the cause of her own father's shame.

219

"Your father has AIDS?"

She waited to see his reaction, which, she hoped, might help her to make sense of her own. Adam regarded her with a look that resembled admiration. She was about to get angry—what was there to admire about her father getting AIDS?—when he startled her by taking her hand in his. He squeezed it and let it go, then wiped his eyes and laughed. "That's pretty bad, your father getting AIDS. I mean, if we were contestants on *Queen for a Day*, you wouldn't stand a chance. But you would definitely come in second."

After that, they had little trouble finding what to talk about. Around and around they walked, past the tennis courts and health club, then back around the pool, Adam trying to make sense of the long, stifled hatred between his parents and his father's affair with Melinda Sung. When neither of them could take another step, Adam asked if she wanted to get some dinner. His mother refused to cook, and the heavy atmosphere in the apartment made him too lethargic to eat more than grilled cheese. "Nothing fancy," he apologized. "Let's just get a bite at one of those innocuous little places in the mall."

For a strange moment, Wendy thought of asking her father to come with them, and telling Adam to ask his mother, as if they could all forget their troubles laughing around a table at Boca Chinese Village. *Sun will shine tomorrow*, Mrs. Haber's fortune cookie might reveal. But Wendy doubted that her father could be persuaded to leave his room.

Sure enough, when she got back to the apartment, he was in his bedroom with the door locked. She was tempted to knock and see if he was all right. But she didn't want to wake him. And she wasn't sure what she could say that she hadn't already said.

She put on a fresh shirt and earrings, took the keys to the Grand Marquis, and went back out. Adam hadn't changed his clothes but he obviously had primped his hair; it rippled above his head like the distorted air above hot asphalt. She drove them to an unassuming Chinese place between a pet shop and a discount shoe emporium.

"Not Chinese," Adam said. "Anything but Chinese."

She turned to him in horror. "God," she said. "I didn't think—"

He laughed a laugh that sounded like a delicate glass object breaking. "I'm going to have to get used to it. It's like someone blind learning not to care when people say, 'Do you see?'"

They drove to a Cuban restaurant in the identical mall across the highway. Only two other tables were occupied; this wasn't the tourist season, and she and Adam were eating much later than most residents of Boca ate. "Spicy," she told the waiter. "We want our food very, very hot. *Muy, muy caliente.*" The waiter, a suave Cuban in his twenties, nodded obsequiously, but their food came bland as pap, the chef refusing to believe that anyone in Boca could eat anything seasoned with more than a single grain of pepper. Silently, Wendy and Adam forked their way through bowls of tasteless rice, chicken, goat, and plantains. The only choice for dessert was Jell-O or tapioca pudding. Wendy tried to joke about the food, but Adam already had sunk back into whatever murky depths he had been mired in before they met.

She returned her father's car to its spot outside the condo, but neither she nor Adam made a move to get out. "How did this happen?" Adam asked, and for a moment Wendy thought he meant their tragedies, but she saw him trailing his finger around the hole in her father's seat. After she'd explained,

Adam described his own reaction to the detectives' revelation that his father had been the one who'd put the dead woman in the drum. "I went around yanking down blinds and knocking over my ex-wife's glass display-cases." He set Wendy's hand beside the hole. "Go ahead. Tear up the whole seat. You'll feel better. Believe me."

She jerked away her hand. The image of Adam knocking over his ex-wife's glass shelves unnerved her. "We can't sit here like this," she said.

"You don't want to be seen with a murderer's son?"

"It has nothing to do with your father." Not in the way he thought. She couldn't very well say that she was drawn to him because his father was a murderer. Her hesitation had more to do with her own father. If he saw her sitting in his car with a man she'd just met, especially after all the hints she'd dropped about Harry, he would consider her a fickle-hearted whore. Which she was. Not a whore, but fickle hearted. Although her father had no business casting aspersions.

"I'd better go," she said. "I have an article I have to work on." This wasn't entirely a lie; she'd promised her editor the piece about the tunnels under Helena the day she got back.

"You're a reporter? That's what this is all about? You got my story, and now you're going to go inside and write it up?"

"No," she said, "of course not." She told him that she had absolutely no interest in writing about his father, and even if she did, she would never get a story under false pretenses. Only reporters who worked for tabloids pretended to be someone they weren't. "I'm on your side," she assured him, going so far as to offer him advice on how to handle the press if any future revelations came to light, a possibility that made Adam jerk in apprehension, given he hadn't considered the possibility of there being any further revelations.

"I can't handle this." He got out of the Grand Marquis. "The first person I trust turns out to be a reporter."

He walked away, neglecting to close the door. Immediately, the car was flocked with moths. Shuddering, Wendy leaned across the seat and pulled Adam's door shut. The car went dark, but she sensed the moths' thick bodies fluttering past her face and heard them smacking against the glass. She powered down the windows, then sat waiting in the dark for the invaders to escape.

Which was how she almost came to miss the call from Harry. Just as she unlocked the door, the phone started ringing. She rushed to grab the receiver, not even bothering to flick on the light in the guest room. "Hello? Hello?" her father croaked on the other end, and Wendy wondered, from the emotion clogging his voice, if he thought the caller was Rosina.

"Dad, this one's for me."

"Oh." Her father hung up. And it did turn out to be for her, although she wasn't sure how she'd known.

"I wasn't supposed to call. But I couldn't stand it another day. You're angry at me for what happened. But darling, Wendy, it wasn't as if you told me to stop. We'd done things like that before."

She wasn't upset that Harry had broken his promise and called. But couldn't he say hello? Couldn't he even ask her how she was? On and on he went in that reasonable, tranquilizing voice. Deep, with a Western rumble and the lofty elocution of a man who has studied Blake. But there was something about that voice she couldn't trust. She felt as if she were a horse in a stall, and the man with this calming voice was holding out a halter and trying to rope her in.

It came back to her then, what had happened in that shed, how Harry had pinned her arms behind her back amid the halters, saddles, and riding implements whose names she didn't know, how he had turned her to face a wall and taken her from behind. Finally, when she'd thought he might release her, he'd pressed her harder against the wall. Slick with sweat, panting harshly, he had breathed in her ear: *Come live with me and be my love . . . and I'll fuck you and I'll fuck you, never the same way twice, every chance I get.*

And she might have said yes. That's what scared her now, that she might have said yes. She was tired of being strong, of having so much freedom. *Yes,* she might have said, *this is what I want, for as long as we can have it. Don't let my life be boring. Don't ever let me go.* But pressed against that wall, it occurred to her that she'd reached some sort of limit. If you spent your life seeking strangeness, this was where you ended up, in a shed in Montana with a man like Harry Yates sweating against your back.

"Darling? What happened that afternoon won't happen again, I promise. I want to marry you, Wendy. I want you to come home and marry me."

His voice sounded sincere. He'd apologized, hadn't he? Hadn't he just apologized and promised never to do again what he'd done to her that day? She was tempted to accept. She would go to her father and bestow the good news. *Dad,* she would say, *I'm getting married.* Her father wouldn't care that her fiancé wasn't Jewish. Past a certain age, all that mattered was that a woman wouldn't grow old alone, that she would have a child before she couldn't.

Except, if she married Harry, she would never have a child. He already had raised two families. He claimed that he and Wendy wouldn't be able to keep making love the way they'd taken to making love if they were responsible for a child. The fact that her fiancé was twenty years her senior and would die or become infirm before Wendy reached sixty would outweigh any satisfaction her father might have taken in her news. *It's your decision*, he would say, shrugging as if she were a patient who refused to follow his advice about a tooth.

"Harry, my dad is dying. That's all I can think about right now." She sat on the fold-out bed. "Besides, I want a child." She'd thrown him off, she could tell. For that matter, she had thrown herself off.

"That's what this is all about? Your father is dying? What is he dying with, might I ask? Suddenly, because your father is sick, you want to have a child?"

What an amazing thing to say. Of course her desire to have a child had something to do with her father's illness. Not to mention her mother's death. "I want a child, Harry. That isn't so unusual, for a woman to want a child."

His voice changed. It was no longer the voice he might use to calm a horse. It was the voice he might have used to argue with a student who was complaining about a grade. "I can't do that," Harry said. "I can't have another child. I can't bear to be tied down."

She uttered such a yelp that she was afraid her father would come in and ask what was wrong. Harry couldn't bear to be tied down! She laughed again.

"Wendy? Are you there? Might you reveal what I said that you find so amusing?"

She wasn't about to tell him. "Harry, I'm hanging up now. The only way I'll marry you is if you agree to have a child. You think about that. You can tell me when I get home. Oh, and don't call again. My father is dying. I don't want you to upset him. Do you hear me? Don't call back."

* * *

Adam stabilized the books beneath his chin and reached for his mother's door. He could have rung the bell, but she wouldn't open the door to anyone who didn't have a key. Sure enough, the minute he was inside, the column of books bowed out and toppled. Colorful if outdated photos of Israel, Australia, Switzerland, and various countries in South America gleamed up at him from the flagstones of his mother's foyer. She had sent him to the library to bring home descriptions of countries they might move to, just as, the day before, she had sent him to the courthouse to find out what she needed to do to legally change her name.

He went along with his mother's plans because he knew she would never carry them out. She hated the unknown—which meant anywhere the natives weren't middle-class American suburban Jews. She didn't even like Florida. If a person left a crumb on the counter, the kitchen would be thick with ants. There were hurricanes, floods, tornadoes, and blasts of ultraviolet light that would give a person melanoma. "The Mouth of the Rat," she said bitterly. "Who wants to live in a place whose name means 'Mouth of the Rat'?" She had agreed to move to Boca only because that was where Jews who'd made it in New Jersey went when they retired. And her husband had sweet-talked her into moving.

What she really wanted, Adam knew, was a project to discuss and someone to discuss it with. Throughout his childhood, his mother had carried home armloads of brochures from travel agencies and swaths of fabric and paint chips from decorating stores. She'd tried to get Adam's father to sit down and help her plan their next vacation or the color scheme of the remodeled kitchen or den. To Florence Haber, planning where to go and what to do once you got there was more enjoyable than the actual vacation, just as planning your new decor was more enjoyable than living in the redecorated house. But Adam's father would take no part in such proposals. "If you want a vacation, take one," he used to say. "I earn the money, I don't have to pick out the goddamn wallpaper, too."

As a teenager, Adam had sided with his father. Neither of them gave a damn which pattern of garish wallpaper his mother selected, which hideous shade of avocado flooring. But it turned out Adam had picked the wrong side. Which was worse, a mother who liked to indulge her interest in decorating schemes, or a father who had impregnated a poor Chinese immigrant then killed her?

With all his mother had been through, it wouldn't do any harm to spend a few hours discussing the pros and cons of countries they would never move to. Together, they admired photographs of brawny Israeli women picking oranges, waterskiing Aussies, and a nattily dressed Alpine innkeeper pouring tea. They debated the relative merits of this climate or that cuisine and the question of whether the Jewish community of Argentina was finally safe from aging Nazis. Sure enough, after they'd settled on Tel Aviv, his mother pushed back the books and said, "Adam, sweetheart, you're a good son, and I appreciate that you would give up your life and move with your old mother so far away, but we might as well stay here. It's too late to start over. Even if we went to the moon to live, we would meet someone who knew what happened. Here, at least we know that everybody already knows. Besides, in Israel it's still a desert. Bombs can go off. Here, there's air conditioning. There's Publix. There's a security guard and a gate."

The doorbell rang, and Adam patted his mother's arm. "Don't worry. I'll take care of it." Wendy's advice about dealing with reporters came back to him. Basically, he wasn't supposed to say anything spontaneous. *We're terribly upset. Our hearts go out to the family of Melinda Sung.* But anything that deviated from the predictable would get seized upon and quoted. As in: *My father was a rotten SOB who made my mother's life miserable. I'm glad he blew his brains out. May his soul rot in hell.*

Adam unlocked the door. But instead of a reporter he saw the two detectives who had been handling his father's case.

"Sir? Mr. Haber? Do you mind if we come in?" This was said by the taller of the two detectives, a gawky straw-haired blonde in mud-brown trousers. The man, who was younger, wore a green short-sleeve shirt and khaki pants. There was nothing formidable about either one, and Adam wondered what they thought when they watched detective shows on TV, whether they were embarrassed to be so drab. Maybe they had deluded themselves into thinking they did indeed resemble James Garner and Angie Dickinson. He ushered the detectives into his mother's living room, then panicked at the sight of the travel brochures, as if these might be evidence that he and his mother intended to flee their crime. The male detective sat beside Adam's mother. "We've only come to tell you that we pretty much wrapped up our investigation. Our operatives up north tell us they've finished tracking down the names in the address book."

Address book? No one had told Adam anything about an address book. His father had kept a list of mistresses? There had been other affairs? Other victims?

"It was in her purse," the female detective said. "Some of the entries at the beginning and the end of the alphabet were no longer readable. And there weren't many entries in between. But we tracked down what names we could."

As it turned out, most of the people in Melinda Sung's

address book were either dead or hard to find. The only fact the detectives had turned up was that Melinda had been an orphan whose uncle had paid to bring her over from China as the prospective bride of an older friend. But the groom had refused to marry her, and Melinda had taken a job at Haber Imports to support herself and repay her uncle. The uncle was twenty years dead, and Melinda seemed to have no surviving relatives, which was a relief to Adam, who had been agonizing about what to do if she had a family. Still, he was surprisingly angry to learn that Melinda had been rejected by the man who'd paid her fare to America to be his bride. A beautiful woman half his age wasn't good enough for the ugly letch? Or had *she* rejected *him* and he'd lied to save face?

"Pardon me." Adam interrupted some small talk between his mother and the detectives. "I was wondering if you ever find yourself getting attached to the victims of the crimes you investigate. If you ever find yourself thinking about them too much."

From their expressions, he realized it was no wiser to speak spontaneously to detectives than to reporters. The male detective made a movement with his hands as though pushing up his sleeves, except he wasn't wearing any sleeves. "Sometimes, if you can't resolve a case, it might bug you that you haven't resolved it. But this case has been resolved. Hasn't it, Mr. Haber? Is there something you know about your father's relationship to Miss Sung that you haven't told us?"

As if Adam weren't already off balance, the doorbell rang, and when he went to open it, he saw his wife—his ex-wife—Barbara.

"Adam. I thought you might be here. It said in the paper . . . But really, I came to see your mother. I was in Palm Beach, visiting my own folks, and I figured she could use some support."

Barbara squinted through the screen. "You don't look so good, Addie. Are you okay? What happened to your hair?"

His hair? At a time like this? His wife was choosing this moment to point out that Adam had stopped using gel to curl his hair? The real question was why he'd ever started using gel in the first place, or what he was doing with a gold bracelet around his wrist or an earring in his ear. He looked at his wife. His ex-wife. Her bangs did this funny circle-thing like a daisy in the middle of her forehead. How did she get her hair to do that? Why couldn't she leave any part of her body the way it was?

"Adam? Aren't you going to let me in?"

"What?" He should have realized that she was waiting for him to open the door, as if she couldn't open it herself.

"Florence, I'm so, so sorry." Barbara pecked his mother's cheek. "This must be horrible for you. Just so, so horrible."

Adam's mother and ex-wife hugged. The detectives left, at which Adam's mother brought out cookies and tea for Barbara. On and on the women went, Barbara saying how horrible it must be to discover that your husband would "do such a thing," and Adam's mother saying, "What can you expect? Men are men."

"Excuse me," Adam said. "You ladies don't need me hanging around. Barbara, it was great to see you. I hope everything goes your way. Mom, I'll be home in a little while." And, smiling and nodding, he went outside and stood in front of his mother's condo, trying to think where he could go and whom he knew in Boca. Only one person came to mind. Well, he thought, why not. He tried to remember her address. Pod Three, Condo what? Then it came to him that she lived in the condo with the naked girl out front.

* * *

Wendy had awoken that morning at eight and been surprised and disheartened not to see her father in the kitchen, eating his Special K. By nine, she was worried enough to rap at his door.

The room was empty, the bed unmade. She doubted that her father had left his bed unmade since he was a boy. The sight of the rumpled sheet choked her throat and made her head spin. Finally, when her head cleared, she searched the condo. Nothing. No note. His golf hat was in the closet; his bike was in the shed. "Sometimes I get a little blue," he'd once confessed, "but I go out and take a walk, and I manage to shake it off." Maybe he'd felt too weak to take a walk and had gone for a drive. Maybe he had driven to Miami to see Rosina.

She passed the morning cleaning the already immaculate apartment and doing a wash so small it barely filled the bottom of the machine. Then she sat at the kitchen table and tried to come up with a lede for her story about those tunnels under Helena. But everything sounded cheap. Everything reminded her of Stu Haber or her dad. She had just crumpled another sheet of paper when she looked out the blinds and saw Adam loitering in front of her father's building as if he wanted to come in but wasn't sure which bell to ring. She checked what she was wearing—gym shorts and a T-shirt; she wouldn't have looked half-bad if she'd remembered to put on make-up—then opened the door and went out.

"Oh. Hi." Adam tugged the waistband of his trousers. "I know this is a little weird, but I wanted to buy a bathing suit and didn't know where to go. I thought maybe you could help me shop." He shuffled his feet. "Seeing as you were the one who suggested I buy it."

"Sure." She felt a flutter of excitement, followed by a twinge of guilt at being so excited when her father was who-knew-where. "I don't have a car," she said, relieved to realize this was true.

But they didn't need the Grand Marquis. Adam had rented a crappy Fiesta at the airport. Wendy ran inside to get her shoes, and Adam went back to his mother's pod to get the car.

"There's a flea market my mother and I used to go to," Wendy said.

"A flea market?"

She explained that the Boca flea market was a local institution—a huge bare-bones warehouse in which hundreds of vendors set up booths. Adam could buy a bathing suit there more cheaply than at a mall.

They parked in the enormous lot and joined the methodical flow of old women with shiny white handbags and their wispy-haired husbands, who, Wendy knew, looked forward to buying tubs of peanut brittle and munching the candy while marveling at electronic gadgets that would have earned their disbelief if they had seen them in *Buck Rogers* half a century earlier.

The market was crowded, but not as packed as it would have been on a rainy day. Wendy and Adam strolled past racks of women's shifts, VCRs and Game Boys, and booth after booth of twelve-dollar watches, some with leather bands. Like her golf games with her father, Wendy's visits to the flea market with her mother had been little more than excuses to talk. Whenever Wendy needed a new watch—she used up watches the way other people went through shoes—she had a terrible time deciding which watch to buy. Once, she had driven her

mother crazy by finding a watch she liked, seeking a better bargain at another booth, then deciding she liked the first watch
after all and being unable to find it again.

"Here," Adam said. "How about this one?" He pulled a pair
of surfer's shorts from a rack and held them against his waist.
When Wendy didn't object, he handed the man some bills. At
a shop selling novelties, he picked up a plastic monkey. "I can't
believe I spent twenty years selling crap like this."

"It isn't crap." Wendy snatched away the monkey. "I love this
stuff. I have an entire collection of monkeys and acrobats like
these on my desk in the newsroom." She pushed up the base
with her thumb and the monkey did a flip around a bar. "I
could play with this for hours. I do, sometimes, when I'm
trying to write a story." She set the monkey down, annoyed at
herself for reminding Adam of her job.

"You know," Adam said, "in all the years of running my
father's business I never met a single person who actually
ended up owning anything I imported, let alone anyone who
got pleasure out of owning it."

They walked the labyrinth of aisles, finally stopping at a
booth where a parrot hung from a golden hoop. As they
passed, the bird whistled and made a comment: "Hey, sailor,
toot toot." Adam backtracked across the bird's electric eye.
"Come up and see me sometime!" the parrot squawked. The
tag on its claw said $35.99. But the store sold cheaper toys. In a
box beside the register, little wind-up noses, dentures, and
corn cobs chattered and marched until they fell, their tiny legs
still struggling in the air. The store was jammed with so many
kids it seemed the kids were for sale and the toys were there
only to keep them occupied.

Well, Adam wondered, if the kids *had* been for sale, which
one would he have bought? How about the little Japanese girl

in the short pink cotton dress? No, definitely not the Japanese girl. Maybe that light-skinned black boy—he looked intelligent, good-natured, calm. Adam would have taken home any of these kids, except the stubby whey-faced boy trying to yank the tail from a battery-powered pig.

"Do all parents love their kids?" he asked Wendy. "What if you get a really ugly or unpleasant one? If it's your kid, do you *know* it's ugly or unpleasant?"

"Beats me," Wendy said. "I have this brother. Joel. He's not really fucked-up, but, well, he's a little fucked-up. I love him. But I don't love him the way a sister is supposed to love a brother. But my parents . . . My mother once told me that you love your difficult child the most. So yes, I would have to say most parents love their kids, even if the kids aren't all that lovable."

"My father didn't love me." He hadn't meant to say it. Talk about whiny. *My father didn't love me.* But there was a parrot in his chest and the damn bird wouldn't shut up. *My father didn't love me,* the parrot squawked. *My father didn't love me. My father didn't love me.*

Wendy touched his arm. "Your father was crazy. He didn't just have sex with this girl, he killed her. You're not crazy. Maybe your father didn't love you, but that doesn't mean you won't love your own kid."

"Oh," he said. "You don't think that kind of stuff gets passed along?"

"Why should it? A guy like you probably picks up how creepy his father is and makes sure he's nothing like him. Probably, a guy like you ends up the exact opposite of his father."

Adam had to fight to keep from crying. "Wait outside," he told Wendy. "Just go ahead, wait outside the booth."

She did as she was told, and Adam studied the racks of toys until he found a wind-up duck that pedaled a bike while twirling an umbrella above its head. The duck came from China, but it wasn't the usual shoddy goods. For one thing, the toy was made of tin. For another, it was hand painted. The toy wasn't manufactured according to some design; the details had been left to whoever made it. And clearly the person who'd made this duck enjoyed designing clever toys.

"Duck, yes, very good purchase." The man behind the register nodded. "You buy this for you kid? Whoever you buy it for, she like."

And, what do you know, she did. Adam tapped Wendy on the arm and held out the duck. "Oh, Adam, this is exactly the sort of thing I love." She laughed and kissed his cheek. "And now I'll buy *you* something. You could use a little pick-me-up."

She took him by his elbow and guided him down the aisle. He saw a carousel of silk ties he liked, not that he had any reason to wear a tie now. But Wendy wouldn't hear of it. "After all you've been through, you deserve more than a stupid tie." She dragged him down aisle after aisle until he started to get annoyed. How could such a confident woman find it so hard to make up her mind?

Finally, she stopped. "I've got it. Wait here. Sit on this bench. I'll be right back."

He didn't need to wait long. Apparently, once she made up her mind, she had no trouble acting on her decision. She returned and sat beside him and held out a plastic bag. Adam reached inside and pulled out a nine-by-twelve sketchbook. He reached in again and came out with a charcoal pencil, a packet of pastels, and a watercolor kit—not a child's toy but a decent set.

"They sold oils," Wendy apologized, "but they were incredibly expensive. I had no idea a tube of paint could cost that much."

Whatever oils he'd owned, he'd thrown out the month before, preparing for the garage sale. Years earlier, Barbara had used his easel to hold a planter. Their jittery short-haired kitten, Winky, had climbed up on the easel and gotten in the dirt; Barbara had come in and yelled, the cat scrambled to get away, the planter tumbled and the easel broke.

"Adam? Are you okay? Adam?"

He picked up Wendy's hand and pressed it against his chest. "Would you marry me?" he joked. At least, he hoped it was a joke. "Would you marry me and have my child?"

* * *

Milt knew he was flirting with dementia, but in his distress he felt justified addressing his questions to Moose, who was sitting beside him at the clubhouse bar, on the very same stool Moose actually used to sit on. So what if Moose was dead now? That didn't mean he couldn't listen.

And that's what Moose did. He listened. He sat on the stool with a patient look on his bovine face and every now and then lifted his beer and sipped. Never mind if Moose was even less loquacious in death than he had been in life. Milt sipped his own beer and wrinkled his lips in distaste; he hated beer, but sometimes, in the clubhouse after a game of golf, a seltzer just wouldn't do.

"It's pointless," Milt admitted. "So what if a man dies without playing a last good round of golf? But it's sort of, I don't know, a sign. He lets me play a decent round, then I believe He's really up there and agree to go out quietly."

The young man behind the bar asked Milt if he wanted something else to drink or eat, and Milt jerked his head no. He had gotten up early and gone out without eating. After playing a quick nine holes, he'd taken a rest, then he'd played another nine. He should have been famished. A rack of hot dogs was going around a case, getting cooked by a light bulb. In the old days, he would have enjoyed sneaking such a meal, knowing how much Greta would disapprove. But the fatty smell made him retch.

"I thought I'd get my swing back in its groove," he told Moose. "Then I would come out again with Wendy. How can I go out this way, her hitting such a long ball and me barely able . . ." Tears welled behind Milt's eyes. Moose held out his thick hands to show he understood. "I could have been a rich man," Milt said, "if I hadn't married and had kids. But what kind of life would that have been? What reason is there to get up in the morning if you don't have someone who needs you? And now? Who needs me now?" He couldn't resist reciting to Moose the list of people who no longer needed him: Greta, who was dead; Wendy, who'd barely needed him when she was born; and Joel, who might be irresponsible in matters of employment but at least had had the sense to marry an obstetrician, a competent woman who not only cooked and cleaned and raised their kids but supported him and paid their bills. Only one person needed Milt's assistance now. And no matter how much he tried to talk himself into it, he couldn't bring himself to offer that person his help.

Two foursomes came in; it must have been after five o'clock and the men had just gotten off from work. One of these men sat on Moose's seat, and Milt figured it was time to go. His daughter, no doubt, would be worrying where he was.

He left some bills and went outside. A good-looking younger man saw Milt and asked if he might like to pair up. He wished Wendy were there. She might have taken a fancy to the man and dumped that horse-riding professor of hers. What

237

did an attractive vivacious woman like his daughter want with an old fart like that? Well, that was what some women did. They looked around too long, then panicked and grabbed the first man who asked them.

"Sir? Did you want to join me, sir?"

Waving, Milt took his leave. He ought to go home to Wendy.

Instead, he surprised himself by getting on the Turnpike and heading south. He glanced at his watch; he would make it to Rosina's just as she was going out for the evening. If she came out with another man, Milt could put his mind at rest. There wouldn't be a thing he owed her.

He turned onto I-95, and just north of Hollywood, a Florida downpour began to fall. He tried not to let the wipers make him dizzy, but for all the time he'd been spending in bed, he hadn't been sleeping. He was tempted to close his eyes. What did he have to live for? But no. If he went to sleep at sixty miles an hour, he was likely to kill an innocent person who had a reason to stay alive. And so, when a roadside diner loomed up from the rain, Milt clicked on his blinker and pulled in. He turned off the engine. The car grew stuffy. Rain beat against the roof. He struggled to take off his cardigan, then folded it beneath his head. The hole in the leather seat was an annoying hollow beneath his ribs. But even with his knees folded beneath the wheel, Milt fell into a sleep so sound it was like being sucked under by an enormous wave and drowned.

* * *

After they got back to the development, Adam said he ought to check on his mother, but he promised that he would try to stop by and visit Wendy later. He dropped her near the pool, and she walked to her father's condo, hoping to find his car. It seemed impossible that her orderly, responsible father had left without telling her where he'd gone. In the old days, neither of her parents would walk to the corner mailbox without leaving the other one a note. And every note, no matter how brief, had started with "Sweetheart" and ended with "Love." Except that her father had disappeared without a word and Wendy had no idea how to find him. There wasn't a single person she could rely on, no one who owed her the obligation a parent owed a child or a husband owed a wife.

She took a shower, then went in the kitchen to make a bite to eat. The freezer was filled with bagels, each sliced in a plastic bag with the excess air sucked out. She defrosted one bagel and toasted it, scrambled two eggs, took her time washing the dish and pan. This must have been how her father felt, trying to pass the time, waiting for someone who was never coming home. She went in his room and sat on the unmade bed, inspecting her mother's portrait. At any moment, the phone would ring and the cops would tell her that her father had been found in his Grand Marquis with a shotgun between his legs. The expectation was so real she almost could hear the shot.

There was a knock at the door and she jumped up and ran to get it. But her father wouldn't need to knock. Would he? Unless he'd lost his keys?

She opened the door and saw Adam. He wore a short-sleeve pink shirt they'd picked up at the flea market and a light-weight pair of shorts. He stepped inside and looked around. Hadn't her father gotten back? Did she have any idea where he might have gone?

He must have driven to Miami, Wendy said. She could poke around in his drawers and find Rosina's number. But calling seemed a violation of his privacy. And she dreaded talking to his mistress.

Adam volunteered to stay and wait. But Wendy didn't want her father to come home and find her on his couch with some guy he'd never met. She didn't want to introduce her father to Adam Haber and watch his face register who Adam Haber was. Then again, neither did she want to sit alone and wait. She and Adam could go out for a little while. An hour. Two, at most. Surely her father would be home by then. The trouble was, you couldn't do much in an hour. She already had eaten dinner. A movie would take too long.

"How about the driving range?" she suggested.

Adam stared at her. "A driver? You want me to hold a driver?"

The image came back to her—Lou Sunshine cocking his club above that cantaloupe. "You can't spend half your life trying to please your father and the other half trying to avoid anything he ever did. Do what you want to do," she said.

"Believe me, I don't want to play golf. What kind of a sport is it if a person can play it while smoking a cigar?" He rubbed his head. "Sorry. I have this memory of my father with a cigar in his mouth, taking swings with this big black driver."

Her heart went out to him—literally; she felt her heart make a movement outward in her chest.

"I have an idea," Adam said suddenly. "If you want to play golf, we'll play golf."

"At night?"

"Don't you trust me?" He affected a wounded look. And the truth was, Wendy didn't care where they went as long as they weren't gone long. She got her purse, and the next thing she knew they were standing outside a huge video-arcade called Boomers. Adam led her through the entrance, and the din was so overwhelming she could understand how the place had received its name. The arcade was filled with teenagers who hadn't yet gotten to enjoy enough real death in their lives and so needed a simulation. It was a relief to go out the back and shut the door against the harrowing clamor of explosions, gun shots, shrieks, and screams.

"See?" Adam said. "Golf."

Above them rose eighteen holes of the highest-tech miniature golf Wendy had ever seen, with waterfalls, flashing lights, and statues of elephants that moved their trunks and roared. Still, the set-up disappointed her. Where were the miniature golf courses of her youth? Why had it become so hard to put the obstacles *on* the course instead of off to one side? She missed the windmill with rotating arms that sent your ball straight back at you unless you timed your shot just right, or the giraffe grazing on the fairway in such a way that you had to send your ball directly up its neck. "This isn't real golf," she said.

"Yeah? Miniature anything is still that thing. A miniature poodle is still a poodle. Hey, I deal in novelties. If anyone should know what 'miniature' means, it's me." He bought their tickets and returned with a scorecard and stubby pencil. "I'll go first," he said. He gripped his club the way a batter would hold a bat.

"You can't even hold the club right," Wendy teased.

"It's only miniature golf."

"You're the one who just told me golf is golf." She came up behind him and circled his shoulders with her arms. She backed her knees against the crooks of his knees and wrapped her fingers around his hands.

"Hey," he said. "I'm beginning to see why people enjoy this game."

"Never mind that." She moved the club straight back along the ground. "The entire game is in the wrists. When you putt, keep your wrists stiff. When you take a swing with your driver, you bring your arms straight back, like this. Then you cock your wrists and bring your arms down straight and snap your wrists at the ball."

Laughing, Adam let go of his club and turned. "That's the whole secret of golf?" He kissed her—lightly, but on the mouth. "Let me tell you, if I'd had you giving me lessons when I was a kid, I'd be Tiger Woods by now."

* * *

A powerful light was shining down on Milt.

"Sir?" The cop rapped on the window. "Sir, are you all right?"

Milt uncurled painfully and sat up. He shook his head at the officer, who looked so young he ought to have been wearing a Boy Scout uniform. "Fine," Milt mouthed, "go away."

The officer clicked off his light and disappeared. The sun was faint but up. Milt had been sleeping here all night, in the lot at a roadside diner. Amazing, given how uncomfortable he had been. He felt refreshed, though dizzy. He couldn't remember the last time he'd eaten.

Never mind, he knew what he had to do. He got back on the highway and turned off at Rosina's exit. By six, he was standing outside her door. She was an early riser, Milt knew. And if someone was in there with her, better to find out now. Milt buttoned his sweater to hide the wrinkles in his shirt. He was tugging up his socks when Rosina stepped out.

"Eii!" She clapped a hand to her robe—a green chiffony

thing that Milt had always liked. Stooped as he was, he figured he might as well pick up Rosina's paper.

"Mil-ton." She drew out his name in two long syllables. He couldn't tell if she was glad or displeased to see him. "I am having my breakfast. You are welcome to share it with me."

He thanked her and went in, surprised at how calm he felt. His hands barely trembled. He followed her to the little round glass table that stood before the balcony, from which a person could just make out, if that person stood and strained, a sliver of the Atlantic. The table was set for one, with a glass of that pinkish juice, half a grapefruit, and buttered toast.

Rosina started to the kitchen. "I still have a box of the Especial K."

Milt shook his head no. He was hungry—very hungry—but afraid to say what he had to say on anything but an empty stomach. "Did you get my letter?"

She returned and sat beside him. "You are waiting I should answer? This isn't what I think. I think, from reading that letter, Milton doesn't want to hear from Rosina anymore." She peered out the balcony. "I am knowing before you know. I am trying to figure out how to tell you. But is hard. Is very hard." Her voice faltered. "I no let you . . . After I know, I no let you. I am hoping you don't have what I am having." She covered her face. Milt wanted to hold her. He wanted to ask her how she had gotten what she had.

Rosina ran one finger beneath each eye. She wasn't wearing make-up. She was still beautiful, Milt thought, but he had never seen her so pale.

"Is amusement," Rosina said, "to get this illness of young people and homosexual." She smoothed her robe's lapel. "I would think maybe to take the medicine, but are very many

243

pills. Very expensive. I am never becoming citizen. I haven't this insurance." She lifted one fluid arm and flicked her wrist in imitation of some forties star like Garbo. "On bright side, I am never getting old, never being burdens on anyone." She laid her palm along Milt's cheek. "You are very nice gentleman, Mil-ton. No questions. No ugly names. I am glad you come to say good-bye." He wanted to press the hand harder to his cheek. He wanted to say that he would take care of her. Pay for her treatment. They would take care of each other until one or both passed on.

"Good-bye," he said, "Rosina," drawing out her name because he loved saying "Rosina" and knew that he would never again have the chance to say it.

* * *

She awoke on the lounge chair in the Florida room at the back of her father's condo. A foursome was teeing off. The night before, she had played miniature golf with Adam. He had kissed her. At the memory of that kiss, her heart did this little arc-and-fall, like a chip shot to the green. But when she thought of the possibility that her father hadn't yet come home, she nearly threw up.

Warily, she searched the house. "Dad?" she shouted. No dad. She might have called the cops, but she knew they wouldn't put out a bulletin until another day had passed. Or maybe she just hated the thought of telling some smirky young officer that her father had gotten AIDS from sleeping with a woman he had picked up at a coffee shop in Miami and he hadn't come home the night before. If only she could guess Rosina's last name. She went back to the patio to sit and think. Eleven foursomes golfed past. Not a single one of them, female or male, could hit a golf ball worth a damn.

The front door opened. She jumped up. Her father staggered in. He wore a yellow sweater smeared with soot. His hair was standing straight up from his head. Even his eyebrows seemed disheveled.

"Next time," he grumbled, "would you mind locking the front door? You left it open all night."

"The next time you go out, would you mind telling me where you're going? I was so worried I nearly—"

"I'm going in to take a shower."

"You're avoiding me. I fly thousands of miles to see you, you tell me you have AIDS, then you refuse to talk about it." He already was in his room but he hadn't shut the door. "Did you sleep last night? Where did you sleep?"

"I slept. Where is none of your business."

"Good. You slept. Now you can talk to me."

He slammed his door. But not many minutes later, he came out in fresh clothes. His hair was wet and combed.

"Dad," she said, "please tell me where you went last night."

He stood for a while without answering. Then he said—so quietly she almost couldn't hear—"I have never read a single true word about getting old. Not in any book. Not in any newspaper. The truth about getting old is that every single person you've ever loved dies. And you're not supposed to care. It's the so-called natural order of things. Well, let me tell you, when every person you've ever loved dies, you feel like dying with them."

She knew it was selfish, but she couldn't keep from saying it. "*I'm* still alive."

He expelled air through his nose. "In two days, you're going back to a state so far away it would take me an entire day to get there in a plane."

She wished she had told him earlier about her plan to move

to Florida. If she told him now, he would think she was saying it to cheer him up. Besides, she wasn't sure she really would.

* * *

On this, her next-to-last evening in his house, her father went to bed at eight. When Adam came to call an hour later, Wendy agreed to go out with him. There wasn't any point in sitting up alone while her father sulked in his room.

"You want to give me another golf lesson?" Adam asked.

"As a matter of fact, I do." She led him behind her father's building, where they wandered along the cart paths. Being on a golf course after dark filled her with the sense of wandering forbidden ground, a landscape of longing and pursuit. She pulled Adam toward the sand trap.

"Here?"

They settled awkwardly, the sand damp beneath their thighs. Somewhere in the distance, sprinklers hissed their sinister hiss. God only knew what wildlife was out there. Alligators were even now shouldering heavily toward them. And fire ants. She and Adam were probably lying directly on a nest of stinging ants.

She unbuttoned Adam's shirt. There was just enough light to discern the general characteristics of his chest. Taut. Well muscled. Dark. She ran her hands across the warm furred skin, then nuzzled her face against it. He had a nice chest. A chest to be rested on and caressed. Maybe, if you had been away from home as long as she had, what once had seemed familiar now struck you as exciting. Or maybe she was finally settling.

Well, so what if she was. You couldn't shop around forever. You had to buy something and take it home.

They kissed. She sucked his lip.

"Wait," he said. "I can't. Not like this."

He pushed her off and stood. Wendy struggled to her feet. She felt insulted. But she had to admit he was right. What was she doing kissing a virtual stranger on the golf course while her father was home suffering from a broken heart and AIDS?

They straightened their clothes and brushed off the sand. Adam unlaced his shoes and poured sand back in the trap. *Good-bye*, they said. *Good night.* But they couldn't bring themselves to leave. They couldn't even bring themselves to stop touching each other. Instead, they slunk around the development making out like teenagers. *This is crazy. We need to stop.* They sat beside the pool and watched the water shimmer beneath the lights. They got up and said good-bye, then talked a while longer.

Eventually, they ended up in the weight room at the club. What senior citizen would be working out so late? They sat and kissed on one of those narrow benches people lie on when lifting weights, then got so carried away they took refuge in the sauna. The steam wasn't on, but in that airless wood cabana they soon grew oiled with sweat. Wendy stretched out on the lowest tier, thinking of all the elderly Jewish men whose saggy hairy bottoms had settled on this bench. Her father must have taken a *shvitz* here with Moose.

"There's no chance you have, you know, what my father . . ."

Adam said he hadn't slept with anyone but his wife in twenty years.

Not since the divorce? Hadn't he even had a crush on another woman?

Well, maybe he'd had a crush, but he couldn't really talk about it.

"You can tell me," Wendy urged.

"No," he said, "I can't. But don't worry. She isn't competition. She isn't exactly available. She isn't even alive."

Wendy tried to think what this might mean, but Adam already had put his hands around her waist and she no longer cared. He pressed one hand against her breast while sliding the other hand up her thigh. For some reason, she was reminded of the flat wood box in which a person could slip a coin and make it disappear. All those years importing novelties seemed to have given Adam Haber the sleight-of-hand required to remove a woman's underwear without taking off her shorts. He could palm her heart and make it vanish, and then, with a sideways smile, lay it back inside her ribs. It was a trick, but not a bad trick. She had missed this with Harry, the way sex could make you laugh.

And, laughing, they took off their clothes. For a moment, sitting opposite on the bench, Adam seemed reluctant to make love to her. Then he muttered, "I don't care" and kissed her breast. "I don't care," he kept repeating, "I don't care, I don't care."

Wendy closed her eyes, and in those final distorted seconds while she clenched her teeth and moaned and dug her fingers in Adam's back, she saw a small red rubber ball swinging up along a string—up and almost in, up and almost in, almost in the cup, the cup on that wooden stick. And then the ball swung gracefully along its arc, and she called his name— "Adam!"—and her cry rebounded from the rough wood walls and the ball fell softly in.

* * *

She was scheduled to fly back to Montana the next afternoon, but she couldn't bear to leave. Back in Helena, she might decide her feelings for Adam Haber were the illusion and what she felt for Harry was real. Not to mention that her father was still so dejected he might do away with himself, if not with a gun, then by refusing to get out of bed. On top of everything, she hadn't spent a minute at the beach. The Rockies were fine, but she missed the melancholy vista of the sea, the glimmering line of light that ran from your ankles to the sun like a magnificent ball and chain.

The problem was, this would also be her last chance to spend some time with Adam. And Adam wanted to spend the day with her. He was tired of staying in. His mother wasn't ready for an outing. Besides, she loathed the beach. But there was nothing to prevent him from going to the beach alone and "accidentally" meeting up with Wendy and her dad.

And so it was that Wendy and her father unloaded the trunk of the Grand Marquis and carried their cooler, an umbrella, and a folding chair up the boardwalk through the dunes. At the crest, by the lifeguard tower, Milt stopped and read the day's conditions. "Waves: moderate to rough. Weather: overcast. Water temperature: 81 degrees. Sea pests: men-of-war." He shook his head. "Sometimes a day at the beach isn't exactly a day at the beach," he said wryly, then lapsed back into silence, trudging across the sand as if weighted with possessions, although in fact he carried only the folding chair.

The only other beachgoers were a party of Hispanic teenagers sunning themselves on tropical-colored towels, flirting and trading quips. Wendy stopped and chose a spot. Her father screwed their umbrella in the sand and positioned his chair beneath its shade. He removed the *Sun-Sentinel* from the back pocket of his trousers, sat on his chair and read, turning the pages at a pace so maddeningly slow he seemed determined to convey that just because he had agreed to accompany her to the beach didn't mean he intended to talk to her.

249

She left him to the goings-on of the Fort Lauderdale city council and walked to the water's edge. Good, the waves were choppy. Her mother had liked rough waves, too. One morning in Atlantic City when Wendy was nine or ten, she and her mother had gotten up early and sneaked out to take a swim. Only a few loners had been on the beach. Wendy and her mother had swum out a long way, then they'd waited for a wave. An enormous breaker rolled toward them. "Watch out!" her mother yelled. But it was her mother who got washed away. Flexible with youth, Wendy was flipped and shaken but regained her feet. She looked back toward the boardwalk, where an empty rickshaw was being pulled by an overweight black man, and, beyond that, to the moldy old hotel where her father and Joel were still sleeping. The lifeguard's tower was empty; the lifeguards, Wendy knew, didn't arrive until much later. She stood looking around the water until she spotted a clump of tangled red seaweed, which, she suddenly realized, wasn't seaweed at all. She ran heavily back toward the beach, lunging against the undertow, then grabbed her mother's hair and pulled.

For the rest of their vacation, Wendy's parents spoiled her in ways they had never done before—dinner at her favorite restaurant, greasy fried twists of dough, roller-coaster rides and games of chance and a giant blue-and-green stuffed squid. She was aware that she had done something out of the ordinary, but until this very moment, it hadn't quite sunk in that she had saved her mother's life.

Now, standing on the beach in Boca, she looked out across the sea and realized that Adam Haber was already in the water; she could just make out his head bobbing on the waves like a curly black coconut. She felt uneasy about leaving her father alone on shore, as if, on dry land, he would be in more peril than she was, swimming out to sea. But she launched herself and swam, boring beneath each wave, until she burst up from the water inches from Adam's face.

"Water witch," he hissed. She laced her arms around his neck. She didn't want to go home and leave him. Then again, how could she be sure that what she felt for Adam was any more real than what she'd felt for Harry, or, for that matter, for Arick, Quaid, or Sam? Surely she had loved Arick. Yet she had left him, for no better reason than he had gotten a little carried away with his newfound intellectual credentials. What kind of woman would leave a man because he had gone on the wagon and lost some weight?

She clasped Adam's neck tighter. How absolutely terrifying to choose any one person and stay with him your entire life. You couldn't tie each other down. You couldn't rely on God. You had to do your own pathetic job of tying *yourself* down. You took a vow enforced by nothing but your belief in the beauty of such a vow. Of course, if you truly were miserable, you could break that vow and leave. But what if you were only a little bit miserable? What if your husband beat you or slept around?

"Look." Adam pointed, and it took Wendy a moment to make out the brilliant blue helmets of three Portuguese men-of-war floating on the next wave. Nothing was quite as painful as the sting of a man-of-war; once, when Joel was small, he had been stung so badly he couldn't stop screaming.

Adam unwrapped her arms from around his neck and started pushing outward with his palms to push away the jelly-fish.

"Adam!" she called. "Be careful, you'll get stung," although she was touched to be reminded that a man needn't live in Montana or be a cowboy to act in a chivalrous way.

He struggled back toward her and lifted her in his arms.

"I could get used to this," she said. "Living here, I mean. Going to the beach."

"I suppose I could, too. Get used to living here, I mean."

Wendy leaned forward and kissed him. Their tongues mated in each other's mouths, salty and slick as mollusks. And they rode the waves that way, the sea lifting them, then letting them drop, lifting them, then letting them drop, slapping their cheeks with brine.

* * *

An apple core flew up from the trash. Then a Kentucky Fried Chicken box, spilling bones across the sand.

Rats, Milt thought. Vermin.

But a fat black raccoon chinned itself above the rim and plopped heavily to the sand. The animal lifted the apple in its small black hands and gnawed the rotting fruit. Pausing, it looked up at Milt and grinned with the corrupt innocence of a beggar.

Milt put down his paper, stood from his chair, and removed his pants. Who cared who saw his sores? Those Spanish kids were too wrapped up in themselves to notice some elderly white guy taking off his pants. There was Wendy, but she was out there in the waves. One could only hope this was the same young man who had been prowling around the house these past few nights, tracking in grass and sand. Not that Milt could object, given how little attention he had been paying her. But what about her professor friend out west? Never mind. Milt was hardly one to judge.

But just because a person was old didn't mean he should be forced to watch something he could no longer have. Fine, he'd take a walk. He looked back at his blanket. He had left his wallet in his pants. But those boys seemed more interested in getting laid than taking his twenty bucks. And if someone did steal his wallet? Twenty bucks wouldn't buy much, especially where Milt was headed.

* * *

Wendy loved the feel of being cradled, weightless, in the sea. But that awful apprehension about her father kept ebbing back with each wave.

"I'm getting out." Her fingers trickled down Adam's spine to the waistband of his trunks. The trunks they had bought together. She kissed him one last time, then started back to shore. The last wave knocked her harder than she'd expected and she ended up on her knees on a carpet of broken shells. Another wave washed in, the water flowing backward to reveal a perfectly intact razorback clam.

She could identify the shell because her father's father had owned a straight-edge razor, which, after Grandpa Leo died, her father had kept in a cigar box with a lock of his mother's hair. Once, when she was young, Wendy had found the box, taken out the razor and unfolded it, at which her father had come in and snatched it back. "Pussycat, that's not a toy." A few weeks later, in Atlantic City, he had handed her a shell that looked exactly like that razor. "Here, sweetheart, you can play with this." That night, in their hotel room, Wendy settled him in a chair, wrapped a steamy washcloth around his face, spurted fragrant dollops of shaving cream on his cheeks, and used the shell to scrape it off. She slapped her father's cheeks with aftershave and brushed Vitalis through his hair. "Shave and a haircut"—he snapped his fingers—"two bits" and meant to a man to remember standing in an overheated store with his father, gulping down a bottle of Dr. Brown's. Milt turned and tread water, looking wistfully out to sea as if Greta were on some rock, brushing her long red hair with a spiny shell, and he was about to swim toward her. But the plane passed overhead right then, and Milt made the mistake of stealing one last look at the banner, reading through salt-blurred eyes the letters that spelled out a brand of sparkling water Milt knew to be no better than seltzer but costing three times the price. He thought of the seltzer he and Greta used to have delivered to the house, and the egg cream his daughter Wendy had concocted for him that morning and stowed in the cooler for his lunch, along with a sandwich of pickled herring on a buttered onion roll, a bag of sweet cold plums, and two Chips Ahoy cookies. He couldn't depart this earth with that delicious lunch still in the cooler any more than he could leave this life without playing one last decent round of golf.

He glanced back toward shore and saw his daughter swimming toward him. She was worried about him; he could see that from the way she swam so hard, without coming up for air. She was thinking he might drown. Ridiculous! He, Milt Rothstein, could take care of himself. He always had been able to take care of himself. Not to mention taking care of everyone else.

That was what he missed. There was no one to take care of. Not his patients. Not his wife. His children no longer needed him. Only Rosina needed him. And Rosina, well, Rosina . . .

Milt grew angry at himself. What did he mean "well, Rosina"? Either she needed him or she didn't. And if she did need Milt's help, what did it matter what she was? If someone needed your help, she needed your help. No law said you had to sleep with a woman to offer her your help. Just as no law prevented him—for once in his life—from accepting help from someone else. From his daughter, for example. From the doctor. From Rosina.

He was farther out than he'd thought. Over his shoulder, a glinting green wave raised its foamy fingers as if preparing to strike him down. Milt got ready and took a breath, and then, when the wave was nearly on him, raised one arm above his head and curled the other along his side, then lifted his feet and let go, a man giving himself up to forces greater than himself, but secure in the knowledge that he was nestled in the palm of a watery forceful God who was lifting him up and weighing him, and whether He found Milt wanting or not, would never let him drop but would carry him along forever, closer in toward the shore.

EILEEN POLLACK is the author of *The Rabbi in the Attic and Other Stories*; *Paradise, New York*; and *Woman Walking Ahead: In Search of Catherine Weldon and Sitting Bull*, which won a WILLA finalist award in nonfiction. She has received fellowships from the Michener Foundation, the National Endowment for the Arts, the Rona Jaffe Foundation, and the Massachusetts Arts Council. Stories from *In the Mouth* have been awarded a Pushcart Prize, the Cohen Award from *Ploughshares*, and the Lawrence Foundation Prize from *Michigan Quarterly Review*. "The Bris" was selected by Stephen King for inclusion in the *Best American Short Stories 2007*. Eileen lives in Ann Arbor and teaches at the University of Michigan, where she is Zell Director of the MFA Program in Creative Writing.